MW00488230

Praise For Shadow's Way

A spell weaver, Shadow's Way, kept me in suspense, which, as a lover of good mysteries is not easy for an author to do. I often guess an ending before I hit the middle. As in her last book, Like I Used to Dance, Ms. Frances' characters are delicious portrayals, richly textured, gradually revealing their good and evil humanity, as her hauntingly realistic settings and surprising story unfolds. To say more might give away the best of her new book. I have thoroughly enjoyed both of her novels and highly recommend them.

Sherry Haskin

Two of the historic forces that still shape American culture, ante-bellum southern ideology and the catholic church, are brought into fascinating and disturbing juxtaposition in this novel. Barbara Frances lays bare traditions that while often enough exposed as decadent in some measure, still retain strong elements of venerability through the usual telling of their stories. Not here. Nothing is embellished or disguised. At its core, like a Russell Lee camera lens, this work shows us marginalized people seeking growth and redemption without filters or touch-up. With all their blemishes, in their stumbling nakedness they emerge as utterly noble.

David Wiener

Shadow's Way

To Cheryl -
Beware, yet embrace the shadow;
Love you -
Barbara Frances
2022

Barbara Frances

Shadow's Way

By Barbara Frances

Published By
Positive Imaging, LLC
http://positive-imaging.com
bill@positive-imaging.com

ISBN 9781944071677

CHAPTER ONE

Her timing was perfect. As she rounded the corner, daily Mass had just ended and the Archbishop was now standing outside the richly carved doors of St. Paul's Cathedral. His followers were tiered below him on the steps. He turned towards the woman allowing his eyes to trace the contours of her body. She was aware of this attention and as always, felt the thrill of that power. A sheer white muslin shift clung to her black swim suit, still wet from morning exercise at the community pool. Despite the heat and the humidity from the Gulf of Mexico, she strolled by as if it were a cool spring day in Vermont.

Elaine Chauvier was a stately woman, aware of her long legs and enticing figure. Some said she was a snob and she would have agreed with them. After all, she was from aristocracy. Her great grandfather and General Robert E. Lee had been close friends. Her family had owned sections of plantation land in the area with nearly a hundred slaves. No one could give this woman a passing glance without being momentarily transfixed. Soft black hair, always a bit ruffled to give a false impression of casualness, framed a face of classic perfection. Piercing dark eyes conveyed the superiority she felt over everyone.

Archbishop Andre Figurant gave hardly a thought to the man who knelt to kiss his ring or the mother holding up her baby for a blessing. His focus was across the boulevard, beyond the wrought-iron fence surrounding the complex which consisted of the Cathedral, the Archbishop's mansion and a striking plaza of mosaic tiles, gardens and statues of Mother Mary and St. Paul.

The gliding presence hypnotized as well as beguiled him. *If only that fence could restrain these desires.* He wanted more and that was his disease, an enduring obsession, perhaps an incurable illness. He watched as the vision of his dreams lightly ascended the four steps to the porch of Shadow's Way, the best preserved antebellum home in the state of Alabama, perhaps in the entire South. When she reached the top, she turned to face him with a look of disdain that flung him back to being a sharecropper's son working on her family's land. She would never see him as an equal no matter his ranking in the Church or the money he now had.

"Your Excellency." He was annoyed by this cry that brought him back to his priestly role. "Will you please pray for my boy to get well?"

A cow-faced woman in a faded cotton dress looked up at him. Kindness quickly replaced his irritation. His flock, his devotees, his faithful evoked mixed emotions. He both reveled in and detested their homage. "Yes, of course, my dear daughter. I bless him in the name of our Lady and implore her to heal your son in the name of her son, Jesus Christ."

He paused to look across the street. Elaine lingered on her front porch admiring the azaleas. Fully aware of the archbishop's compulsive gaze, she tilted her head and smiled flirtatiously at the flowers. "You are my lovelies," she purred, then flicked her wrist as if dismissing them as well as him.

An elaborate easel by the front door held a sign, written in large Gothic letters, "Bed & Breakfast." Underneath in smaller print were the words, "Gourmet Dinner Upon Request."

You're nothing more than the overseer of a rooming house, he wanted to shout, *and all because of me.* The impulse was subdued by a humble request. "Please bless these, your Excellency, jest so's I don't fall down no more." Archbishop Andre looked down at the make shift crutches the old man held up. A deep grief overcame him. "Mother Mary and Brother Jesus," he prayed as he gently took the crutches, made the sign of the cross over them and rested his hand on the parishioner's head, "bless and protect this man as he walks."

Gratitude glistened in the old man's eyes. "Thank you, your Excellency."

Abruptly, Andre turned back toward the Cathedral doors, disgusted that he'd always been a man divided by conflicting natures. The love he felt for those in need and the desire to relieve the suffering of others were as real as his longings for a life of freedom, a life devoid of moral obligations.

Elaine picked up the mail inside her door slot and pulled the heavy door shut. Immediately she set about inspecting the large foyer and winding staircase, all polished to a gleam. She glanced to her right into the dining room and admired the perfectly placed china settings on the table and then to her left into the living room. She smiled at the portrait of a severe-looking man in a Confederate uniform perched over the mantel piece. "Bonjour, Grand-pere Henri." She quickly scanned the fluffed sofa pillows and precisely placed magazines on the coffee table.

Well, it looks like Lily Mae has been doing her job. Miracles, miracles. These two rooms, the foyer and the three bedrooms directly overhead were exactly as they had been one hundred and thirty-five years ago. Elaine was very careful to see that not one little detail was changed. When the wallpaper, draperies or upholstery had to be replaced, she paid exorbitant prices to get the exact duplicates.

A sharp nasal voice shattered the quiet. "Oh, Ms. Chauvier, good morning, good morning." Elaine turned her head towards the stairway and forced a smile. Mr. and Mrs. McCrether, a Boston couple, middle-aged, dumpy and plain, began their descent. They wore matching Bermuda shorts with flowered tops.

Elaine wanted to spit. It was so unfair that someone of her stature should have to accommodate people of this sort. Nevertheless, she donned the veil of dripping politeness she always used with paying customers. After all, she reminded herself, *I need these uncouth individuals for my livelihood.*

"Why good morning, Mr. and Mrs. McCrether. My, my, don't you look all well and refreshed. Lovely outfits." Her lilting voice with its buoyant flow bubbled up from the time of Southern refinement laced with hypocrisy. She pushed a strand of hair behind her ear. "Before I went for my morning swim, I left precise directions with Lily Mae. I pray she provided your breakfast and all your other needs to your satisfaction."

"It was wonderful. Those muffins were… well, we couldn't have asked for more," Mrs. McCrether tittered.

Elaine giggled demurely, aware of Mr. McCrether's unrestrained glances and tugged at the see through wrap now clinging to her swimsuit. "Please, do forgive my unfitting appearance," she purred. "If you'll excuse me, I must make myself presentable but before I depart can I in any way, be of service to you this fine morning?"

Elaine's past acting career served her well in this business. Very few ever detected the manipulation and deception under her well-constructed mask. "I know good and well she'd have gotten an Oscar someday if she hadn't had to come back here to take care of the mess her no-good daddy left," old Judge Davis would say every time her name came up, and it came up quite a bit. Elaine Chauvier was the sort of person people liked to talk about.

"We couldn't have asked for more," Mrs. McCrether bellowed. Elaine glanced at the wall paper around the woman's head as if expecting to see scratch marks left by her strident tone. "And for our last night," Mrs. McCrether went on, "we'd like to order the gourmet dinner. I know it says on your brochure to order when making the reservation, but could you make an exception for us? Pretty pleeease."

Damn Yankees, pushy, impertinent, always feeling entitled. Elaine nodded with a syrupy smile. "Do you all know what ya'll would like? I offer three entrees. Do ya'll wish to see a menu?"

"No that won't be necessary." Mr. McCrether waddled down the remaining steps. "Our mouths watered over the review in your local paper about the Shadow's Way Prawn Dinner."

"Oh, did it ever," Mrs. McCrether interjected. "You must have paid that food editor a pretty price." Both McCrethers laughed louder than what would have been considered appropriate in polite society. *They don't begin to know how unrefined they are.* Elaine tried not to shudder. "Very good choice," she cooed. "I'm sure every course will be pleasing to your palates. Now you must forgive my crudeness, but I have to require in advance the three hundred and fifty dollars plus ten per cent gratuity."

The couple stared in disbelief. "Oh, the prices weren't in the article," Mr. McCrether gasped.

"Higher quality eating establishments don't usually list prices, plus this is a last-minute request." Elaine reveled in their distress. It was as if she were a girl again watching frantic fireflies trapped in the upside-down jar on her bedroom's window sill. "It is after all, five courses, prepared with all fresh, natural ingredients."

"Of course, of course, that's fine." Mr. McCrether reached for his wallet, took out the bills and handed them to Elaine.

"Hors d'oeuvres and aperitifs at seven in the sun room and then you can retire to the main dining room for your dinner. You will be dining alone this evening, so romantic by candlelight."

The couple exchanged a quick glance seeming embarrassed. *Oh yes, these two are finished with passion, at least for one another.* After giving directions to the Fine Arts Museum and graciously bidding them farewell, Elaine walked down the foyer, through the small sitting/library room and into the large kitchen. A broad breakfast nook overlooked a backyard gushing in greenery and pink, yellow, red, and white flowers. A gazebo for weddings and a carriage house, now called the honeymoon bungalow, sat at the bottom of a slight slope.

Elaine had turned Shadow's Way into a money maker and she knew her great-grandfather was proud of her. Even though he was long in the grave he still wandered through the rooms and gave her advice, praise and sometimes admonishment. Occasionally, guests would tell her about footsteps in the hallway and doors opening. She would smile warmly and say, "Isn't it somethin' how these old houses can make one believe in haunts?"

As the rumors about ghosts spread, her business increased as well as her prices. "People are so interested in the supernatural. I pray you have an encounter," she would whisper to those who specifically came for such a contact.

"Good mornin', Lily Mae. The front rooms are perfect."

"Mornin' Ma'am. Yessum, I done vacuum too." Lily Mae, a black woman in her mid-forties, stood at the island rolling out biscuit dough. She was very short and very round, with a round face and round bulging eyes that registered a state of perpetual fear. "The blowfish" is what Elaine called her in private.

"Not quite so thick." Elaine impatiently scooted Lily Mae over and began rolling the dough. "I swear, how many times do I have to show you?" Standing slightly behind, Lily Mae stuck out her tongue at her.

"Listen, that Boston couple has decided here at the last minute to have the prawn dinner tonight. There goes my free evenin.' I should have just said no, but I can't lose good references even from the heathen land of Boston. After all it is another dollar comin in."

She held up a perfect biscuit. "Lily Mae, see this. Now that's how you do it. Do you think you can do that?"

"Yessum." Lily Mae shuffled back to the board.

Elaine rinsed her hands and looked out the kitchen window towards the two cabins situated down a paved lane to the right of the main house. These were all that remained of the slave quarters. Elaine had renovated them into lovely cottages painted white with navy trim, still quite small and simple. Years ago, her father had had bathrooms put in. She rented these mainly to guests with children in order to avoid noise in the main house. However, now one was being occupied by a nonpaying intruder. "Where's Ofelia? I'll have her go to the market."

As if hearing her name, the handsome Ofelia emerged from her cabin. She could have passed for Elaine's twin except she was chocolate brown and a good twenty years younger. Like Elaine she was tall, moved regally and held her head high, yet she possessed none of her sister's arrogance. Elaine detested her.

"Good mornin' everybody," Ofelia's deep velvety voice settled into the corners of the room. "Lily Mae, honey, I do hope that coffee is strong."

"Ofelia, you'll have to go to the market and get some fresh prawns," Elaine commanded. "That Boston couple wants the gourmet dinner this evening."

"I'm singing at the club tonight and I've got to rest and rehearse this afternoon." She took down a cup from the cabinet.

Elaine flinched at the rebuff. "Well that's too bad. You need to contribute to the upkeep of this business."

Ofelia pretended not to hear, "Oh, dear sister, I just can't. Besides I'm beat. My baby worked me over good last night." She winked at Lily Mae who almost dropped a biscuit between quiet snickers. Ofelia's mischievous streak delighted in unnerving Elaine's phony prudishness.

Elaine quickly flipped through the cards in her recipe box. *She's just like her mother, a whore breaking up a family.* Elaine knew Greg Wallace, Ofelia's lover. He was one of the richest white men around and was married with two daughters.

Elaine's father had also been married with two daughters, yet he had kept Monique LeBlanc, his Brown Sugar Queen, at the exquisite Elysian Hotel in the center of town. After Elaine's mother died, he had moved Monique and their bastard daughter, Ofelia, into Shadow's Way. By then, Elaine had already turned her back on the family and was well on her way to a notable acting career in New York.

Ofelia sat down with her cup of coffee. "Just have everything delivered. I know ole Carlyle would love to see you," Ofelia teased. "He practically slobbers all over his shirt every time he gets near you."

Ignoring her, Elaine saw the letter sitting on the counter. "Where did this come from, Lily Mae?"

"This mornin's mail while you was out."

Elaine tore it open and began reading catching her breath. "Oh God, no. Rudy's coming." She'd almost forgotten she had a nephew. "Without so much as an invitation."

"Oh, but I invited him. I guess I forgot to tell you." Ofelia was delighted. "He's actually coming?"

"How dare you invite someone to my home?"

"It's our home, remember."

Elaine glared at her. "That's not true and you know it. How dare you."

Ofelia picked a strawberry from the fruit bowl on the counter and bit into it. "When will he be getting here?"

"Week after next."

"It's been years," Ofelia moved her fingers as if counting them off. "Oh, the fun we had."

Elaine slumped down on the nearest chair. "Lily Mae, bring me a cup of coffee." Her energy had drained into the floor's wooden planks. Her lifelong goal had been to be free of her family and she had succeeded in this area until over a month ago, when Ofelia showed up at her front door. And now this nephew.

After ten days Elaine had commanded Ofelia to leave. "This is my home as much as it's yours," Ofelia shouted back. "So I'm staying till I get ready to go back." She had left New Orleans to escape memories and heal a broken heart. Five months before, her fiancé, Roderick, had broken their engagement. Six weeks later, her Grand-mere died. These losses had toppled her emotional well-being. She had to get away from the sorrow and chose to revisit her childhood home and become acquainted with her estranged sister.

Unfortunately, Elaine didn't care about Ofelia's pain. Neither did she care about any relative who wanted to establish a relationship with her. She had seen Rudy only three times since he was born and that was enough for her. His mother, Gabrielle, had been her bothersome little sister who had died in a plane explosion over the Atlantic Ocean. Elaine hadn't bothered going to the memorial. *He's probably comin' to get even with me*. The color drained from her face.

"Elaine, you okay?" Ofelia asked. "You aren't looking well."

"I was too busy with this business, this bed 'n breakfast," Elaine snapped, "and couldn't go to Gabrielle's services. It was too much to ask of me."

"What does that have to do with Rudy? Sometimes Elaine, you..." Ofelia didn't want to go on. Elaine was staring into space, into another world. Ofelia continued, "I had just twisted my ankle while rollerskating and couldn't go either. But Grand-mere went." She paused taking another strawberry. "Grand-mere said Gabrielle was the kindest of the kind."

"Well, your Grand-mere didn't have to raise her," Elaine spat out as she stuffed the letter back in the envelope.

Ofelia sipped her coffee. "Why don't you want to have family around you.?"

"I've got things to do." Elaine stood up.

"All you have," Ofelia raised her voice, "is this old house and some fantasies about that great-grandfather hanging over the fireplace. That scoundrel Henri the first Chauvier."

"Don't you dare!" Elaine cried out. Lily Mae disappeared into the walk-in pantry.

Ofelia watched her sister move from the stove to the refrigerator and back again, aimlessly, lips moving in silent speech. Despite Elaine's hatefulness Ofelia felt sorry for her. She had no life outside of her business and "barely tolerable" customers, as she generally described them. This old house and the spirits who roamed its halls were the only things she cherished.

Wanting to make things better Ofelia suggested, "Close Shadow's Way for a week or so. Let's show Rudy a good time."

"There's the huge Carlyle wedding next Saturday. We'll be filled with wedding guests from Thursday till Sunday." Elaine flipped her head and declared, "And I may just go to New York for a few days."

"You're not going to New York and you know it." Ofelia leaned back with a laugh. "You're as stuck to this place as flies are to glue paper."

"And you're as frivolous as our father. Like him, all you want to do is live off others and have a good time."

More wide-eyed than usual, Lily Mae peeked out from the pantry. Ofelia remained undaunted. She shrugged her shoulders and announced. "Okay then, go to New York. Rudy and I will have a great time. Be sure to take your ghosts with you." She tossed the rest of her coffee in the sink. "This is bitter. Lily Mae, would you mind making me some of the good coffee that's reserved for the guests?"

Lily Mae stuck her head out again and looked at Elaine. She knew who the boss was.

Ofelia waited a moment. Lily Mae didn't move. Ofelia sighed and headed out, letting the screen door slam shut behind her.

Elaine forced her face into a placid expression and put the envelope in the letter holder next to her phone. Her hands shook ever so slightly. Her halfsister frightened her. Unlike everyone else, Ofelia wasn't in awe or afraid of her.

CHAPTER TWO

Archbishop Figurant gazed down the extended maple table, luminous from layer upon layer of bee's wax. Soon they would be arriving. It was going to be a hard-hitting but necessary meeting, long overdue. Abandoning protocol, he would be going against the Church's hierarchy to expose a long-lived charade of denial and hypocrisy. No longer was he going to hide the truth behind haughty self-righteousness. He was going to act.

Lanita entered the room with a large tray of chicken sandwiches and fruit pastries. "Oh, 'cuse me, your Excellency. I didn't know you were already here. I'll be out of your way in no time." Her words hummed with the rhythmic cadence of a Caribbean island. Neat as a pin in a freshly starched uniform and hair tucked away in a plain white turban, she slipped from point A to point B, with smoothness and efficiency.

"You're fine, Lanita. I'm trying to get my thoughts in order. You'd best put out some ashtrays. I anticipate Monsignors Flannigan and Murphy will burn up a field of tobacco when they hear what I've got to say."

She laughed out loud. "Maybe I should put out the whiskey, too, yes?

"No, they'll have to survive on coffee or water today." He smiled at her. "Be good for them."

He and Lanita had a comfortable relationship. She had been his housekeeper for six years. He knew some of her secrets and she knew some of his. Late afternoons he often watched her from the upstairs window as she rode her bicycle home, hair fanning out in an Afro halo and a colorful skirt billowing in the wind.

He knew only bits and pieces about her. He'd hired her right after the death of an old woman she had been caring for, a woman she loved like her own mother. Not long after that, she told him that she had run away from her island home by posing as a waitress on a cruise ship. "We docked in Miami and I've been sort of looking over my shoulder ever since." She paused and looked off in the distance. "I can still picture the place of my childhood." She spoke matter-of-factly as if she were telling him what was for dinner.

For reasons he couldn't explain, he felt a link connecting them. It seemed that they had known each other for eons, in many other lifetimes—even though he didn't believe in reincarnation.

There was a knock on the door. His secretary, Brother Damien, entered with a stack of papers. He was a tall, thin man who projected intelligence, competence and calmness. He wore a brown Franciscan robe which seemed to be the only appropriate attire for a man with his presence. "Here are all the reports, your Excellency." He turned to leave. "I'll be in the foyer greeting everyone."

Archbishop Andre sat down. He noticed that he was alone and wondered when Lanita had left. With a sigh he began perusing the pages. *Holy Mary Mother of God, what a mess.* This scandal could easily topple the whole Roman institution. Six cases had already been reported in his diocese alone. The grapevine buzzed that there were perhaps hundreds across the United States and thousands more across the world.

He dropped his head and felt the anger surge through him. He knew first-hand what this abuse could do to a small child, innocent and defenseless. He wished he had the power to defrock every pedophile priest out there, but he didn't. And unfortunately, the Pope was weak and controlled by a College of Cardinals who believed that denials and cover-ups were the absolute, infallible rights of the Roman Catholic Church.

Hours later the room was thick with curling smoke and floating distress coming from the six diocesan council members. Monsignor Rodin nervously tapped his pen on the table top, "Where's the proof?" he spewed out of a face, fat from years of over-indulgence. "Mother Church is always under attack by Her enemies."

"We have letters, testimonies," Brother Damien quietly interjected. "This has been going on for years, perhaps forever." He paused before continuing with emphasis. "The lid is beginning to be lifted and the truth is only going to get worse."

Archbishop Andre poured a glass of water. He raised his voice in authority. "Brother Damien is right. We all know the Church has always been the perfect haven, or rather hide-out, for deviant behavior." He adjusted his Roman collar and continued, "The ignorant masses trust their priests. Why? Because we've taught them that we are above them, better than they are." He emptied the glass. *God, how I could use a shot of whiskey!* "They've been told it's a sin to even question a priest, much less accuse one of molesting their child."

"Are you saying, Andre, that we don't have a Divine calling which separates us from the masses?"

Andre erupted, "I don't know. Do you?" Monsignor O'Malley leaned back as the words struck him. "Divine calling or not doesn't give any of us the right to abuse our power."

"So, you're proposing that we remove these priests from their duties?" Monsignor Schoon exclaimed in disbelief. "We already have a shortage of priests in the diocese."

The Archbishop rose up to his full six feet, four inches. "I'm not proposing. I'm demanding," he shouted. "Several large parishes have assistant priests. Those assistants can fill these vacancies."

Monsignor O'Malley spoke with hesitancy, "That will...greatly...impact...the work load of priests who have assistants."

"How can any one of you stand by and allow this to go on and still refer to yourselves as shepherds for Christ?" Andre sighed with disgust. "How can you pretend we don't have a serious problem here?"

A dead silence, sticky and dank, saturated the room. Finally, Monsignor Clarkson cleared his throat and said, "I commend you, Archbishop, for wanting to take care of these children."

What an ass-kisser, Monsignor Rodin thought.

"But what will we do with these deviants?" Monsignor Schoon asked. "Turn them over to the authorities?" They all faced Andre waiting for a response. He remained still.

Everyone in the room respected the Archbishop for being a strong and positive leader. True, some detested his methods and some bitterly resented his popularity, but each had to acknowledge that he had raised their diocese from near poverty to being one of the wealthiest in the country. Plus, the number of converts had tripled, and fallen-away Catholics began returning from the day he took this position. Unlike other hierarchy, he didn't hide in the mansion but went out among all the people, the poor as well as the rich. He broke with the tradition of clerical aloofness.

Monsignor Rodin looked directly at the Archbishop. "And after we expose these accused pedophiles, are we going to expose those priests who break their vow of celibacy?"

The Archbishop returned an icy stare. "Don't change the subject, Monsignor." The Monsignor's face turned red with embarrassment. Had he stepped over a boundary? *Perhaps those stories were mean-spirited rumors.*

"Besides," said Monsignor Baldeo, another Archbishop supporter, "these pedophiles are abusing children, the least among us. With consenting adults, whether it's a priest or lay-person, it's a matter of conscience."

Some looked away to stifle a chuckle. Monsignor Baldeo had long ago abandoned the constraints of celibacy. He and his secretary had been in a relationship for years and had, in fact, produced two children. It was rumored that they had gotten married in Mexico with the Archbishop's approval. However, they maintained separate households, and everyone looked the other way or pretended not to know.

The Archbishop stood up. The meeting had run its course. He leaned over the table and firmly planted his palms on the shimmering wood. "These priests are to be removed from their duties immediately. If anyone questions our actions, you tell the truth. I will not allow this great archdiocese to be mired in lies and cover-ups. This is 1985, for the love of Jesus. It's time."

He straightened up and looked at each of them. "We must, at the very least, give the impression that we care about our children. Our parishioners need to see that we're not a bunch of frauds." He lowered his voice just above a whisper. "No longer will this be swept under the carpet. We've all known that this was going on. I for one have known about it since childhood." He paused and looked up with sad and tired eyes. "Let this diocese be the pioneer in bringing this awful wickedness to the light. Others will follow."

The stillness was intense as each man sat frozen in his own knowledge of the Church's abuse of children. Finally Monsignor Williams spoke. "And what do you propose to do with these priests? Have them arrested?' His tone was cynical. You may be looking for a job as

I'm sure Rome won't sit still for that." Some murmurs and a snicker or two traveled around the table.

The Archbishop turned away disgusted and looked across the street at Shadow's Way. "Rather than have them incarcerated, I'd prefer to rehabilitate them, but until I get those plans worked out, I want you to inform these priests that they are being stripped of all pastoral duties that bring them in contact with children." He turned back to them, looking drained. "You can assign them to clean the grounds, help with secretarial duties, drive the elderly to Mass, or any other chore that doesn't put them in contact with children. Understand?"

He went back to his desk and dropped down in his chair. "And prepare yourselves for more cases. Once people know that we are no longer in denial, they will start coming forward with more accusations."

He looked directly at each of them in turn. "Understand? Understand? Understand?" Except for Monsignor Rodin, they nodded their heads in agreement.

"You are dismissed." Without another word he rose and left the room.

He hurried down the wide hallway to his private chambers. He wanted to get away from all the corruption, the Church's as well as his own. He recalled Monsignor Rodin's innuendo and wished he had remained on the farm, obscure with few or no responsibilities.

He entered the living room area of his apartment and headed straight to the bar where he poured amber whiskey from an elaborate cut-glass decanter into a coffee cup. He downed the drink in one gulp, then crossed over to his desk and picked up the phone receiver. He hesitated struggling with his demons. Finally giving in to his lower nature, he dialed a number.

"Yes, hello Madame Claudine."

He laughed, "I've been dealing with cover-up artists all afternoon, so I could certainly use a diversion this evening. Could you send Dominique over?"

A look of disappointment came over his face. "Oh, I'm sorry she's not feeling well."

He listened, then sighed. "I suppose Lydia will do but tell her tonight I don't want any talk about revolutions."

The Archbishop listened and then laughed. "You do that. No talking."

He hung up and waited, debating what to do next. With a determined nod, he dialed another number. It rang a long time before being answered.

"Hello, Elaine, this is Archbishop Andre. Could you meet with me Thursday morning around eleven? Something urgent has come up which we need to discuss."

CHAPTER THREE

Bastien Figurant sat on an overturned bucket outside his shack and administered first aid to a fox's rear leg. "The sorry-son-of-a-bitch that shot you should have his balls cut off. There, there, you'll be okay."

The fox, calm for a wild animal in the hands of a person, looked up into the kind face worn by alcohol and the outdoors. Despite the ravages of hard living, this man clearly was the exact duplicate of Archbishop Andre. True, he was frayed and coarse, whereas his twin was refined and distinguished. Yet both were handsome men with olive skin and dark brown hair and eyes. Bastien was thinner than his brother but maintained a good solid frame.

Bastien picked up a vial and cursed under his breath when he saw that it was empty. "Dammit," he said to the fox. "You have to have this medicine, but I done drunk the last of my allowance which means I have to go begging again to my holy brother."

Unexpectedly, the fox lurched forward just before Bastien heard the distant sound of a car motor. The lane to his cabin was still empty. "Don't worry, don't worry. I'll put you back where you'll be safe." He quickly carried the fox over to the assortment of pens holding animals in various stages of healing. There were four dogs recovering from starvation, two kittens he had found in a tote sack by the side of the road, a brown rabbit whose front paw had been mangled in a trap, and an orphan fawn, only a few days old.

Now the car was turning onto his lane. "I'll be damn if that ain't a police car," Bastien froze for a moment. "What did I do now?" Then he flung a checkered blanket over the fox's cage. "Now, you just relax. You're safe."

The car stopped next to the rusted shed with "Figurant's Car Repair" painted in once bright yellow letters, now weather faded and dull. An officer climbed out and yelled in a heavy Cajun accent, "My friend, Bastien, how you be?" White teeth gleamed like wet pearls in his black leathery face. Bastien exhaled relief and with a big smile limped towards him. Bastien's right leg had been as stiff as a board all day, a sure sign that a big rain, maybe even a hurricane was forming somewhere.

"My friend, Leone. What brings you out to here? That police car gave me a fright. For some reason I didn't think it'd be you." The friends hugged each other warmly. "Sorry I can't pour you no drink, but I got some chicory coffee still from this mornin'. It'll put hair on your chest, I guarantee."

"Too hot and sticky for coffee." Leone took off his hat and wiped his brow on his shirt sleeve. "Just come out to warn ya. That Bradley boy, you know that ole bastard Colonel Reggie Bradley's boy? Well, he be campin' out nite 'fore last and says someone stole his fifteen-hundred-dollar rifle from outta his truck. Being everyone knows how you hate people killing animals, he's going around sayin' you stole it.

Bastien thought of the orphaned fawn, hardly a day old, lying on the ground in a pool of blood next to its dead mother. He had carried the baby back to his cabin and fed it formula water, all the while feeling his anger grow into a rage too great to control. He had emptied the last bottle of whiskey on the shelf and left. But now his mind was jumbled up with chopped up bits and pieces from the evening: a man snoring loudly in the tent, the huge pickup, two large ice chests packed with cut-up deer, a rifle glinting in the moonlight on the back rack. Wanting to kill the man in the tent, but then his mother whispering, "No, no, my sweet Bastien. Remember Jesus."

Then the bend of the river and the rapidly flowing current. Striking the rifle against a tree trunk time and time again until it became shattered beyond use. Making sure all the parts were picked up and thrown into the flowing water. Watching them being swept far away. Bastien sat down knowing that if he told Leone any of this, his best friend would have to do his duty and make out a report. And Bastien knew Leone wouldn't do that. But still he wasn't going to put this good man into such a predicament. Bastien shook his head and looked away. "No, I hadn't gone much of any place, not far at all. Can't get around with this leg, you know."

Leone smiled. He didn't care that his friend was lying. From the time they had begun walking, they'd been partners, roaming these low lands, pretending to be explorers. Leone had come out here only to warn Bastien of possible danger. "Okay, then you watch out for that Bradley trash. And oh, listen, Darlene told me to tell you come by for some jambalaya. She love to cook for you." He laughed. "It do make her feel good cause you eat so damn much."

Bastien swallowed the lump in his throat as he watched his good friend get back in his car and drive away. It made him want to ask God why the hell He didn't create more men like Leone. Life would be so much safer and easier to get around in. But most people said God knew what He was doing. *"And God, why can't I be like regular men and not give a damn if a baby deer's mama gets killed?"* As if reading his thoughts, one of his hounds wandered over, licked his hand and whined softly.

The 1980 black Mercedes sped down the road. Every five years the Archbishop would get a new car and give Bastien his used one. In return, Bastien kept both cars in excellent condition. He was a genius when it came to car repair and maintenance. He was also a self-taught and gifted veterinarian. Yet only the old timers brought him their cars and animals. Unlike the newcomers, they weren't put off by his alcoholic behavior or the squalor of his living conditions.

Bastien parked in his brother's driveway and hurried to the back door. After several loud knocks, Lanita opened the door. "Mon cher Bastien. Take those dirty shoes off on the steps. I just mopped. Now wait here." She disappeared and soon returned carrying a pair of clean socks.

"Darlene's doing my wash this week." Bastien sat on the top step and removed his filthy socks.

Lanita held the door open and smiled. "That's good. Remember you soak 'em good in hot water before takin' 'em over. Don't want you ruinin' any more washers."

Bastien stood just inside the door and watched Lanita. She reminded him of one of his stray animals, so beautiful and so innocent. He wished he had the courage to ask her out for coffee or a catfish fry, but she might say no, or even worse get insulted. Besides, he was too shy.

"You look nice, Bastien. You shaved, yes?"

"And even scrubbed my teeth." He laughed at his joke.

Lanita liked this man. Yet she also feared him. Through closed doors she had heard the anger and contempt he harbored against his brother. Both men confused her. Bastien could be gentle one moment and violent the next. Andre could be caring one moment and cold the next. Bastien's behavior could be blamed on drinking but Andre's was a mystery.

"Go on down, your brother's in his office." She shooed him with a dishtowel. "I still got an oven to clean."

Andre was sitting at his desk as Bastien opened the door without knocking. His brother's sudden appearance startled him, but he quickly recovered. "Bastien, how good to see you. You must be out of money? So soon?"

Bastien felt his stomach tighten. He hated needing help from this man who had turned away from him when he needed help. He clenched his teeth. "Yeah, I got a fox that some son-of-a-bitch shot and no medicine and I need to get food for all of them. I ain't been gettin' much work. Only two paying ones in eight days, Mr. Lou Tantene's German Shepherd and then ole' lady Clarise's junky Ford."

Bastien began nervously swaying back and forth in his chair. Andre knew what this signaled. "It's okay, Bastien, it's okay. Would you like a glass of ...?"

"Yes," Bastien interrupted. "I don't have no more whiskey either. You never give me the rich stuff like you pour down your throat. I like what you drink."

Andre poured his brother a drink and handed it to him. "What are you talking about? I gave you three bottles of this exact whiskey a couple of weeks ago."

"No, you didn't. You pour the cheap stuff into your empties and then give 'em to me."

Andre didn't respond. His brother had not had a drink today, so it would do no good to say anything. He removed a picture of Jesus with little children hanging on the wall next to his desk and began turning the combination on the safe.

Bastien watched his brother count out a number of bills and suddenly felt bad about his behavior. "Andre, you are good to me and I'm sorry I'm ...." He stopped, afraid to go on. "You know the other night I think I did a bad thing."

Andre sighed, praying to maintain his patience. "How bad was it?"

"It's some demon shadow that I don't see a-comin.'" Bastien poured more whiskey into his glass.

"You want to tell me about it?"

Bastien shook his head.

"Is it something that could put you back in prison?"

Bastien gulped down his drink, grabbed the bills in his brother's hand and scooped up several unopened bottles on the bar and walked out of the room.

Andre closed the safe and gazed at the picture as he put it back in place. "May those child molesters rot in hell."

CHAPTER FOUR

Lydia closed the door to the Archbishop's bedroom and tiptoed around the dimly lit study, admiring the artwork and décor. No matter how many times she came here, she was always amazed by the riches. Her long tie-dyed skirt and t-shirt embossed with a rainbow peace sign confirmed less materialistic values. "Oh man, so much needless opulence," she spoke just above a whisper. "It's downright decadent." She lit a marijuana cigarette and flung the flower-entwined plait of auburn hair over her shoulder. "But he does help the poor." Madame Claudine had told her that there was always some beggar hanging around the backdoor getting a handout and about his weekly trips to the poor sections with baskets of food.

She inhaled deeply and blew a puff of smoke at a medieval icon of the Virgin Mary and reflected, *he's got his own karma to deal with,* she stifled a drug-induced giggle, *and who am I to get all judgmental? I've just spent two hours with this wealthy man of God, pleasuring every inch of his body.* She inhaled deeply, *wealthy man of God! That's what's called an oxymoron.*

Madame Claudine never tolerated criticism from any of the "Archbishop's four girls" as she called them. "Always remember he provides for you so that you don't have to go anyplace else. Complain and go back to the streets and forget about this cushy life." This threat had kept Lydia and the others in their place, but tonight Lydia sensed this comfortable life could be coming to an end. Something was obviously bothering the Archbishop.

He said softly, "I may not be seeing you again." As she was about to leave. Then with a hint of scorned laughter, "But who knows? I'm the weakest of men."

Lydia knew very little about the Archbishop's other three ladies. Madame believed in keeping them separate to avoid jealously and bickering. "Am I his favorite?" or "Who does he like best?" Madame never answered such silly questions and would add, "His requests depend upon his mood and his needs in that moment."

Lydia removed a tiny covered ashtray from the cloth bag on her shoulder and carefully snuffed out the joint. She slid the ashtray closed before dropping it back in the bag. "Time to go, I guess. Come and go and no one knows a thing." She reached behind one of the books on the shelf and pressed the button. A wall next to the bookcase opened three to four feet. She slipped through and disappeared into the darkness. The wall slid back into place.

Lydia was the Archbishop's only American lover. She was his free spirit, vibrant and full of stimulating ideas. Each of the others provided their own form of amusement. Dominique, a French singer, charmed him with her beautiful voice and invigorating massages that culminated in untold ecstasy. Camilla, a Spanish woman his age, pampered him with poetry readings and quiet intercourse. The last was Gayla, an Irish lass and former nun, who would pray with him before discarding her habit in an exotic strip tease and lap dance. Of the four, Dominique was the most requested because she was the most like Elaine, his inexplicable obsession.

Years ago, when Andre was first introduced to Madame, he contacted her almost every week requesting one of the ladies. Lately his passions and interests were tapering off. In the past year, he had called her only three times.

Elaine descended the front stairway in a flowing antebellum gown, carrying a lighted candelabrum. She stopped midway to look down into the foyer, the dining room and living room, just to make sure she would be all alone with her G-G-Daddy, the family patriarch. It was well after midnight, but she never took a chance on being discovered. She generally avoided the main stairway, but tonight there were no guests to intrude upon their privacy. Just two weeks ago, a Michigan woman came in late from bar hopping and caught a glimpse of this lady from the Old South. The next morning when the woman asked about the woman, Elaine exclaimed, "Oh my great-grandmother inspects the cabinets to make sure the servants haven't made off with any silver or precious things." Due to this woman's spreading word of a ghostly sighting, Elaine had booked four reservations within three days.

As Elaine entered the living room she smiled at the portrait of her great-grandfather, Monsieur Henri Chauvier the first, regally standing over the mantel. She set the candelabrum on the corner table and when she turned back she saw that her G-G-Daddy was now sitting in the Queen Anne armchair next to the fireplace. "Oh Grand-pere, you've arrived." He smiled. He loved seeing her in this dress, which fell over her shoulders exposing creamy white skin.

"You are looking well, mon Grand-pere." She smiled and seductively fluttered a black lacy fan in front of her face. "Guess who's coming to visit? No, silly, not Robert E. Lee." She sashayed around the room. "Someone you haven't met. Your great-great-grandson, Gabrielle's boy." Holding her skirt up ever so slightly, she tiptoed towards the coffee table. "Perhaps you would like for me to introduce you to him."

She stopped abruptly, startled. "Oh, yes, forgive me. You're right. I forgot. That wouldn't be a good idea." Her voice and facial expressions became those of a small child, a child who's being scolded. "I know, I know. This is our secret. No one must ever know. I promise to never to say a word." She crossed her heart.

Then the grown-up Elaine recovered, curtsied and sat across from him on the Chippendale sofa. She listened attentively as he spoke. After a few minutes she sat upright, a bit indignant. "Of course, I'm still your Virgin Queen, just as pure as Queen Elizabeth the first." She looked away, peering into the past. "Of course, when I was an actress, I sometimes pretended to be a wayward woman, but that was only play acting, long ago." She waved the fan vigorously. "But there's no more role playing, except when you advise me to do so."

The little girl once again, she listened and giggled quietly. *You are my Queen, my Virgin Queen. You are the best one in this family. The rest have all been great disappointments, but not you.*

Suddenly Elaine stood up. "Where are my manners? Would you care for a sherry or do I have to ask?" She glided over to the cabinet bar, humming "My Darling Clementine" and poured the amber liquid into aperitif glasses. She placed one on the small table next to the Queen Anne chair and sat down across from the chair with her glass. Deep in thought she sipped and twisted at a bow on her skirt. Finally she cried out, "You have to help me. I don't know what to do. I've worked so hard to keep Shadow's Way in the family, mainly to please you. And now it seems..." Her voice broke into whining sobs as her mind went back to that morning's awful encounter.

Since the Archbishop's call she had been anxious about this meeting. At eleven sharp, Lanita had led her into the Archbishop's office. "Would you like a cup of coffee?"

"I think not," Elaine snapped rudely. She had always harbored an animosity towards this lowly servant woman from the islands who would look Elaine in the eye as if she were an equal.

Calmly Lanita stared at her for a moment before leaving the room. *Something's not right with her.* She had once tried to warn the Archbishop. "Be careful of her. She walks with shadows." He dismissed this with a chuckle. "No need to worry. I understand her."

Andre entered the room and paused for a moment, fascinated as always by Elaine's beauty. He took her outstretched hand and kissed it gently. According to protocol she should have kissed his ring, but such formality was out of the question with this one. Andre's family had worked the land that once belonged to her family. She was and always would be superior to him. His success and wealth were no match when compared to her breeding.

Her pretense annoys me, yet she still controls me. With an exaggerated flourish, he offered her an overstuffed chair. She was the queen approaching her throne, aided by a faithful servant. Once she was settled, he sat down across from her. His brilliance, his wealth, his strikingly handsome face always impressed her. She smiled sweetly and thought, *if only he had been born into a better family, perhaps, I could have....*

She shook her head ever so slightly at this thought and glanced out from the formal living room window at the marble plaza in front of the Cathedral. A glorious statue of the Virgin Mary reigned at its center. She felt comforted. She had always been devoted to the Virgin and the Church. On the mornings she didn't go to the pool she attended Mass, drowning herself in the ritual, losing her identity to an even greater degree than when she was with her G-G-Daddy. And then at Sunday High Mass, she became the voice of the choir, the perfume of the incense, the light of the candles, a powerful goddess melting into the blood and sinews of the high priest. The altar was her Athenian temple, her sacred stage.

"Before we get down to business, how about a glass of your favorite sherry?" Andre got back up and took down his most expensive Venetian glasses from the shelf above the bar. He knew he'd have to use the best and be on his best to manage this meeting.

"That would be wonderful." She forced a laugh. "It's almost the afternoon so I suppose if I imbibed I wouldn't be terribly naughty, would I?" She arranged herself into an alluring pose, crossing her long legs and allowed her skirt to slide above her knees. As far back as she could remember her legs had delighted him.

As a girl she would often come with her father to check on the rentals, the family property since the plantation days. Gabrielle usually refused to go saying it was a blot on their souls that their ancestors had owned people and forced them to work that land. "I don't want to set foot on such unholy ground." While her father praised Gabrielle, "I feel a lot the same way, my dearest," Elaine kept silent and thought, *I'd still own them if I could.*

As soon as they arrived at the tenet farm, Elaine would skip off with Andre. His strange twin, Bastien, usually hung back and watched. He was terribly sweet, but different in a way she couldn't grasp. Yet she was never nervous around him, whereas Andre frightened her a bit. She suspected Andre could see her secrets.

"When you come out here," Andre told her one day, "I like to look at your legs. But you already know that, don't you?" He smiled slyly and handed her the small bouquet of wild flowers he had just picked.

From the beginning they were bound by a power struggle. Andre excelled in school whereas Elaine couldn't be bothered. When on the brink of failing her classes, she demanded that he let her copy off his papers. "Or else, I'll have my father kick your family off the farm."

"I'll tell you what," young Andre laughed, knowing that Henri the second would never do such a thing, "I'll let you copy my homework and sometimes off my tests if you'll pull up your skirt all the way to your panties and let me look for as long as I want, whenever I want." So, she held up her skirt and felt powerful because he was doing as she wanted. And he felt powerful because he was getting what he wanted.

On her sixteenth birthday, Andre had another request. "You're out of your mind to think I would kiss you much less be your girlfriend." Elaine was indignant. "You think just because I let you see my legs I'd let someone like you, a common renter, do more?" The stinging words stayed with him and spawned a vow to get even someday.

The homework copying and the leg showing ended as did all communication between them. A year and a half later he left for the seminary. She flunked out of school and left for New York. She never saw him again until the day she came begging him to save Shadow's Way.

"Elaine, Elaine, come back." Andre's voice pulled her back to the sweet-smelling sherry. "You were off again in one of your worlds."

One of my worlds? She detested even a mild reprimand. *My vivid imagination is what puts me above people like you.* "Oh, I'm afraid the sand man couldn't find my bedroom last night," she faked a yawn, "so I'm a little weary."

She was acting and generally he had enjoyed figuring out the reasons for the show; however he had since grown tired of the performances. He cleared his throat. "I want to discuss our arrangement." He noticed some of the color drain from her face and smiled. His time for getting even had come. *Am I just the sharecropper's son now?*

"We have a problem in the Church. As you may have already heard, cases of priests molesting children, mostly boys, have been surfacing. As the Archbishop of this diocese, it is my duty to take care of the children."

He paused. She stared at him, not sensing where this could be going.

"I want to have these priests confined, incarcerated if you will, in a place where they can receive psychiatric treatment." He took a few sips of sherry. "And it seems that Shadow's Way is the perfect place for that."

Elaine placed her hand over her heart as she struggled to breathe. Andre continued, "You can remain there, rent free as before, but instead of having your regular customers, you will have these pedophiles as your guests. You'll be compensated as an employee of the Church."

She sprang up. "You are a sordid, hideous creature." She shook her fist at him. "I shall tell everyone. I will."

"What shall you tell, Elaine?" Andre was amused. "You have nothing to tell."

Elaine steadied herself and slowly walked over to the window. "I have the papers."

She turned to face him and dropped into a Betty Davis impersonation. "Priests are holy men, incapable of such hideous acts. All priests that is, except you. Years ago, I refused to be your mistress and now you're having your revenge by stealing my home, my soul's refuge."

Andre was impassive. Her personality changes no longer surprised or even interested him. She raised her glass in a mocking toast and then emptied it in one long gulp. The glass clanged as she set it on the bar's marble counter. "Once again, I've been betrayed."

She bowed her head and folded her hands in a prayerful mode. "Now I must go to the church authorities, pray for your soul and ask God to forgive you for all your lecherous ways."

Andre could not contain himself. "Elaine, just stop with the act. You don't fool me."

Her memory joggled back to high school when her English teacher had humiliated her, "You're not on the stage in my classroom, so stop acting." The whole class had laughed at her.

The hall clock chimed several times. Elaine sat alone in the dark. The candles had burned down to clumps of wax spilling onto the table. From the street light outside the front window, she saw that her great grandfather was once again in his picture frame. *Is he sneering at me?* She looked away. Everyone was turning against her, just as they had on her mother. She could be homeless. No she was too smart for that. The plans had begun. She pulled herself up and screamed at the portrait. "Save your judgment. No one will conquer me like the Yankees conquered you. You're the one who lost, not me." She ran up the stairway, stumbling, pulling off the gown, stepping out of the petticoats. A flowing river of lace and crinoline cascaded down the steps.

CHAPTER FIVE

The flight to Savannah had been pleasant enough. He had avoided flying as much as possible since his mother's death, but when he got Ofelia's note, he knew he had to go and so he crossed his fingers and boarded a plane heading south. He planned to spend a few days in this beautiful Southern town and get acclimated to this peculiar part of the world, then go on to the deep, deep South to visit his Aunt Elaine. But first, he wanted to look up a college girlfriend now living here and who knows—perhaps reignite a flame. While at the car rental counter, he decided he'd drive the remaining four hundred and fifty miles down to the ancestral home. The road trip would give him time to fortify himself against his Southern roots.

Rudy Chauvier Landon laughed inwardly as he recalled the debacle at his grandfather's funeral. He'd been nine-years-old and the whole thing could best be described as a third-rate horror flick. Even before his family had set off for that foreign land, he'd overheard his mother on the phone begging her doctor, "You have to prescribe some tranquilizers for me. I can't make it otherwise." The boy Rudy knew that only kooky people took those pills. His friend's mom took them all the time and she never knew what day it was and didn't give a damn if her son and his friends trashed the house or not. So he assumed and rightfully so, that the days ahead would be different if not downright fun.

The entertainment exceeded all his expectations when the prescribed pills had the opposite effect on his mother. Rather than calming her, they wired her to the extreme. She couldn't sit still and was constantly moving about, and she talked nonstop. She cooked-up platters of meats and pots of vegetables, cleaned the bathrooms twice a day, and swept the floors at all times. On the other hand Aunt Elaine, whom he had only seen twice before, slunk around like a feral creature who gazed at everyone with laser eyes and a squished mouth. She seemed like an alien, beamed down from some far-off planet. The sisters argued over everything–what the obituary should say, which suit Henri the second should be dressed in, where he should be buried.

"He doesn't deserve to be buried in white ground," the alien hissed. "Put him next to his whore."

"He married his whore," his mother had screamed. "And she was your stepmom."

"That's a lie, a lie spread by vile people."

Bernie, Rudy's dad shook his head and remained silent when Rudy asked, "Dad, what's a whore and where is white ground?" After that, Bernie took care to get his son as well as little Ofelia out of the house as often as possible. He carted them downtown to an old fashioned ice-cream parlor where they tried every flavor. He took them to a museum where they chased one another from one exhibit to another. They roamed the parks and slid down the slides. And Rudy fell in love. Ofelia was beautiful, smart, fun and his junior by ten months. She was perfect, and on the ride to the airport to go back home, he announced his intentions to marry her.

Upon hearing this, his mother turned all the way around in her seat. "What are you thinking? She screamed. "She's my half-sister."

"Gabrielle, calm down for Christ's sake," his dad yelled, having had enough. "And throw away those goddamn tranquilizers." He grabbed the bottle, rolled down the car window and pitched it out.

In the end, the sisters came to an agreement. Their father was cremated, and his ashes were divided between his first wife's white grave and his second wife's black one. After the memorial Ofelia sat in a corner of the kitchen and cried, "Grand-mere says daddy's with mommy now and is happy. Do you think that's true?" Rudy couldn't answer.

He left Savannah after wandering the streets alone for two days. The college girlfriend had gotten married over Christmas and wasn't even interested in meeting him for a drink. The expectations of a love-making marathon had evaporated into the sticky humidity. While roaming through the city, he managed to pick up a smattering of Southern English like fixin'ta, galldern, sure'nough, muchabliged and pitchin'afit. There were other words and phrases he hadn't been able to translate.

The closer he got to his destination the more anxious he became. His mother had never liked the South. "The hypocrisy and spitefulness down there'll dry out your bones." According to the map, he was only ten miles from Shadow's Way when without warning, steam began billowing from the hood of the car. The temperature needle was flat over in the red section of the dial. Just ahead he spotted a faded sign, Figurant's Car Repair. Although an unbeliever he blurted out, "Thank you, Jesus," a common expression he'd heard dozens of times since crossing the Mason-Dixon.

The car crawled down the lane and died next to a rusted shop surrounded by junk in varying degrees of decay. Rudy swallowed. *My years of karate training might come in handy.* He saw Bastien walking up from some animal pens, wiping his hands on a rag. He was dirty, but he didn't look like a retarded inbred, an observation that both surprised and pleased him. The man was rather handsome and seemed intelligent.

Rudy smiled and called out, "I think I've killed this rental car. I hope you can bring her back to life."

"Well, I have raised some that would've been put six feet under by other mechanics," Bastien mumbled dryly.

Rudy put out his hand for a shake. "I'm Rudy, Rudy Landon. Rudy Chauvier Landon. You may know of my relatives."

Bastien started to put out his hand, but then pulled it back. "You related to Elaine Chauvier?"

"The very one. She's my aunt."

"You're little Gabrielle's boy?"

Before Rudy could nod, Bastien enthusiastically went on, "Oh, she was a pretty girl. Pretty and sweet, not a thing like that sister of hers." He stopped and took a step back. "Oh, don't mind me and my mouth."

"No offense taken." Rudy laughed. "I haven't seen my aunt since I was a boy, but what I do remember is a little scary."

"And oh, I was sure sorry about what happened to your mama. I cried when I read it in the paper. I'm glad you weren't with her."

Rudy paused thinking about this. "Yes, I guess that part was good. She was coming back from a conference on crimes against children."

This touched a nerve in Bastien. "You don't say. She was a good one alright." His hands shook as he popped the hood of the car. He reached in his back pocket for his flask and took a long swig. All it took was one look. "Wooeee," he whistled. "What I figured. Busted radiator hose. But I can have her purring like a kitten in a few days."

After a short discussion, they arranged for Bastien to drive Rudy over to Shadow's Way and come back to get him as soon as the job was finished. Rudy insisted on giving him money in advance. Bastien liked him. "You're like your mama," he said shyly, then added,

"Your granddaddy was a nice man too, though some folks was down on him cause he was married to a ... oh well, never mind that. Like me, your granddaddy never cared 'bout what comes off people's tongues or rots in their minds."

On the ride into town Bastien talked nonstop. Some of the family stories Rudy had already heard from his mother. "Remember, little Ofelia? Well, she's at Shadow's Way too."

"Yeah, I got a letter from her a few weeks ago."

"Been living with her Grand-mere and Grand tante. Finished that college there in New Orleans and is all growed up, really something to see. Pretty, you know."

"She was always beautiful, even as a little girl." Rudy smiled recalling that past time.

"But then, some months back," Bastien continued, "her Grand-mere died, God bless her, and so she showed up at Shadow's Way. I hear Elaine didn't like it one bit, but Ofelia stood her ground, waved some papers in Elaine's face and says, 'This is as much my place as yours.'" Bastien laughed. "She told her alright."

He removed a whiskey bottle from under the seat, took a swallow and handed it to Rudy. Rudy shook his head. "That's the truth alright." Bastien cleared his throat and spat out the window. "Lily Mae, her maid, always tells me what's going on. The thing that chapped Elaine real good was those papers, I guess a will, saying one third of everything was hers."

"Yes she wrote me about that."

Bastien took another swig from the bottle. "Yeah, and she moved into one of the cottages that used to be the servant quarters cause 'that's where my ancestors lived,' she said, but I think she just don't want to be under the same roof as Elaine. That's damn smart, too."

Rudy was silent. Before receiving Ofelia's letter, he had never given a thought to any inheritance. His mother had told him that his grandfather had spent everything. "He would take his new wife and daughter to Paris and stay for months barring no expense, and when he ran out of money he'd sell off another parcel of land or one of the businesses. He did what he wanted, God bless him. Shadow's Way was mortgaged to the teeth when he died."

Rudy had been with his grandfather for short visits when he was one, four, and five, yet he always felt a bond with him. He liked this grandfather who didn't follow the customs.

That night Rudy lay in bed, staring at the high ceiling of imprinted tin and an enormous cut-glass chandelier. *All that weight could pull down that old ceiling.* He scooted over to the edge of the bed. *I'd be cut to shreds.*

Aunt Elaine had insisted that he have the room where Robert E. Lee had stayed. "Who knows, he may visit you." She winked at him, then resumed gushing about the grandeurs of Shadow's Way. Rudy noticed that she always used the name Shadow's Way, never once saying this house or this home. "Shadow's Way is so wonderful to me," she whispered. "Shadow's Way always looks out for me." She seemed to be talking about a lover rather than a structure of wood, tin, plaster and tile built around a hundred and fifty years ago. Rudy detected a flirtatious tilt of her head when she concluded that "Shadow's Way loves me like no other." There was a dark shadow hiding in plain view.

Earlier that day Bastien had dropped him off at the end of the sidewalk with his suitcase and duffle bag at his feet and began driving off. "I would help you to the door," he called out from the pickup window, "but your aunt treats me like I'm something she'd like to squash under her shoe." Rudy began the trek towards the porch, all the while intuiting something closely akin to horror. He paused to gather his composure before climbing the four polished steps to the entrance.

Before he could push the bell, the door flew open and Ofelia wrapped her arms around him with laughter and loud exclamations. Finally, she released her hug and stood back. "You are all grown-up," he said with surprise.

Ofelia swatted at him. "Well, what did ya expect, Goofy Goo?" He'd forgotten she always called him that. "You've gotten a tad bit bigger yourself."

Rudy heard an exaggerated throat clearing. Aunt Elaine was descending the stairs, more beautiful than he had remembered. Now that he was grown, he sensed a magnetism within her that could draw someone into what could only be called a web. He drew back inwardly protecting himself.

"My dearest Rudy," she hummed, kissing both his cheeks.

Rudy turned over in the bed and listened closely. *Are those footsteps?* They stopped just outside his door. "Yes, who is it?" he called. No one answered. Only deadly silence. *Is there really such a thing as a haunted house?* An outside streetlamp cast long shadows across the room. Then he heard a strange noise like someone or something with long claws scraping across the door's wooden panels. He pulled the cover up to his chin, self-conscious at being so terrified. Not since he was a little boy going through a carnival's haunted house had he been scared like this.

Once again he called out, louder this time, "What do you want?" He thought he heard a slight moan and then silence. "That house has a dark soul," his mother had said. "I believe it affected all of us in some ways."

In an effort to settle his nerves, Rudy reviewed the grand tour his aunt had given him that afternoon. "The back portion had to be rebuilt after the war," she explained, "because the damn Yankees were using Shadow's Way as their headquarters and set it on fire." She shook her head several times in disgust. "Can you imagine? They had a bonfire going in the back yard and their tale was that the wind shifted, but your great great-grandfather told me himself it was deliberate."

She inhaled quickly, "I mean that's what he wrote in his diary." Stunned, Rudy stared at her. She had meant what she said, "your great-great-grandfather told me." The room seemed to get darker. His impulse in that moment was to take off and he might have if Ofelia had not been standing next to him.

He turned over in bed with new courage. *Maybe my great-great grandfather is still walkin' and talkin,'* he thought, then shouted, "Come on in, you old geezer, you sorry old slave owner." He heard a soft scuffling sound moving away from the door and down the hall. He was too frightened to get up and have a look. *What would my frat brothers say if they saw me now?* Mimicking one of his friends, he called out, "Rudy, you're a pussy!"

Another strange incident occurred during the tour. At the very back of the house they came upon a door secured by at least a half-dozen locks and bolts. "My gosh, is this your Fort Knox?" he blurted out.

"No, dear nephew," Ofelia mocked, "that's Sista Elaine's lair where she hides the bodies. No one has ever been in that room and, according to Lily Mae, if you try to get in she'll put a curse on you."

Elaine glared at Ofelia, but Ofelia just glared right back at her. It was obvious that Ofelia wasn't afraid of this woman which helped Rudy relax a bit. "In this family we do love drama," Elaine smiled radiantly, "and I'm afraid my dear half-sister is not lacking in this respect." She tapped one of the locks. "There are always guests snooping around, so you can understand I have to ensure some privacy for myself."

She turned back to Ofelia. "And you know I have a cleaning girl from Bottom county who comes in every three weeks and gives it a thorough cleaning. That sneaky Lily Mae can't be trusted with my valuables."

By dinner that evening the whole atmosphere had changed. Elaine was so charming and entertaining that Rudy enjoyed being with her. She told hilarious stories and was more than kind towards Ofelia. "Rudy, you are so blessed to have an aunt as talented as Ofelia. She can sing like a lark." Rudy was confused. Had his earlier impressions and observations been wrong? But now in the dark he felt his first hunches had been correct. No one else was in the house besides Elaine and there had been footsteps and scratching outside his door. Tomorrow he would insist on staying in the other servant quarter next to Ofelia's. And if his aunt objected, he'd check into a hotel.

CHAPTER SIX

Elaine paced around her bedroom while whispering spirits swirled around. "You're going to lose your Shadow's Way." Ever since Ofelia had landed on her doorstep, fanning that later will in her face, Elaine had begun to feel as insecure as she had as a child. Now Rudy was also here claiming his share and that loathsome sharecropper's son was breaking his promise, "You can stay there forever."

From the shadows G-G-Daddy scolded, "Put your mind on something else before you become as crazy as your mother." He was right. Tight spots were a part of life, and they had never gotten the best of her before and they wouldn't this time either.

"G-G-Daddy, you can't let Shadow's Way be taken away again," she cried, but he was gone. She had to put her mind on something else.

Looking around the room, she resolved to bask in her surroundings. As with the rest of the house, she had spared no expense for her apartment. This space had originally been the outdoor kitchen, separate from the main part of the house because the summer heat coupled with wood burning cook stoves made for very unbearable living conditions. When window-units and then air-conditioning came along, her father added a section connecting the kitchen to the house. He reconfigured the space putting the new kitchen closer to the dining areas. He turned the old section into an area for entertaining his cronies with liquor, cards and lively intellectual conversations. Elaine grudgingly gave her father credit for these innovations, even though they were done after her mother's death, all for his beloved Monique.

When Elaine took over the house, she converted the poker parlor into her own area with a sitting section and bedroom. The walk-in pantry was divided into a bathroom and storage area and the storage space was converted it into a closet and dressing area. The large window was replaced by a stained-glass scene of a waterfall cascading down a mountain. It tinted the room in blues and greens and the cut-glass transom above the outside door altered the sun's rays into prisms of gold and yellow. The silk canopied bed, indeed the whole room, dazzled with colors. Elaine was proud of the transformations and felt beautiful and secure in this room.

But still the goblins invaded her private sanctuary. "Your beloved Shadow's Way is going to be snatched away. First it was the Yankees, then Ofelia and the bogus will and now Andre."

She raised the lid on a humidor and took out a cigar, the same type she imagined her G-G-Daddy smoked. Twisting it under her nose she inhaled the pungent aroma and decided she'd wait till later. Overcome by her worries, she leaned back on the chaise lounge and closed her eyes. *Of course, the main person to blame is my father, Henri the second.*

Her father's drinking, gambling and frequent trips to Frances and God knows where else with his nigra mistress and illegitimate brat had drained the family fortune down to nothing. True, everything had been lost in the Civil War but Henri the first, being the entrepreneur that he was, had recouped a great deal of the family's wealth as a pioneer in the ship-building industry, which his son, Gerard, successfully ran until his premature death at fifty-five from a brain hemorrhage. At the time Elaine's father was a twenty-one-year-old Harvard man. He had learned nothing about the family business and Gerard never interfered with his son's lifestyle, which was nothing short of prodigal. Henri the second was young and rich with no responsibilities except to keep his grades just above passing.

Henri the first had also been able to recover most of the family's land and when Gerard took over, he sectioned it into tenant farms. Most of the older poor whites in the area had rented and worked these parcels. However, once Henri the second took charge he began selling the parcels to cover his expenses. Then came the summer day just after the tail of a hurricane when his beloved Monique was strolling barefoot near the creek at one of their properties. She stepped on a water moccasin riled up from the storm and died before he could get her to the hospital.

Mrs. Connelly down the street said she'd never seen a man grieve like him. "Why, he'd walk the neighborhood all night long cryin' and callin' out, 'Monique, Monique.' It was a wretched thing to hear."

He took to going to the various creeks and streams at all hours of the day or night wielding a machete and hacking into bits all the snakes he could find. Finally, after several fearful calls from residents who witnessed the half-crazed man's behavior, the sheriff came out and confiscated his execution weapon. Two months later, Ofelia's Grand-mere LeBlanc took little Ofelia to her home in New Orleans. Henri then barricaded himself inside Shadow's Way where he stayed in seclusion for three years.

Elaine had just left the stage after her third curtain call when the stage manager rushed up. "Your sister called. Says it's very important." Elaine waved him away. Purposely taking her time, she removed her stage makeup and costume. Her friend, Lance and his lover were waiting at a swank bar on 45th. After enjoying a midnight breakfast with them, she hailed a cab to her apartment, put on her nightgown and then at two fifteen in the morning, dialed her sister's number. "This is for calling me in the middle of my standing ovation."

The receiver was picked up, dropped, and picked up again. A shuffling noise before a groggy, "Hello."

"Good morning, Bernie. Is that sister of mine around?"

Elaine heard him mutter, "bitch", before Gabrielle said. "For God's sake, Elaine, at this hour. I should have known." She paused hoping for an apology to no avail. "Dad's attorney, Mr. Dawson, called this afternoon. It seems that Dad is very ill. He found him lying in the back yard." She paused waiting for her sister to say something. After several seconds, she went on, "He's in St. Jerome's Hospital. We're leaving in the morning."

"Well, I'm in the middle of a Broadway show and then I have a call-back for the movie in Los Angeles, so…"

"Elaine, he's dying, in pitiful shape. If that won't get you there, then maybe you'll come to rescue Shadow's Way. Mr. Dawson says it's going to be auctioned off. The taxes haven't been paid in years."

Elaine blurted out, "That sorry scoundrel. I knew he'd lose it."

"Listen, Elaine, I don't want so much as a floorboard from that place. You can have it, lock, stock and barrel, but you'll have to pay the taxes."

Elaine tightened her grip on the phone. "I have to get up in three hours," Gabrielle said with a yawn, "so I'm saying goodbye. If you don't show up, I'll see it's auctioned off."

Elaine slammed down the receiver. She would have to go back. It was her duty to save Shadow's Way. She spent the rest of the night packing and by noon the next day was ready to leave, never to return to this life again. "You're going back home where you belong," G-G-Daddy whispered as she locked her last suitcase.

Despite the pleadings of agents, directors and producers, both in New York and Hollywood, Elaine never wavered. It was her destiny to live out her life with her great grandfather in the place and the time designated for her. In the beginning G-G-Daddy had not followed her to New York; however, when her career had been threatened he once again stood at the foot of her bed and told her exactly what she had to do. In a time of crisis he was always there.

His visits had begun when she was a little girl. Awakened by her parents' loud arguing she would crunch up into a ball terrified by what she heard. "I'm going to kill myself. You're a no-good whore monger." She would put a pillow over her head, but still she could hear her mother's shrieks and threats. Just when she thought she could take no more, G–G Daddy would appear at the foot of her bed. "Go to sleep, my little daughter," he soothed her." I'll stay here. Nothing will harm you." He looked just like he did in the picture over the mantel.

When the backdoor slammed, she knew her father was off to his whore. Then she'd hear her mother scream, "I'm going to end it." But G-G-Daddy continued calming her until she drifted off to sleep.

Gabrielle usually slept through the noise, but one night she bolted into her sister's room. "Elaine, Elaine, I heard mama in the kitchen. She's going through the knife drawer and she says she's going to cut out her heart." In a sleep stupor Elaine staggered downstairs. Her mother wielded a sharp steak knife and caught Elaine's upper arm.

Elaine looked at the blood seeping from the gash. Then someone else took over. Trixie was her name. G-G-Daddy had sent this girl years ago to help Elaine survive. Trixie was very strong. She threw their mother to the floor. With the uninjured arm Trixie drew back her fist and knocked their mother senseless. A tooth lay on the floor near her ear. Trixie picked up the knife ready to slice the unconscious figure's throat wide-open. "She's not worth it," G-G-Daddy was standing near the stove. "You can go now." He nodded, and Trixie vanished. Dazed Elaine saw the knife in her hand, dropped it and prayed that her mother would kill herself before Trixie did.

As Elaine tended to her bleeding wound G-G Daddy counseled her. "You must leave Shadow's Way for now. Go to New York and become a famous actress." So right after her seventeenth birthday and almost a year before high school graduation, she was on the train headed northward. No one came to see her off, and the scar on her upper right arm never went away.

Sometime later her mother finally succeeded in killing herself. Her father was making love to Monique, Gabrielle was rubbing her pregnant belly with coconut oil and Elaine was rehearsing her second lead. The telegram was waiting on her dressing table. *Your Mama's gone and done it all the way. Cut herself up good. God rest her soul. Lily Mae.* Elaine dropped the message in the waste can with a smile, relieved that the albatross around her neck had finally dropped into the sea. Her mother was buried the day her play opened so of course, she didn't attend the funeral.

She also missed her sister's funeral. "People make such a big deal out of funerals and what's the point?" she ranted to Mr. Carlyle at the fish market. "Besides, my sister's dead. I can't do a thing about that." But when her father died, that was different. "Shadow's Way belongs to you," G-G-Daddy whispered. She went back to claim what was hers.

A light knock on the door awakened Elaine. She had fallen asleep holding the unlit cigar. Another knock. "Yes, what is it, Lily Mae? It better be important."

"Aunt Elaine, sorry to bother you, but I just made a pitcher of passion daiquiris and thought you might like one."

It took her several moments to register that Rudy was the one delivering this invitation. "Oh, why, why yes, darlin'. I would love one. Be there in a minute," she said gaily, infused with new life.

"We're out on the gazebo."

Elaine's ebullience quickly faded. "We" meant that Ofelia would be there. Those two had hardly spent a moment apart since he arrived. Elaine saw Rudy at breakfast and sometimes at dinner, but the rest of the time he was off with Ofelia. It was true that they often asked her to come along. "Can't you see I have work to do?" She would decline and then feel left out.

She had wanted to tell Rudy to go back home during his very first breakfast when he announced, "Aunt Elaine, I hope it's okay if I move out to the other quarter." Elaine stopped buttering her biscuit. "You want to stay in the old slave quarter? You don't belong there." The tone of condescension irritated him.

"That room upstairs is too fancy for me, and ah," he cleared his throat, "when I come in late, I might disturb the other guests. But the main thing is I don't like to be spooked and well, I believe I heard scratching on my door and footsteps in the hallway last night." Before he could go on, Elaine got up, took her plate and went into the kitchen. A moment later, she returned and slammed down the cottage key next to his coffee cup, turned and walked out without saying a word. She didn't speak to him for two days.

Rudy knew he had to take her moods and childish behavior with a shrug and even humor. His mother's stories about growing up with a Mad Hatter sister still made him laugh. Then just before he left on this trip, his dad had warned, "Everyone has to walk on eggshells around Elaine or else there's hell to pay." Rudy wasn't about to walk on eggshells and yet he was determined to stay a few weeks since Ofelia was also there, and both wanted to get things settled with the latest will.

Elaine was pleased that Rudy and Ofelia wanted to have a drink with her. She put on a new sundress and matching sandals. While admiring herself in the floor length mirror, G-G-Daddy stood in the corner. "You are still the most beautiful. No one can begin to match your loveliness."

Armed with this compliment, Elaine glided outdoors to the gazebo. She was greeted with joyful shouts of "Welcome" and "So glad you're joining us." Elaine felt almost as loved as she had in front of an adoring audience. *Perhaps they do care for me. I must remember that they are still quite young and self-absorbed.* After a few sips of the delicious drink, she began to feel cherished by her handsome nephew as well as her bothersome half-sister.

The descending sun highlighted the yard in warm shades of gold and orange. Rudy and Ofelia had set a lovely table with yellow and red roses, her favorite flower. On top of that, they had ordered a lavish meal from Une Fleur's, one of the finest French restaurants in the area. She wasn't allowed to lift a finger and her glass was kept filled with the numbing fruit drink. Elaine felt spoiled, cared for and even loved in ways she had seldom experienced. For most of her life, she had been isolated, alone and neglected. G-G-Daddy was the only one who had really loved her, and even he would sometimes criticize, scold and make demands.

It was now dark. The daiquiri pitcher was empty. Very little remained of the salmon, crab salad, asparagus and potatoes au gratin. Lightning bugs competed with the twinkling lights strewn around the gazebo, flower beds and tree trunks. Elaine looked over the grounds, her fairyland, with pride. The effects were mesmerizing, and she was responsible, responsible for all the renovations and all the beauty. *I've done it all myself with the help of no one, absolutely no one.*

Hmmm, what about Andre? Don't you call that help? She twisted in her chair and wished she could have another drink. Opposite from her, Ofelia and Rudy sat quietly, smiling and looking her. She began to feel frightened. Something was closing in on her.

Ofelia began softly very kindly. "Elaine, you've turned this place into a paradise."

The compliment touched Elaine. "Thank you, my dear. It's been a labor of love."

"All these years you've worked so hard." Ofelia leaned in towards her. "Maybe it's time for you to realize your dreams and visit France or go back to New York, your old stomping grounds. Spend time in places you love."

Sparks of fear sent charges through Elaine. "What's going on?"

Rudy scooted his chair closer. "Wouldn't you like to be free of all this, the demanding customers, the constant work?"

Panic was bubbling up. Elaine sat up straight.

"I've talked to an appraiser," Rudy continued, "and was blown away by the amount of money we could get for this place." Rudy inhaled deeply and continued, "Ofelia and I are willing to let you have fifty percent since you're the one who's made the improvements and kept it up."

"And you can keep all the money you've made off this place, which legally is partially ours." Ofelia hurriedly added, "With the prices you charge I'm sure you've put away quite a bit."

All at once, the Furies were unleashed. Elaine shoved hard at the table toppling over bottles and glasses. A hardly recognizable malevolent creature now sat before them. "So that was your plan. You are despicable ingrates," she spat at them. "Yes, bribe the silly old lady with good liquor, delicious food, and charming conversation. Pretend you care for her, distract her and then take her home away from her. You'll be in hell before that happens."

She had kicked off her sandals earlier and now she had to crouch under her chair to find them. She slipped them on and stood up. "You've been deceived. Henri the first bequeathed Shadow's Way to me alone. No one else shall ever have it."

"Henri the first has nothing to do with this," Rudy said with a slight laugh. "Your father and my grandfather, Henri the second was the owner and in his last will, he left the estate to you, my mother and Ofelia or their heirs in the event of death."

"You pathetic boy, so much like your mother." She then turned all her force on Ofelia. "I know you're behind this and you'll pay. You'll pay." She practically ran to her apartment, all the time murmuring French. Echoes of door locks snapping into place bounced around the yard. Rudy and Ofelia were immobile. "Well, that didn't go as planned," Rudy sighed.

Inside, Elaine turned on a lamp draped with several scarves. In the dim light she sat at her dressing table and stared in the mirror. She could see the shadow of G-G-Daddy standing across the room. "What are we going to do now? Everyone is determined to take our home away."

G-G-Daddy whispered, "Your daddy's whore had a horrible death."

Elaine thought about this for some time and then laughed. "Why, yes. That's perfect."

"But not the whore's daughter. The holy one across the street. He's got the deed."

Elaine went to the center of the room and pulled back the rug covering a trap door. Swinging it open, she began to descend a steep stairway.

"Come with me. We have to prepare," she called to the shadow by the bed.

CHAPTER SEVEN

Lanita sashayed down the narrow dirt path to her tiny shotgun house. It was painted in island colors, seawater turquoise with sunshine yellow trim and a scarlet front door. The yard was enclosed by a low chain-link fence that kept critters out but allowed passersby to take in the beauty of all the plants, vines and flowers. She smiled realizing that her place looked like something from a child's picture book, perhaps a book from her own childhood.

Lanita loved her little dwelling. Since her mother's death, she had never been as peaceful or content as she was here. As she unlocked the front door her cat, Jangles meowed loudly, stretching and yawning from his porch chair.

"Oui, je suis ici. Bon soir, mon cher."

Jangles jumped off the chair and began rubbing against her leg.

"As-tu bien dormi?"

Only with Jangles did she speak French, her native tongue, and he alone shared her home. Sometimes she missed the Caribbean island, but she was never sorry she had run away. It had been a long journey from the island to Miami, to New York and finally to Alabama.

Her previous life had to remain a secret, or so she thought. On occasion, she had been tempted to confess to her benefactor, the Archbishop, about her birth name and what had happened. However, she kept her lips sealed and also lied to him about having a man in her life. The Archbishop had never been improper with her, yet she didn't fully trust him. He had his own secrets.

While cleaning his bedroom she would sometimes breathe in various perfume or lotion fragrances as she changed the stained sheets. There might be a long black hair on the pillow and at other times a few tightly permed red ones or an occasional short brown strand. "So, he entertains women. It's none of my business as long as he leaves me alone," she told Jangles as they sat on the front porch in the late afternoon sun.

The Archbishop's duplicitous nature as an ordained man of God and a morally errant one bothered her, but also gave her leverage, bargaining power if he ever discovered and then perhaps threatened to reveal her identity. "I know his kindness and generosity far outweighs his shadow side, but I still have to be careful." Jangles mewed as if he understood every word. "His twin, Bastien, on the other hand exposes his darkness to the world and hides his gentleness except with the animals. I don't know which I prefer." No longer interested in listening, Jangles jumped down to chase a field mouse into its hole.

Later that evening, Lanita fried plantains and wiped away tears that wouldn't stop. She was a motherless child with no family. She wished she could return to her island. She wished her mother had not died. She wished she could do something besides house cleaning. Once the last dish was washed and in the drain rack, she took off her apron. "Jangles," she announced as he followed her into the bedroom, "tonight, I have to shake my blues or else I'll end up in the bayou." The cat jumped up on the bed and watched her put on a yellow sundress with clusters of red and blue flowers on the skirt. "I'm going to the club, listen to the music, maybe dance some and maybe have a rum."

She parked her bicycle at the side of the building and walked around to the front. Gutsy blues music streamed out through the walls and lifted her spirits immediately. Just inside the door she waited as her lungs and eyes adjusted to the smoke and darkness before locating an empty table close to the dance floor. She was barely seated before a cocktail waitress hurried over and took her order. Even though it was still early, the place was beginning to fill up. Two tables over, she recognized the beautiful black woman staying at Shadow's Way. They had chatted briefly one morning while Lanita picked up a beer can someone had thrown in the Archbishop's yard. She was with a white man, boyishly good looking.

Ofelia noticed her and waved her to come to their table. Lanita cringed, *What the hell was her name? It started with an O, Olivia, no, it was an unusual name.* She grabbed her purse. *I need to be with people. So what, if I can't remember.*

Ofelia greeted her with a warm smile. "Hey Lanita, this is my nephew, Rudy."

"Your nephew?" Lanita blurted out.

"It's a long story, Ofelia said with a laugh. "Rudy, this is Lanita. She works for the Archbishop across the street."

Rudy stood up and shook her hand. Lanita felt an instant attraction. *Me and a white boy, ooh-la-la.* Lanita shook her head dismissing the idea. *I've been without a man for way too long.*

"Something wrong?" Rudy asked.

"No, no, I'm very happy to meet you."

"That's an island accent, isn't it? Love it. Keep talking." Rudy held out the chair for her to sit next to him. The music changed to a different tempo. Ofelia stood up. "Well, that's my cue. You kids have fun." Ofelia got up and headed for the stage. When the announcer said her name, Lanita sighed with relief. *Ofelia.*

Ofelia played a few chords and then electrified the audience with, "Somethin's Got a Hold On Me." People jumped up and hurried to the dance floor. Lanita inhaled, dumbfounded by the power and quality of her voice. Rudy leaned over, "She's great, right? And to think she's my aunt."

Aunt and nephew, the same age? Then she remembered the evening Lily Mae had filled her ears while basting a leg of lamb for Elaine's dinner party honoring Andre. "Why is Ms. Chauvier goin' to all this trouble for the Archbishop?" Lanita asked. "They hardly speak to one another."

"Well you sees," Lily Mae began, "rumor has it that the Archbishop kept Miss Elaine from losin' this place and bein' on the streets." Lily Mae chuckled. "That be all I can figure out. She feel she owe him somethin'. She do this 'bout ever three years or so."

Then later while the guests were having their cake, cognacs and coffee, Lily Mae filled her in on the story about Henri the second, Monique and their daughter Ofelia. And about Gabrielle and her death, and Rudy. "Henri's wife and daughter had babies just about the same time, only months apart."

After a couple of rum and colas, Lanita felt carefree and giddy. Rudy was a great dancer and she was able to follow his lead without a hitch. When Ofelia finished her last number, the crowd cheered. "More, more!" they cried. After several bows she gave in. "Thank you, thank you, my friends. I'll close with one for my Grand-mere who is watching me from up there." She pointed to the ceiling. The crowd got very quiet. Her soulful rendition of "Summertime" made Lanita cry.

"It's the rum," she told Rudy as he handed her his handkerchief, then added, "I think Ofelia and me must have been sisters in a previous life."

"Now the rum's talking," Rudy teased.

When Ofelia finished, a distinguished-looking white man in his mid-forties stood at the bottom of the steps leading up to the stage. He guided her down the steps and then kissed her cheek. Lanita caught her breath and looked over at Rudy. *What's going on with us black girls and white men?*

Ofelia introduced Greg to Lanita. Even though he was several inches shorter than Ofelia, he exuded an air of arrogance that defied his lack of stature. A receding hairline didn't hamper a face kept youthful due to the skill of a plastic surgeon.

Lanita silently gasped. T*hat suit of his is worth months of my salary and the Archbishop pays me good.* Ofelia started to sit down, but Greg stopped her by putting his arm around her waist, saying, "The champagne's waiting." It sounded more like a command than a statement. Lanita didn't like him.

"You two have fun now," Rudy said with a grin. Ofelia seemed to force a smile and then allowed Greg to escort her away. At the door, she turned and blew them a kiss.

"He's an ass," Lanita said.

"Yeah and she told me she came here to recover from an asshole in New Orleans." Rudy looked back at the door. "She's got so much fire, but she's like putty around him."

Lanita clicked her tongue, "A lot do that, go from the frying pan into the fire."

"Sad but true." Rudy put his arm around Lanita's shoulder and pulled her to him. "But let's forget about them and have some fun. What do you say?"

Lanita decided to throw caution to the wind. Rudy's youthful enthusiasm thrilled and prompted her to surrender to an evening of pleasures she hadn't experienced in some time. After a short drive, they were in the lobby of the hotel where Lanita had once applied for a maid's position.

Rudy told her that his grandfather had kept his mistress in this same hotel. "Ofelia was probably conceived here." They giggled loudly until the elevator doors opened to take them to the third-floor room. Lanita had never been a guest in a room like this. Several hours later, she awoke and looked over at the lovely man next to her. *You're something else.* She giggled softly noticing the crinkled and matted bed sheets.

Careful not to awaken the sleeping prince, she dressed quietly and slipped out. A cab took her to her bicycle. She peddled home on clouds only to be greeted by an unhappy Jangles who hissed and darted out the door to relieve himself. "Alors, desole, mon doux."

Forty-five minutes later she was in the kitchen at the Archbishop's. She offered no explanation for her lateness and thankfully, no one seemed to have noticed. She cleaned and cooked with a new zest, smiling while humming island tunes.

A little after three Lanita was peeling potatoes at the kitchen sink when the front doorbell rang. It rang again. *Brother Damien must be out.* Lanita wiped her hands on her apron. As she hurried through the dining room, library and parlor, it rang several more times. "My God have some patience." she said under her breath. Just as she got to the front door, the Archbishop came out of his office with a perturbed look. "I forgot that Brother Damien's on hospital rounds," he explained.

She opened the door to Rudy's smiling face. "Hi again." His exuberant greeting filled the foyer. "You disappeared this morning."

Andre came into the foyer. Lanita, bowed her head, embarrassed to the core.

"Oh, good afternoon, Sir." Rudy backed away.

"Don't tell me." Andre studied his face. "You must be Gabrielle's boy. I see the resemblance. Bastien said you were here." He continued with increased enthusiasm, "Come in, come in."

Andre led him to the parlor. "I had hoped that you'd drop by. Your mother was a very sweet soul." Lanita had already slipped out of sight. Rudy wanted to kick himself. "If you want to see her," Ofelia had instructed, "go around to the back."

The Archbishop offered him a chair. "I was and still am so very sorry for your loss. I pray for her but seriously doubt that she needs it." Andre sat down across from him.

"A day doesn't go by that I don't think of her."

"Yes, your mother, your aunt, Bastien and I grew up playing and getting into mischief together." He paused sensing that Rudy was uncomfortable.

"Mom never said much about her childhood." He wanted to add *she never mentioned any of you.*

"Well that's true for most of us." He went to a corner table and called Lanita on the intercom. "Could you please bring us some refreshments. Lemonade and those ginger snaps you made yesterday would be good." He smiled at Rudy. "I always knew your mother would have a wonderful family, so if you don't mind I'd like to hear all about you."

"Your brother is repairing my rental car and told me to drop by. He really liked my mom too." They paused as the hall clock chimed and Andre said a silent prayer. Lanita entered without a sound, set the tray of refreshments on the coffee table and left without a word or glance in their direction. "You seem to have already met Lanita?"

Rudy didn't want to cause any problems. "Ofelia introduced us."

Without waiting for a comment he nervously began a litany. "I graduated from Columbia with a degree in finance, but after working at it for a couple of years, I realized I'm not cut out for that line of work. I'd built up a little cushion for myself and decided to take off a few months, explore my heritage you know. Hadn't seen my Aunt Elaine since my granddad's funeral. Then after this visit, I plan to go to France and England and find some more relatives." He stopped to take a drink of lemonade.

"But first, I want to help Ofelia, Aunt Ofelia," he paused with a slight laugh, "launch a singing career. She's really good you know, and what I know about business I think I can help her."

Andre then asked him a series of questions. "How is your father? Are you enjoying the reunion with your Aunt Elaine?" He talked about the importance of family and the Church while Rudy drank lemonade, ate cookies and half-way listened. Finally, he decided he could take no more and blurted out,

"Mom and Dad thought it best that I not be raised in any religion, so, I'm not a Catholic and I don't even believe much in a God."

Andre nodded knowingly as he got up to bid Rudy goodbye. "Well, perhaps we have more in common than you think." Rudy shook his hand and mumbled words of thanks and flew off the porch two steps at a time. *Now I know how those poor bastards felt during the inquisition.*

Lanita had already left for the day. "All that goddamn talk. He wouldn't shut up," he vented to Ofelia. "Do you know where she lives?" Rudy swore again as Ofelia shook her head, then dashed over to his cabin to take a shower. Even though Ofelia wasn't singing tonight, he'd go back to the club on the off chance that Lanita would show up again.

CHAPTER EIGHT

Elaine pulled onto the narrow dirt lane leading to Bastien's place. Tall weeds scraped the sides of her flawless 1984 Audi. "Any scratches on this car and he'll pay," she muttered. When the repair shop came into view, she figured that the sagging structure would topple over if it weren't for the dozens of thread-bare tires and rusting car parts packed against the sides. The soothing classical music coming from her car stereo didn't relieve her disgust. "I bet dozens and dozens of rats call that home."

She parked a distance from his cabin. The place looked and felt deserted. "Hello," she called out. "Bastien, you have company." A couple of hounds sat up and looked her over. One got up, wagging his tail as he came towards her. "Stay back, you flea bag."

With a mournful look the dog turned around and went under the cabin porch. Elaine glanced towards the creek, only partially visible through the thicket of tall grasses and cypress trees weighed down by hanging moss. The air was sticky and stifling. She took some deep breaths. Finally her eyes were able to make out a figure sitting at the edge of the creek on what looked like a fallen tree trunk. He was holding a cane fishing pole with one hand and patting a floppy eared hound with the other. To her left, she saw a path leading down towards his location.

Once she was practically on top of him, she called out, "You havin' any luck?"

Alarmed, Bastien sprang up jerking the line into the air.

"Oh, my dear, I didn't mean to frighten you. Forgive me. She needed to be careful around this man who had spent five years in prison for nearly killing two people even though G-G-Daddy had assured her that he was safe and added, "Being an ex-con, no one will believe him if he were to try to implicate you."

"Oh dear, I had forgotten how very handsome you are," she began confidently. She felt she could charm any man even a backward nincompoop like this one slouched before her. "Even more so than that twin of yours." She tilted her head with a flirtatious laugh. "He's way too soft and clean, looks more like a sissy, if you ask me." Bastien kept his eyes on the ground and didn't say anything. "Of course, you better never tell him I said that. After all, I do have to live across the street from him." Silly giggles trailed off through the high grasses.

Bastien didn't move an inch. He wasn't better than his brother at anything and everyone knew that. Except his mother did tell him once, "Bastien, you have a kinder spirit." Besides he was smart enough to know that Elaine considered him no better than an earthworm. She was after something.

Elaine tried to avoid the perils of her surroundings, but the swamp grass scratched her legs and left streak marks on her beige skirt and the soggy ground oozed into her open-toed pumps. She began to feel anxious and heard the shrill voice, *you're getting your clothes all dirty.* The rains had swelled the creek waters into a fast current stirring up another disturbing memory. She was three and all alone in the bathroom sitting in the huge tub with water gushing out of the faucet. Try as hard as she could, her small hands weren't able to twist the knob to stop the flow. "Mama, Mama," she had cried. Finally, someone was lifting her up to safety, but it wasn't her mother.

Suddenly a frightened girl's voice whimpered, "Just look, I'm getting all soiled. Mama will be so mad. Oh, Mama will get so very mad." The desperate little girl's voice caused Bastien to look up. Elaine was wiping her hands over her skirt again and again trying to remove the wet grass marks. His heart opened and the same empathy he felt for his injured animals filled the space.

"It's okay. Don't fret. I'll get you a towel and you'll be as good as new." The tone and kindness touched something in Elaine. She forgot her skirt and gazed up at him with a vacant stare. In the next moment however, the old Elaine was back, arrogant and hateful.

"I'm perfectly fine." She waved her hand as if dismissing whatever had just happened. "I have a business proposition for you, Bastien. One I know you'll like." She started back to the cabin stepping high with her shoulders thrown back. "Come on, now. I don't have all day." Over her shoulder, she called, "I suppose you have lots of snakes around here?"

Bastien was thrown off kilter. *What the hell's going on?*

She smiled sweetly and continued, "I bet cottonmouths are everywhere, especially after these rains. You know my father's whore died of a bite from one of them." Her piercing laughter alarmed the birds in nearby trees who chirped wildly and took to flight. Bastien could feel his anger coming up to the surface. She further provoked him when she twisted around and demanded, "You got lots of them vipers around here, correct?"

He took several deep breaths and didn't answer. His prison doctor had told him to breathe slowly to control his temper. That advice generally worked when he was sober and fortunately for Elaine he hadn't had a drink that day. "They're everywhere around here, but they don't never come up to the house cause of my dogs..." He stopped in mid-sentence, wondering, *What's she doin' talkin' bout snakes?* He turned towards his animal pens. "Got to see 'bout my animals, now. You go on and get out of here."

Elaine was shocked and started to put him in his place for walking off from her but then stopped. G-G Daddy was standing among the trees. Suddenly unable to abate his anger, Bastien came back towards her. Elaine put her hands in front of her face for protection.

"Don't you ever be callin' Monique a whore, you hear me? She was the sweetest woman I ever knew." He leaned in so close that his spittle sprayed her face. "Her and your daddy paid for that good lawyer and got me out of prison. And then they made me the best man for their wedding."

A paralyzing terror knotted Elaine's stomach. Her heart began to beat so rapidly she had to lean back against a tree truck. She remembered her father's funeral. People going out of their way to tell her what a good man he was. *"A good man,"* she wanted to scream. *"He was a lazy good-for-nothing who drove my mama to suicide and wasted the entire family fortune satisfying his whims."* Now she was finding out that her father had squandered money not only on his whore and brat, but also on getting a murdering villain out of prison. How many others had profited from her inheritance, money that should be hers? And now here's someone else talking about that illicit marriage between her father and his whore. Such a union was forbidden in this state and yet, everyone was acting like it was legal even though the ritual had to have taken place in some godless place up north.

She had to get away. She was rushing towards her car when G-G-Daddy's whispered, "I sent you on a mission." For a brief moment she hated G-G-Daddy always expecting her to take care of everything, but then she remembered that he was the only one who cared about her. Instead of getting in the car, she removed the bottle of whiskey and the two glasses from the seat. The thought of drinking from one his glasses had prompted her to bring two clean ones. When she returned, Bastien had already settled on a bench near the fox pen. "Andre tells me that you're fond of fine whiskey."

"What you two doin' talkin' 'bout me?" He didn't look up. "Ya'll don't even like one another."

"Oh, he wasn't talking about you," Elaine spoke softly hoping to placate him. "I went to him with this business plan and he said you'd be the best at helping me and when I asked him what you'd charge, he said, 'Oh a bottle of good whiskey should be enough.'" Bastien stared at her, suspicious. Could he believe anything she was saying?

"I'll tell you all about it, but first let's have a drink," Elaine continued. "The liquor store owner said this is the best." She held up the bottle for him to see.

The thought of tasting fine whiskey weakened his mistrust. The last bottle from his brother sat empty on the kitchen counter. "Well, I guess. Don't mind if I do." She started for the cabin and he followed at a distance. Two folding chairs and a tray table set on the cabin porch. "Oh, this is quite lovely," Elaine said as she placed the glasses and bottle on the tray.

Bastien quickly wiped off the chairs using the threadbare towel hanging on a nail. "I got some ice," he offered. "I like to drink mine plain, but I can get you some ice and water too." He rushed towards the door.

"No, no, no. You're a man after my own heart. I like mine straight too." She filled one of the glasses. "I hope you don't mind drinking this good stuff out of these old jelly glasses." Her laughter floated like a dirty fog. A shudder inched down Bastien's spine, but after the first swallow that uneasiness began drifting off to the ethers. *Maybe I've been wrong about this woman.*

After the third glass, he knew he'd been wrong. This stuff was better than his brother's and she wasn't at all stingy with her servings. Before his glass could get close to empty she would be refilling it to the top. He drank, and she chatted nonstop about their childhood days. He didn't remember one incident she related, but then he didn't remember lots of things from those times, and the years of booze and trauma had sent most memories into a locked chamber of his mind. Elaine occasionally took a small sip providing Bastien with the lion's share. She prayed the alcohol would induce him to help her. Once the bottle was nearly empty, she began talking about the medical research being done on snake venom. "Did you know that the venom from poisonous snakes like the moccasins, is worth a small fortune?"

Bastien shook his head, dumbfounded.

"These scientists are usin' it to cure all sorts of diseases, diseases like high blood pressure, stroke, kidney disease, Parkinson's and, oh my, the list goes on and on." She took a small sip. "Bastien, with all the snakes around here, you could be rollin' in dough."

Sensing something was terribly wrong, he ignored her and picked up a kitten and petted it back and forth, back and forth, gently. He wanted to escape to another world where people like Elaine didn't live.

Elaine cleared her throat several times to get his attention. "You could use that extra money, couldn't you? And you'd be helping people, helping them to get well." Bastien stared at her through dazed eyes.

She spoke softer, "I know you're the best when it comes to catchin' things. We could be a team." He put the kitten down and took another swallow.

Elaine spoke as gently as she could, hoping she would remind him of his mother. "You'll get fifty dollars for each one you catch. Just poisonous ones, like water moccasins and copperheads if they're around. I'll pack them off to the research lab and collect the money."

That was a lot of money for very little work. He sat up straight in his chair and tried not to slur his words. "We're gettin' on into the tail of summer, so there won't be as many like in the spring, but now these rains and then a hurricane, that'll stir things up." He became enthused as he realized that he may not have to go begging to his brother anymore. "I could maybe make some money now. But come spring when they're all comin' out, why that'd be a haul." He was silent for a moment. "You sure their poison can help those sick people?"

"Oh yes, I'll be happy to let you see the reports."

Bastien laughed out loud, took another drink and scooted to the edge of his chair. "That could turn out to be a damn good job." Elaine would have jumped up and hugged him if he hadn't been so dirty.

G-G-Daddy stood at the edge of the porch and smiled. She knew he was proud of her.

"I've got to get something out of the car." Elaine jumped up and left. When she came back, she was carrying an old-fashioned doctor's kit made of black leather and covered with tiny ice pick holes. "Put them in here and I'll be back in a week for the pickup." She set it down. "Take care, now, and make sure you don't get bit."

As he watched her get in her car, the same uneasiness once again began to creep into his gut. "Snakes and medicine? Somethin 'bout it just don't seem right." He stumbled into the cabin, fell on his cot and passed out. In his dream, the police were taking him away while his mother stood by the door crying, "Bastien, I know you try to be a good boy."

CHAPTER NINE

In his dream, Andre was running his fingers through Dominique's long black hair. "You are beautiful," he said softly. Using her delightful French accent, she asked, "Even more beautiful than Elaine?"

"How do you know about Elaine?"

"Oh, Madame Claudine talks, and she says Elaine was your first love."

"More an addiction than love," he mumbled, becoming agitated

"No, you loved her. You always did. But I please you more, yes?" She snuggled down under the sheets. "I will please you."

"It's time for you to go now."

Dominique looked out from the covers with tears in her eyes. "You no longer want me?"

Andre turned over and cried out. "Yes, leave me for good." For a while his rest was undisturbed, then once again he cried out, "No, no." This time the all too familiar nightmare clawed through his sleep.

A groundskeeper was showing Bastien, a boy of seven, how to plant new rose bushes. After finishing the chore, he handed Bastien a box containing a pair of brand-new shiny black shoes. The young boy giggled with astonishment. He had never owned shoes that weren't already worn. Then the groundskeeper led him into the guest house, exited and locked the door. Within five minutes, Father Rene approached the guest house and went inside.

Andre stood outside in the shadows, still in his altar-boy surplice from the morning's Mass. Father Rene finally emerged followed by a downcast Bastien clutching the gleaming shoes to his chest. Andre stood frozen. Time after time he watched his brother enter the chamber of abomination and never once lifted a finger to help.

Bastien said nothing, not even to his twin. There were the many gifts, the compensations for service. Bags of fruit and candy, a new rifle, nice school clothes, a bicycle and most importantly, money. Their father lay dying of consumption; their mother washed clothes for the city ladies, but the few dollars she earned were barely enough to put food on the table, much less buy medicine. However, the gifts and money from Father Rene kept coming. "If it weren't for that saintly priest, we'd all be starving," his mother would say.

Kicking the bed covers to the floor, Andre shouted out in his sleep, "Bastien was the sacrificial lamb."

Then the dream became even darker, more frightening. The young man Bastien was chasing the groundskeeper with an ax. Their mother was crying and begging him to stop. Father Rene lay semiconscious on the freshly mown grass. A foot away, the saintly priest's severed right hand twitched as if still connected to its arm. The other hand clasped his blood-soaked crotch, mauled with jagged cuts. Bastien ran faster and slung the ax. It lodged squarely between the groundskeeper's shoulders, instantly paralyzing him from the neck down. Their hellish screams and cries pommeled Andre's sleeping ears.

Still the nightmare continued. Bastien's face floated above his, eyes burning into his eyes, nose almost touching his nose, screaming, "You stood in the shadows in your altar-boy dress and let them do that to me. And when I got too old, he went after the younger ones, and I had to protect them. And what did you do? You stood in the shadows and ducked into your priestly cassock. You never tried to help me, you bastard?" The iron bars of a prison door slammed shut, again and again. The clanging jarred Andre awake.

He sat upright in the bed, eyes wet with tears and wild with panic. He had never told anyone what he saw that priest and his pimp do to his brother. He became a priest and still remained a coward and a hypocrite. He clutched his chest as his body shook in a palsy of shame.

He looked at the crucifix on the wall and fell to his knees beside his bed. "I am no better than Father Rene and the groundskeeper. I deserted him. Didn't go to the trial and never visited him in prison. I was a coward. Is there forgiveness for this?" He looked at the figure on the cross and felt an overwhelming disgust strangle him. "Yes, I pretend to be a man of God, to be the good brother, charitable with my handouts of whiskey and money."

Lying prostrate over the bed, Andre gave in to all the self-recriminations. *It's all been a sham. The contributions to the needy and all the rest have been nothing more than attempts to reduce my guilt.*

His legs nearly collapsed under him as he rose from the bed. He made his way to the bathroom using the furniture for support. Standing before the lavatory, he faced himself in the mirror. "Now is the time." He turned on the hot water. "I will rectify the wrongs."

He wrapped his face in a hot towel, *those pedophiles don't deserve a place as nice as Shadow's Way, but the church's conservatives are more likely to go along with my plans if the detainees are housed in a beautiful home rather than a prison.* He sighed. *I"m still a master manipulator.*

He lathered his face, picked up the straight razor, and began the ritual. *You were willing to let your brother rot in prison, but not these priests.* The blade slid down his cheek with such force he had to jerk the razor away before it sliced his jugular. He gulped panting like a wounded animal. *And if Bastien had killed that priest and his helper, he would've gone to the chair without so much as a peep from you.* Once again, the blade came dangerously close to his throat nicking his chin. He watched the blood drip into the basin. "Am I trying to kill myself?" he asked out loud. "Cutting my throat would be easier than doing what I must do."

The church bells were chiming. In an hour his Mass would start. The ceremony had become nothing more than a routine habit, delivering no solace, no connection to the spiritual. He came out of the bathroom and stood before a statue of Mary lit up by several vigil candles. "Dear Mother, I will leave the priesthood after this is all taken care of. I no longer choose to be one of the chosen."

Later that day, Elaine called Andre, "Can you drop by this afternoon. I'd like to finalize our plans for Shadow's Way." As far as he was concerned everything had been finalized yet he agreed, somewhat reluctantly. He arrived wearing casual slacks and a sport's shirt. "My, my, have they already defrocked you?" she asked as she offered him a seat in the parlor. He didn't reply.

"Andre, my dear," she smiled sweetly and handed him a cup of freshly brewed coffee. "I'm afraid you leave me no choice but to enlighten the Church officials how you used Church money to rescue and then renovate this place."

Andre leaned back in his chair and remembered the beautiful Sabrina. He was a young priest in his first parish; she was older, widowed and very rich. Every morning she knelt and watched him say Mass, a lace mantilla hanging over her eyes, and every night he lay with her, savoring an all-consuming passion and love he had never experienced before or since. Then one day the tumor appeared, and he wrapped his arms around her as the monster devoured her body, bit by bit. Heartbroken and angry at God above all, he told his Bishop,

"I'm not cut out for this life." The Bishop laughed. "Nonsense my son. You are in grief."

"Did God punish her for my sin?"

The Bishop put his hand on Andre's shoulder. "You're not the first priest who has fallen in love and broken his vow of celibacy? If the truth be known, most..." He stopped and changed course. "Take a leave of absence. We can't afford to lose smart men like you. You'll go far."

Elaine moved her chair closer to his. "Andre are you listening?"

He gazed at her and asked himself, *how could I have been so weak as to fall for your proposition?*

She raised her voice to a threat. "Also, I'm sure the Church's hierarchy would be delighted to hear how you used their money to satisfy your lusts. What would they think of Madame Claudine? And the girls?" She sat back, a satisfied smile on her face. "You'll lose that Archbishop's title. You may even be driven from the priesthood."

Unmoved he looked at her and remembered the goodness and sweetness of Sabrina. A month after she had died, her lawyer informed him that he was a rich man. "She's left two-thirds of her entire estate to you. And the Church gets one third with the stipulation that you be made a Monsignor." After that, Andre continued to rise until he became Archbishop.

Elaine was encouraged by his long silence. He would perhaps be able to finagle his way out of the money issued for Shadow's Way, but he wouldn't be able to dodge a sex scandal.

Andre leaned in towards her. "You are such a fool." His body and voice reflected a deep exhaustion. "You really think I'd use the church's money on something like this place? Go ahead and do what you will but remember this place still belongs to me."

Elaine was so stunned she couldn't move. Nothing was working.

"And here's the icing on top, Elaine. I don't care about this Archbishop's job. Archbishop or not, you'll still be out of here in two weeks." He walked to the foyer and turned back, "And, by the way, I won't be needing Madame Claudine or the girls any longer." He walked out, not bothering to close the door behind him.

By the time she reached the foyer Andre was already crossing the boulevard. She walked over to the mantel and looked up at G-G-Daddy. "Well, that's that. He's left me with no choice, but to do as you've ordered." Her Southern Scarlet O'Hara voice sailed up to the portrait. "Yes, I know you'll guide me through."

CHAPTER TEN

The last guests had left and now there was only one more booked reservation for the following night. She still had so much to get done before this play ended, but for now she was going to sit outside and enjoy the morning sunshine. Little did anyone know what lay ahead. Like her father, Elaine wouldn't tolerate being used. She could still hear him yelling at her mother. "You may have forced me into this marriage with that pregnancy, but I'll make sure you don't get a red dime from my inheritance."

"There's as much blue blood in my veins as in yours," her mother had screamed back, yanking at his shirt. He pulled away and grabbed her wrists. "Everything's going to the girls, already set in an air-tight will. You'll be as penniless as the day I picked you up at that bar."

"My ancestors owned as much land and had as many slaves as yours. But unlike yours mine were honorable people. My grandfather didn't make deals with the Yankees so he could profit from the war." Her mother was running around the room in a frenzy, pulling at her hair. "Traitors, traitors, that was what your family was and your grandfather, Henri the first, was the biggest traitor of all."

Elaine shook the thoughts away. *Had G-G-Daddy collaborated with the enemy?* Elaine hated her mother for putting those slanderous ideas into her head. She knew better. "G-G-Daddy was a very smart businessman and recovered Shadow's Way and its land by honorable means."

"You talkin' to me?" Lily Mae came out to shake some rugs. Agitated, Elaine exclaimed, "Don't creep up on me like that and get me a cold glass of water? With a slice of lemon?" The maid dropped the rugs and went back inside, returning five minutes later with the iced water.

"Lily Mae, you remember how deranged my daddy was before he died? You told me he scared you."

"Yessum, those empty eyes and that long stringy hair. He was a mess, alright."

"Well listen, Rudy and Ofelia claim that part of Shadow's Way belongs to them, so I'm gonna need you to testify in court that my daddy was in fact off his rocker, making that piece of paper they have null and void."

Lily Mae stopped shaking one of the rugs. She wanted no part of this. "Well, ma'am, I can't swear to that 'fore a judge. My mama work more for him."

"You stupid piece of coal. You better start looking for another job." Lily Mae went back into the house with a chuckle.

"You'se threaten me all you want. No one else will work here for yo'r crazy self and you knows it."

Elaine couldn't understand the backtalk but never mind that, she had other more-pressing issues to deal with. The validity of the will could wait, but Andre's threat to Shadow's Way was imminent. "I cannot allow such a desecration of this hallowed edifice," she said and began visualizing the final scene where all her enemies would be destroyed. She smiled. "Trixie will be thrilled to work again."

Rudy came out of his cabin, picked up the daily paper on his step and went back in.

Elaine sneered, "Without so much as a hello. I know he saw me." The hatred she had harbored for his mother churned up against him. Elaine still puzzled over the fact that Gabrielle was even conceived, given the fact that her father detested her mother. Nevertheless, at age five she was presented with an ugly pink thing. "This is your little sister." She hated Gabrielle from the start, but as the little sister grew, she came to hate her even more because she was the spitting image of their father. She had imagined that she was a bastard child. If that had been so, then perhaps things would have been different. Loud parental commands still echoed in Elaine's psyche. "Watch out for your little sister." "Stop being selfish and let little Gabrielle have that." Elaine had been compelled to resort to cruelty. When Trixie shoved Gabrielle into a ditch filled with sticker plants, her father came running. "I saw you do that, you little monster." After that, Elaine was watched and often treated like an unwanted stepchild especially by their father.

Ofelia came out of her cabin and waved at Elaine. "Want some company?" Elaine didn't answer and fiddled with the potted geraniums sitting on the table beside her glass of water. Ofelia began crossing over to her. "You still aren't speaking? And here we wined and dined you like royalty," Ofelia's sarcasm cut through Elaine.

She flopped down on the other lounger. "Elaine, we'll settle this one way or the other. Do you really want a legal battle on your hands?" Elaine remained silent pruning the geraniums.

Ofelia decided to try another approach. "Why don't you come to the club? I would love your input, your coaching. After all, you were a great actress."

She's making fun of me. Elaine's paranoia had begun snowballing these last few weeks. She was convinced that everyone was out to get her. "How do you know I was a great actress?" She snapped. "You've never seen me perform."

Ofelia took off her blouse revealing a skimpy bikini top. "Well, I've seen you play the Southern Belle for your guests and those performances have been amazing."

"Have some decency," Elaine commanded, "and cover yourself."

"God are you for real?" Ofelia laughed. "Remember, one-third of this patio belongs to me, so I'll sit on my one-third in whatever and however I choose."

Elaine pulled her wide-brimmed hat lower over her face. If she dared to stay out for just a few more minutes, her alabaster skin would become as red as the feathers on a scarlet ibis. Crow's feet were forming at the corners of Elaine's eyes and wrinkles were lining her neck. *What will happen once her looks are gone?* Ofelia wondered. *She has nothing but a fading beauty and Shadow's Way.*

Impulsively Ofelia blurted out, "Sometimes I sense that you have a lover." Shocked by her outburst, she added, "Which would be wonderful. We all need someone."

A long icy stare and then a quiet hiss, "I'm not a whore. Like some people."

Ofelia wanted to cuss. She could hear her daddy telling her mother, "Elaine can be cruel like no other, scary cruel." She had been perhaps five at the time. "Daddy, you didn't know the half of it," she mumbled.

"What?" Elaine looked at her.

"Just talking to myself. It runs in the family, you know." Elaine ignored her and drank some lemon water.

The first encounter Ofelia had had with her sister's unbridled cruelty occurred within weeks after her arrival. She had been in the breakfast area arranging flowers where she could easily hear Elaine's raised voice in the next room. "Lily Mae, that half-breed sister of mine is just like her mother, a regular whore. She, too, is breaking up a nice family. That man she's seeing is the father of two lovely girls, just like my father was."

For several seconds Ofelia held the vase with shaking hands. This was intentional. Elaine knew where she was. Ofelia stomped into the dining room and smashed the costly vase at Elaine's feet. Shards of glass flew in all directions while water ran into the cracks of the hardwood floor. Elaine jumped back with a slight scream. Fresh flowers were scattered around her shoes.

Ofelia picked up a large piece of glass and pointed it at Elaine. "Don't you ever, ever call my mother that again, or I swear to God I'll scar up that pasty white face of yours." Elaine was more frightened than she had ever been. "You can call me a whore if that makes you feel superior, but don't ever again call my mother that. You understand, you mean disgusting bitch."

Staggering back a step or two, Ofelia dropped the shard stunned by the fierceness within her. "You bring out the worst in people," she snarled in Elaine's face and walked steadily out of the room, feeling that a kindred wolf spirit was within her.

For the next two nights she had stayed in a hotel, not wanting to be on the same property as her sister. She felt she could have murdered Elaine in that moment and that frightened her. It was true that Greg was married and had two daughters just like her dad, but her dad had a far different relationship with his "other" woman. "Never have I seen two people more in love than those two," her Grand-mere told her many times. "I do believe they had one soul and your daddy couldn't go on living with just half of one."

On the other hand, her relationship with Greg was nothing more than a diversion for each of them. Greg had hired Ofelia before he ever heard her sing knowing that her beauty alone would attract a crowd to his lagging Club Novella. But then as his luck would have it, she was also a great singer. Not a good one, but a great one. She quickly became a local celebrity. Sister Francine's years of voice training had insured a repertoire that ranged from angelic classical to swampy blues. After a week, Greg lured her to his bed. The successful job and the infatuated lover began to restore Ofelia's crushed ego and lift her sadness.

Suddenly Elaine sprang up from her chair with a loud "Oh yes." Ofelia was jolted back to the present and saw Elaine hold onto the table to steady herself. "My goodness. I feel a bit dizzy." Once her head cleared, she began prattling hysterically, "The news has been saying a hurricane is forming out in the Gulf and I can feel it. Let's have a party. You know, a hurricane party? I bet Rudy's never been to one of those." She looked across the yard. "Why yes, that's a good idea. A very good idea. We can all go to the club to hear you sing. You've been wanting that, haven't you? Yes, that would be nice, and then we can all come back here for a celebration."

Abruptly she turned and hurried to the back door, calling out over her shoulder, "There will be so much to celebrate, so very much." Ofelia watched her disappear into her apartment and wondered about the extent of her madness. Another distant memory bubbled up. Ofelia was sitting in her daddy's lap at the kitchen table in Shadow's Way. He stared out the window as in a trance. Her Grand-mere Le Blanc was talking. "I'm going back home now Henri, and I'm taking the child with me. She can't see you like this. Losing one parent is all the burden she can carry. When you pull yourself together, you come get her."

Her daddy turned his head. "You're right, Estella." He hugged Ofelia close to him. "I'm no longer a good dad for this one either. Just like the other two, especially Elaine. I've loved this sweet baby as no other, even more than Gabrielle." Her Grand-mere lifted her from his lap and Ofelia saw him only twice after that. He never came to get her. That was very sad for her, but she knew he had loved her and that made all the difference. Had Elaine ever felt his love?

"Hey girlfriend, you daydreaming again?" Lanita was walking across the yard. "Where's Rudy?"

The cabin door burst open and Rudy hurried out. "I've been at the club every night looking for you."

"Bastien says your car's ready," she said ignoring his comment. "He's over at the Archbishop's ready to take you to get it and he's in a hurry"

She turned and began walking at a fast pace. "I got to get back, lots still to do."

Rudy followed her. "Wait up."

Lanita was upset. She had been in the middle of cleaning the conference room when Bastien burst in, begging her to go get Rudy. "Can't you see I'm busy?"

"Please, I don't want to run into Elaine. She…she…"

Lanita gave in, seeing how nervous he was. "Well, alright." Bastien took the vacuum from her. "I can finish this for you."

Rudy caught up to Lanita as she waited for several cars to pass on the street. "I want to see you again. How about dinner tonight?"

"Rudy, it's not a good idea. I really like you, but it's just not a good idea. There's stuff…"

Rudy felt perplexed. "Listen I'll be gone in a few more weeks. Why can't we have fun for as long as I'm around, and then you'll never hear from me again?"

Lanita was tempted by this proposal. Perhaps that would work. She looked at him and smiled. "I'll think about it. If I decide yes, then I'll see you at Marty's Seafood around seven. It's about three miles down the coast.

Bastien waited in his pickup and watched. Watched Lanita and Rudy as they talked. *They acted like they like one another?* Bastien felt a deep pain, and then he felt like he wanted to hurt Rudy.

CHAPTER ELEVEN

"It took longer than I said to fix your car cause a part I needed wasn't in stock," Bastien said as soon as Rudy crawled into the cab. For several miles they rode in silence. Rudy had made a few attempts at conversation, but Bastien merely grunted keeping his eyes on the road. Finally, Rudy could stand it no longer. "Bastien, have I done something to make you mad?"

"She's too different for you. And not in your class either."

Rudy was confused. "Are you talking about Lanita?"

Bastien glared at him. "Who else would I be talkin' about?"

Rudy became nervous. The barber had told him about the attempted murders. "Yep, it was that guy fixin' your car. Crippled 'em for life, real good. Both that sorry priest and his gardener. Not that they didn't deserve it." Rudy had felt admiration for Bastien on hearing the story but now, being alone with someone who had come close to killing two people, he decided to use caution.

"You're sure right about her being different. She treats me like a dumb kid and here I'm only five years younger than her. Today she told me I'd better watch my step at Shadow's Way. I told her I could take care of myself and she just smiled like she knew something I didn't."

Bastien's hands relaxed their grip on the steering wheel. Rudy swallowed a few times. "She says evil lurks in that house. I guess she must have grown up with voodoo around her."

Bastien chuckled, "Boy, you better listen to her if you know what's good. She's an island woman and they do know about things like evil."

The tension inside the truck was easing out the windows. But at the same time the dense trees and overgrowth on either side of the winding road reminded Rudy of a land of warlocks and witches. He had to get the hell out of this state before he ended up as peculiar as his aunt and this man. Perhaps he would head out in a week or so, especially now since Bastien had gotten between him and Lanita having some fun.

Bastien remained silent the rest of the way and Rudy was no longer interested in striking up any sort of camaraderie. When they reached the garage, Rudy was in a hurry to get to the safety of his car. He gave Bastien an extra twenty dollars and was about to say good-bye when Bastien said, "I don't mean to give you no bad feelin.' It's just that people like Lanita need takin' care of. You're a big rich city guy and she don't have much except what's right here." Bastien's heartfelt concern for Lanita touched Rudy. He hadn't given a thought as to what Lanita might feel once he left. His focus had been on his pleasures and good times.

The car ran better than it had when he first got it. The old timers were right about Bastien's mechanical abilities. "My friend, you couldn't have left your car in better hands, no you couldn't," the barber had testified.

The sweat covered his forehead as he drove through the overgrown lane. The clammy humidity, the still air and a doomed heaviness seemed to weigh down on everything. Rudy found it hard to move, breathe and even think down here. Yet in spite of the atmosphere and Bastien's non-verbal threats, he wasn't ready to leave. He was enjoying his time with Ofelia and he was excited about the inheritance and possibly other fortunes. Out of curiosity, he had gone to the library several afternoons and researched the history of Shadow's Way only to find out that pirates had built smuggling tunnels under many of the old houses. He was curious. Did such tunnels exist under Shadow's Way?

Even though he was in desperate need of a shower, he first stopped at the library to copy more information about this area. In a few hours he would most likely meet Lanita, and he wasn't looking forward to that. What would he tell her? *I don't want to end up with an ax lodged in my back, so I've decided we shouldn't see each other.* Perhaps she wouldn't even show up. That morning she had been hesitant about his proposal. Whatever fun they may have had, he wasn't going to risk his life for a woman whose name he wouldn't remember a year from now.

By five o'clock he was on his way to his cottage with a packet of information and drawings. The elderly librarian was also interested in the history of these places and was fascinated by this handsome young man so passionate about his ancestral home. She almost ran to help him when he came through the doors. Rudy shamefully flirted with her, calling her Gorgeous and Lovely. Even though Rudy didn't give a flip about ancestry or history, *I'm after the treasure,* he didn't dare disappoint her. "Rudy, look at this," she hurried to his table holding a newly discovered document. "I just found this for you. It seems that both Shadow's Way and the Archbishop's mansion are sitting on a spider web of tunnels."

He could hardly wait to share this with Ofelia. When he knocked on her screen door mouth-watering aromas made him realize he hadn't eaten since the tedious breakfast with Aunt Elaine.

That morning Elaine had chattered non-stop, pausing only to sip coffee from an elegant demitasse.

She seemed to be fully recovered from the backyard dinner and the conversation about selling Shadow's Way. The talk was all about her as usual. This time it was her European tour while performing in "A Streetcar Named Desire."

"I know you must be thinking I had to be much too young to play Blanche Dubois." She giggled coquettishly.

Fishing for a damn compliment again, he thought, and continued eating his eggs Mornay with brandied fruit.

"Oh, I was able to create the illusion of advanced age, thanks to the skills of makeup artists and lighting engineers and as my director said, 'my superb acting abilities.'"

"I would give anything to have seen you perform." Rudy lied with a mouth full of buttered croissant. Delighted by this comment, she babbled on. Rudy was finishing his coffee by the time the tour got to Italy. "The lighting system was appalling, simply appalling."

Lily Mae stuck her head in from the hallway. "The church ladies is here. Somethin' 'bout using some of your stuff for the fall bazaar."

Rudy wanted to run out and kiss those church ladies on their white-powdered noses.

"Oh, for heaven's sake. Will you excuse me, dear?"

As soon as Elaine left the room, he was out the back door violating he was sure, some cardinal rule of proper Southern conduct. He could hear her high pitched voice, "How dare you walk out in the middle of a story without so much as a goodbye! I've a mind to banish you to a hotel for your uncouth Yankee behavior."

"Come on in. The door's open." Ofelia called from inside.

Rudy loved Ofelia's pretty cottage, now filled with wonderful smells. It reminded him of his home before his mother died. "It's not the same anymore," his dad kept saying. "It won't ever be the same." Rudy still worried about his dad. "Stop fretting over me. I took a lady out to dinner the other night. Now, you go on and see your aunts."

Ofelia's one room had been transformed into three areas: a bedroom hidden behind a hand-painted screen, a small sitting area at the front with a dinette and in the corner, a basic kitchenette with a half-refrigerator, hot plate, toaster and coffee pot. Open shelves contained food staples and pottery dishes. "Elaine didn't throw a fit when you changed things up?"

Ofelia cocked her head. "Before she could say anything I reminded her that it also belonged to me and my people had made this their home and so would I." Ofelia poured jasmine tea into two mugs and slid one towards him along with a jar of raw honey. "I wouldn't be comfortable in the big house. It was okay when I was a kid with my mom and dad. Elaine was more than glad to let me have my way. I don't think she felt I belonged in the 'big house' either."

She snuggled down into an oversized chair among a herd of zebra-striped pillows. Her long legs stretched over the bamboo coffee table. "Sometimes I think I feel them around," she said. "You know, the ones who lived and suffered here." Her tone was melancholy. "It's like they're in the walls, wanting to let me know how hard it was."

Rudy dumped several teaspoons of honey into his tea. "Not to be mean, but I've had my fill of spooks for now. What are you cooking?"

"Cajun rice 'n beans. About once a week I have to have some of Grand-mere's food." Ofelia folded her hands around her cup, deep in thought. "Elaine once said that the Chauvier slaves didn't want to be free.

'They were so well taken care of,'" she mimicked Elaine's drawl, "'and were so loved by my great-grandfather that they refused to leave after the war.'" Ofelia shook her head. "You know, I think she really believes that bullshit."

"Oh yeah. I've heard other people down here say stuff like that." Rudy got up and looked in the pot of beans. "Have you ever thought she might have you evicted?"

"She threatened once, but as soon as I reminded her of the will and the lawyer, she backed off and hasn't mentioned it again." Ofelia spooned some rice and beans onto a plate and handed it to Rudy. "I continue to look over my shoulder. I know in my gut I can't trust her."

"Before we eat, I have something to show you." He spread out some drawings on the table. "I've been doing research on this place for days. Did you know this area was a major smuggling spot for pirates in the 1600's?"

Ofelia laughed. "Oh yes. My dad told me that a long time ago."

"Well did he tell you they dug tunnels to hide their booty? There's probably still a labyrinth of tunnels under Shadow's Way and the Archbishop's mansion. Some of those treasures could still be there. Just imagine."

"Oh, Rudy, that's a stretch, don't you think?" She wanted to laugh but couldn't. He was serious.

"If there's treasure down there, we might be wealthy beyond our imaginations. I'm going to show all this to Elaine. We need to find out." He glanced at his watch. "But now, I have to get dressed to meet Lanita and end our relationship before it even gets started."

"I thought you really liked her."

"It seems Bastien fancies her as his gal, or at least someone who needs protecting from people like me."

He told her about their conversation and finished off the food. "That was more than yummy. Thanks." He pecked her on the cheek and headed out the door.

CHAPTER TWELVE

Elaine sat at her desk in the former butler's pantry now converted into an office. All that remained from the 1800s was the large mahogany cabinet once filled with the home's best china, crystal and silverware. Even though it was now empty, Elaine was keeping it locked. She didn't want that meddlesome Lily Mae finding out that she was getting rid of things. For days now she had been shipping boxes.

Elaine was stunned, still recovering from an earlier phone call. A Denver woman had requested two nights. In a state of agitation Elaine exclaimed, "I can no long let decent people stay here because the Archbishop across the street is forcing me to keep pedophiles here so there won't be a scandal in the Church." Before she could go on, she heard a loud click. *Did she really hang up on me? Everyone is turning on me.*

She immediately called Carlyle and told him the same story. "So, I won't be calling you anymore as there won't be any more fine foods served at this establishment. The Archbishop has ordered only vegetable broth." Carlyle dismissed the call as one of Elaine's illusions. Over the years she'd told him quite a few tales. Like the one about a Prince in Denmark killing himself because she refused his marriage proposal.

Elaine replaced the phone's receiver and rocked back in her swivel chair looking out the window across to the Cathedral. *I have to let Madame Claudine know what's going on. Those poor girls, no longer needed.* Elaine had introduced Andre to Madame Claudine during the negotiations. It was decided that Madame Claudine would arrange to have all Andre's sexual needs satisfied if he kept Shadow's Way from being auctioned. "I seem to remember that you had massive cravings," Elaine had whispered in his ear.

At first he balked at the offer. "I'm not that person anymore." But after Madame Claudine explained how the trysts could take place without anyone ever knowing, his objections began to lessen. Finally, after she introduced him to her four girls and gave each one the opportunity to explain her special talents, he accepted. Elaine patted herself on her back. "I knew he was just like every other man who needs a woman from time to time," she confided to G-G-Daddy who could not have been prouder of her for effecting such a brilliant plan to save Shadow's Way.

The spoken contract was finalized. Elaine would reside at her beloved Shadow's Way for the rest of her life. If Andre died first which she assumed would happen, then she would regain the title. At least that's what she believed even though she had nothing in writing. Over the years, she never worried about being cast out, because at any moment she could destroy his life by exposing his sex life. But now he didn't care if she exposed his sins to the world. She cursed under her breath and threw the bronze antique letter opener across the room. It stuck in the wall right next to the antique clock. An inch over and she would have shattered the glass and perhaps broken the precious timepiece. Elaine bit her lip. *I'm losing control.*

As her agitation became more severe, she took a thick rubber band from the desk drawer, pulled up her skirt and began popping her thigh. A wide red blister began to rise. She chanted to the snapping cadence, "Bastien isn't going to help. I can't count on anyone. It's like always. There's G-G-Daddy, but..." She stopped, terrified, and looked at the whelps of self-mutilation. "Who's doing this to me?"

Two days before, she had driven out to Bastien's for the pick-up. She saw his car in the yard and banged on the wooden slat-door. "Bastien, I know you're in there. Now answer this door." One of the blood hounds came from the back of the cabin and growled, low and menacing.

"You're nothing but white trash," she screamed, backing off the porch. "I should have known that the likes of you wouldn't want to work." Later that day as she was coming out of the beauty salon, she saw him walking into the drug store with Darlene. He glanced in her direction and turned away quickly.

Elaine massaged the swollen spots. She sat up, once more in control. "Madame Claudine can't help with this." G-G-Daddy had introduced her to Madame Claudine a few months after her move to New York. Elaine's acting wages never quite covered her expensive tastes and so Madame Claudine came in to help with finances. Whenever a money problem arose, Madame would simply send one of her four girls to a rich client. The girls—Lydia, Dominique, Camilla and Gayla—never complained about having to hand over their earnings to Elaine. After all, Madame was kind and took care of all their needs. They knew about girls on the streets with their pimps and considered themselves very lucky.

Once Elaine explained her need to keep Shadow's Way in the family, Madame and her girls moved from New York to serve the Archbishop, now their only client. *Really, it's a win-win situation for everyone,* Elaine often mused. The work load and stress were relaxed, and Elaine had a free home with no worries about paying a dime back to Andre.

"Only Trixie can help now." The evil one had been with Elaine since childhood. Trixie removed the obstacles that arose in Elaine's life. She had followed Elaine to New York and helped her in ways Madame couldn't. Now, Trixie was going to be needed more than ever.

"Aunt Elaine," Rudy called out from the kitchen screen door. "Can I come in?"

Elaine swore under her breath, "Damnit. Why can't I be left alone?" Yet when she saw her nephew peering through the screen, her face brightened. *He's good looking, alright, like my father. And like him, a good for-nothing.*

She unlatched the door. "You look awfully chipper today. You didn't let me know that you wouldn't be here for breakfast this morning."

"Yeah, I'm really sorry. I didn't get in until the early hours of the morning." He walked in and gave her a slight hug. "Unfortunately, I slept through breakfast." He looked directly into her eyes with an appealing grin, "You forgive me?"

"Naughty, boy, of course I do. But you got to know I'm not botherin' with preparin' anything for you anymore. You'll just have to forage for yourself from now on," she scolded sweetly.

"I don't want you doing a thing for me. I came as a visitor, not a lodger." He could be so charming. "In fact, I don't think you should be lifting one precious little finger for me or anyone else."

"Not that again, please," she said sharply. "I don't have time for that foolishness."

"Are you one of those people who can't be happy unless they're working." Rudy held his arms out, "Come on, let's dance and enjoy life."

"Idleness is the devil's workshop," she shooed him away. "Your granddaddy was the idlest man I've ever seen, and you know how he ended up."

"He wasn't idle," Rudy shot back. "A publisher in New York is considering his books."

"What books?" Elaine wanted to laugh. "What are you talking about? He wasn't a writer. You're trying to make him into something he wasn't."

"He wrote three novels and countless short stories." Rudy tried to keep his anger from showing. "He left them to Ofelia and she's sent them off to various publishers."

Silence filled the room. Elaine rubbed her neck, suddenly exhausted. *What had he written about? All the secrets of the family? That G-G-Daddy was a traitor?*

Rudy cleared his throat. "Listen I'm sorry, but from what I remember and what I've heard about him, I like my grandfather and I don't like hearing you talk about him."

Elaine sank down at the kitchen table and wound the rubber band around the salt shaker. Rudy put his briefcase on the table and pulled up a chair. "Let's not argue. I've come across some information that could turn out to be a great fortune for all of us."

He stopped, waiting for a response. An icy stillness sat between them. "I've been doing research." He pulled a folder of papers from the case. "There are tunnels under this house, as well as the Bishop's mansion? Tunnels built by pirates for hiding their loot. Some of which could very likely still be down there."

Elaine glared at him. "Those tunnels don't exist anymore," she sneered. "Our Confederate boys found out they were being used to smuggle out slaves and had them all dynamited."

"Some were dynamited, but not the ones directly under these two structures because, according to what I've read, my great grandfather had made a deal with the Yankees and ..."

"You shut your foul disrespectful mouth." Elaine knocked over her chair getting up.

For an instant, Rudy thought she was going to hit him. "Hold on, hold on," he said leaning back. "I think it's great he was a traitor. I always figured him to be nothing but a sorry piece of humanity."

"Stop it. Stop it, now!" Elaine yelled at the top of her voice. She hurried over and jerked the screen door open. "I want you to leave now and get out of my cottage and go back to your Yankee Land." She wagged her finger at him. "And listen carefully. You stop sticking your nose into where it doesn't belong."

"You could be sitting on a gold mine. Why be stupid?"

He was outside the door starting down the steps, when he heard someone else speaking softly. "Listen dear." He turned to face a new Elaine, this one sweet and kind. "I really appreciate your wanting to look out for me, but I have enough money. There's nothing under this house, my sweet child." She came forward and patted his hand. "That's a fantasy that's been around forever. Now I must get to my chores but do come by for dinner at eight. I so enjoy your company."

Back in his room, Rudy knew he had to get to a bar. He wouldn't have believed someone could shift their personality, their whole appearance so smoothly, so convincingly if he hadn't seen it himself. *She was never an actress. She's just different people by nature.*

CHAPTER THIRTEEN

The Mercedes pulled onto the driveway beside the house. Bastien saw Lanita looking out the window, but she disappeared before he could wave. When he got out of the car she was standing on the stoop.

"Bastien, I have fresh coffee and lemon cake. Would you mind joining me on my break?" She had the sweetest smile.

He beamed with joy, feeling special. "I made sure my shoes were clean 'fore I left."

She laughed. "Thank you. Now come on in and sit down."

A small table covered in a checkered oilcloth was tucked in a corner of the kitchen. *This is where she eats while my fancy brother has the long gleamin' table in the dinin' room. It should be the other way around.* He eased down in the chair, careful not to disturb anything.

She poured his coffee, black and thick, just the way he liked it. His mouth watered when he saw the huge slice of bright yellow cake. Lanita sat down catty corner from him. She took a small bite of cake and then a long sip of coffee. Bastien followed her lead, but he was not able to pause between bites as she did. Within several seconds he was scraping the crumbs from his plate.

"Let me get you some more." Lanita set the cake dish in front of him. "Better still, just help yourself." She handed him the knife. "You don't have desserts very often, do you?"

Bastien looked up at her, somewhat startled. "I only get nice baked things when I go to Darlene's or if I stop at the coffee shop on Jackson."

"Bastien, I've sent things home with you."

"That's right, and yours are the best." He gave her a quick glance and smiled.

Lanita took another sip of coffee and sighed. "There's something I need to talk to you about." She took a deep breath before going on. "Bastien, I'm touched that you want to protect me, but you don't need to. I'm a big girl, and I've seen my way through lots of bad stuff."

Bastien stopped eating and looked away. He was afraid of what was coming. "Rudy done talked to you?"

Lanita didn't answer. She put her dirty dish in the sink and ran water over it. "You're a good man, a nice man, Bastien, but it's best if we don't pry into each other's lives. Keep things the way they've been."

"He's gonna hurt you! Can't you see that?"

Lanita turned to face him. "Please don't talk to me like that."

She wanted to shout back at him, *"Stay the hell away from me and my life. I deserve some fun and I'm going to have it whether you approve or not."*

When Rudy told her about the threatening conversation he'd had with Bastien, she became quite angry. "But I don't want to end up with an ax in my back," Rudy joked but Lanita could tell he was really frightened. She assured him she would handle the situation. "I'd like to be with you until you leave for Europe." They ended up at her place spending the night together.

Lanita picked up Bastien's plate. "I'm tired of being alone."

"You don't have to be alone. I'm here." Bastien could hardly believe those words had come out of his mouth. He had never said anything like this to a woman.

She pulled her hands out of the dishwater and faced him. "I don't want to be cruel, but you have to know this. With the life I've had, I don't want to be with someone who drinks. I owe it to myself to have peace." The soapy water dripped on the linoleum floor, but she didn't notice. "I know you probably can't help yourself, but that's where I stand and where I'll always stand."

Bastien felt like a skinned critter hung up to dry. He grabbed his hat and headed for the door, not looking at her, not wanting to look. His shame was beyond measure. He let the screen door slam. He forgot that he had come to get money and whiskey.

Lanita sank down at the table and looked at the half-eaten cake. *You've destroyed that poor man.*

The intercom buzzed. Her hand trembled as she pushed the button. The Archbishop's voice was magnified over the system. "Lanita, did my brother just drive off?"

"Yes, your Excellency."

"Well, what did he want?" His tone was harsh.

She reflected a moment. "I don't know. I served him coffee and cake and he left."

"Well, I just saw him run a stop sign and almost get hit. If he gets arrested he could go back to prison."

"I told him I wouldn't be with a drunkard."

There was a deep sigh. "I'll call Leone and see if he can get to him before someone else does." He switched off immediately.

Lanita and Rudy walked along the beach. "Afterwards I really felt bad. You should have seen his face, covered in sadness."

"Just remember, you're not responsible for his happiness." Rudy winked at her. "I read that somewhere." He skipped a rock across the outgoing tide.

"Bastien couldn't be any more different from his twin, could he? But then my mother was the total opposite of Aunt Elaine." He picked up another stone. "Did Leone find him before he got into any trouble?"

"Yeah, he found him in front of his favorite bar, just sitting in his car. He took him to his house. I'm sure Darlene's jambalaya made him feel better." She looked out over the water. "You know what he did then? He promised both of them he was going to stop drinking."

Rudy was moved. "He's doing that for you, you know?"

"I wonder what he'd be like sober."

They walked along digging their bare feet into the warm sand. "What was she like, your mother?" Lanita asked.

Rudy gazed at the white birds flying overhead. "She was fun, sweet as coconut pie and always relaxed, never up-tight about anything. The only time I can remember she was mean and angry was at her dad's funeral. On the way home, she apologized to my dad and me saying that being with her sister and in that house made her feel like some evil spirit was taking control. I'm getting to where I feel that way sometimes."

Lanita spread a beach towel on the sand. "Let's sit for a while and watch the sun fall into the Gulf."

Lanita pulled her long skirt up to her knees. "I should have worn shorts like you."

"Yes, and I should have brought some wine and cheese, but then I wasn't thinking about a stroll along the water."

They sat in silence, each lost in their own thoughts. Finally, Lanita spoke. "Sounds like your mom was a lot like Ofelia."

"That's right. In fact, the other day, I almost called her Mom." There was a catch in his voice. Lanita took his hand.

Rudy shrugged with a laugh. "Damn glad I caught myself. I don't think she would have appreciated that."

Lanita lay down on her stomach and propped herself up on her elbows. "I really miss my mom, too."

Rudy nodded his head several times. "It was the worst thing I've ever been through. I can't imagine anything worse coming up in my life...except maybe losing a child or a wife, I suppose."

Lanita spoke just above a whisper, "Six months after my mom died, my dad married again and...," she took several deep breaths. "He was weak and broken after mama died. His new wife and her two daughters controlled everything and when he wasn't around, they made my life miserable. After so long, I ran away. I've never contacted him."

Rudy gently massaged her back. "Maybe it's time to do that."

"I can't, and I don't want to." She watched the waves and remembered her step-mother with the razor strap and the intense pain as it cut into her back. Just a girl, she reached out and grabbed the pot of boiling water on the stove. Lanita could still hear her stepmother's screams as the boiling liquid scalded her face, arms and hands. The step-sisters came running in and she splashed the last on them and threw the pot hitting one of them on the forehead. Then she ran out the back door and ran until she came to the entrance of a convent miles from her home. She told the nuns that her step mother wanted to kill her and the deep cuts on her back and buttocks was proof enough for them. They protected her and helped her get to the States.

Rudy began to talk which brought her back to the present. "For a while after mom was killed, I was deathly afraid I was going to lose my dad to depression. He went from home to work, from work to home, day after day like a zombie. He's better now, but not back to his old self.

Once again, a deep silence fell between them as they watched the evening sky change from yellow to gold to orchid. Suddenly a convertible roared up and parked a few hundred yards away. A cadre of teenagers bounded from every space in the vehicle. Madonna's "Like A Virgin" blasted from the radio. Joyful screams and laughter blended in with the rolling waves.

"We're being evicted." Rudy got up and held out his hand for her. "Let's get to the Crab Cradle and have some soft shells and beer."

"I never got to be a carefree teenager," Lanita said as they walked off.

Rudy put his arm around her shoulder and led her to the outdoor restaurant. "It's never too late. Let's be teenagers again. It won't be that hard for me since I've never really grown up."

Lanita rested her head on his shoulder. "You can show me how."

A few minutes later two tall frosty glasses of beer sat before them. Three small children were running on the beach chasing the gulls. Rudy and Lanita were content to sit in silence, sip beer and observe the surroundings. They had been together only a short time, yet they seemed like an older couple sharing a beer after years of end-of-the-day beers. Lanita leaned over and spoke just above a whisper. "I want to tell you something, but you must promise you won't repeat it."

Rudy smiled, crossed his heart three times and repeated three times. "Cross my heart and hope to die."

Lanita laughed. "You are a little boy."

What? After all these nights, you call still me a boy? I believe I've proved to be a man with a capital M."

"Oh, shut up! Now you're being an annoying teenager."

He took her hand and kissed it. "I love secrets, so tell me, tell me."

Lanita took a deep breath. "I like my job. I really do. The Archbishop is good to me, pays me very well and isn't controlling or demanding like some I've worked for. I like him, but there's something." She stopped, debating whether to go on. "I believe the Archbishop has lovers." She drank some beer. *Now I know how Judas Iscariot must have felt.* "Listen, never mind. I shouldn't…"

Rudy burst out laughing at her serious expression. "You act like that's a crime."

"Rudy, he's a Catholic Archbishop. They aren't supposed to do that."

Rudy thought for a moment. "Oh yeah, I'd forgotten about that. But, come on, don't you think that's a ridiculous rule? I bet nearly all of them have something on the side."

"I shouldn't be gossiping." She brushed the table with her napkin as if to clean her mind. "It's none of my business what the Archbishop does."

But Rudy's curiosity was piqued. "You say lovers, plural?"

Lanita twisted in her chair.

"Come on, you can't throw out a tidbit like that and then drop it."

The weight of keeping silent all these years overpowered her desire to be discreet. "There are four, I think." She hesitated before resuming, "According to what I've picked up, it appears that a different one comes every month or so, sometimes more often, sometimes less."

"Have you ever seen any of his ladies?"

"No, but I've come across things while cleaning like red lipstick on a pillow case, a long black hair, a short blonde hair, a broken fingernail with pink glitter polish, rumpled bed sheets. And then there are the four different fragrances, each has her own perfume."

The waitress set a stacked platter of crabs between them and handed out large bibs. "There's corn on the cob and fried okra comin'," she said as she turned back to the kitchen.

Rudy got up, fastened her bib and kissed her neck several times. "Speaking of special fragrance. You've got the sweetest."

"Just wait. Dessert will come later." She relished the affection.

Peach and pink tinted the landscape as the sun was leaving for the day. The soft colors painted Lanita in a happiness she had not felt in a long time. She looked across the table at Rudy, so carefree, open and lovable, even with butter dripping on his chin. She prayed she wouldn't be too depressed once he left. But for now, she wasn't going to think of that. *Just be in the moment. Be a teenager.*

"Now I've got a little secret to tell you." Rudy whispered as he wiped his chin. "Oh, I guess it's not a secret. But it's sort of a funny coincidence. The other day Ofelia told me she thinks Elaine has a lover." He grimaced at the notion.

"No way, Rudy."

"She's an ice queen," I told her. "But she insisted her intuition is hardly ever off."

"Well, I think Ofelia is off on this one. Besides, Lily Mae says she calls herself the Virgin Queen."

Rudy drank his beer. "I don't give a damn if she is or isn't. I can't imagine any man wanting to bed her."

Lanita took a hot towel from the container the waitress had left. She wiped her hands and mouth. "God, this food is oh so messy. I'll have to take another shower."

"On yes, we'll have to shower in your tiny shower. Such fun." He shot her a boyish grin.

Lanita smiled shyly and turned her attention back to the lapping waves just yards away.

CHAPTER FOURTEEN

Alone in the club, Ofelia sat at the piano bench playing notes from the score in front of her. "That's not it." She picked up a pencil and jotted a revision. The back door swung open flooding the room with sunlight. The night bartender stopped at the sound of the piano and squinted in her direction. "What are you doin' here so early?"

"Hi Jeremy. I was hoping to finish writing this song. My muse seems to prefer this place." Ofelia stretched her back. "Probably because I don't have a piano where I'm staying. What time is it?

Jeremy looked at his watch. "It's five straight up. In four hours you'll be on."

On his way to the back of the bar he stopped and turned to her. "My aunt is having a fit cause I'm working with Elaine Chauvier's sister. She says Elaine was one of the greatest actresses ever. I guess talent must run in your family, huh?"

"Looks that way. Did she get to see her perform?"

"She's never been to New York, but she's seen the two or three movies she was in. She's tried to get me to watch them, but they're too old for my taste. People acted funny back then."

Ofelia couldn't keep from laughing. *Elaine still acts pretty damn funny.* "The style of acting was different then, more melodramatic." Ofelia picked up her satchel of sheet music and headed for the outside door. "I'll see you around 8:30. Please have a vodka tonic waiting."

"Right-on." Jeremy saluted.

Ofelia decided to walk the six blocks to her cottage. She needed the exercise and the time to think. The similarities between Greg and Roderick, her New Orleans' boyfriend, were becoming more apparent and thus more disturbing. Both men were self-centered, controlling and somewhat abusive. What was worse is that she allowed them to be. *I'm afraid of being abandoned, especially by a man.* Just the other night while returning from the bathroom, she had overheard Greg bragging to a country club buddy, "There's nothing like having some of that brown sugar to make your juices flow." Both men laughed loudly. She felt cheap and used and had wanted to run away.

In New Orleans she had wallowed in a cave of misery after Roderick had dumped her. She would listen to Billy Holiday's recordings all day and began imitating her idol at the nightspots where she sang. Then life dealt her the ultimate blow. Grand-mere died. As soon as Grand-mere knew that she was dying, she told Ofelia about the inheritance and gave her the name of the lawyer who had the will. "You've got enough sense now to know what to do," Grand-mere had said. "And honey, you deserve a man who'll treat you the way your daddy treated your mama."

Three weeks after the funeral, Ofelia told Grand tante that she needed to get away for a while and that she wanted to visit her home place. Her estranged sister turned out to be a huge disappointment, but then she met Greg. He was charming, rich, and fun. She knew from the outset there was no future in the relationship but now she was embarrassed about being "the brown sugar on the side." *I'm better than that.*

"A storm's brewing out there for sure," an elderly woman called out across the yard as Ofelia walked past. She sat on her front porch fanning herself with a folded newspaper.

Ofelia smiled, "Afternoon, Mrs. Harkins. There's sure not much breeze, is there? You take care, now." She waved and picked up her pace.

Her other worry was Rudy's obsession over a buried treasure underneath Shadow's Way. "We could be rich beyond our imaginations," he had said. "I want my share of this place and all it contains." She was tired and a little afraid to continue confronting her sister. She was ready for some peace. Maybe it was time to go back to New Orleans.

Early the next morning, Ofelia went into the kitchen to get some sugar. Elaine was putting fresh baked oatmeal cookies into a cookie jar. "They smell wonderful," Ofelia commented reaching out for one. Elaine turned and began waving the spatula in Ofelia's face backing her in the corner between the refrigerator and counter. "You only came here to live off me and steal what belongs to me." Ofelia felt trapped and shoved Elaine as hard as she could. Elaine fell to the floor hitting her head on the edge of the table. She sat up rubbing the back of her head and moaning. When Ofelia saw that she was okay, she grabbed a couple of cookies and rushed out. Later that afternoon, she composed a note. "I'm sorry I shoved you. You frightened me and I over reacted." Ofelia stuck the note on a box of pecan pralines from Angelina's, Elaine's favorite candy, and placed it just outside the kitchen door.

The very next afternoon Elaine knocked on her door. "A peace offering." A smiling Elaine held out a large cereal-sized bowl of bread pudding. "And thank you for those delicious pralines." Ofelia's heart opened in forgiveness and love. "How sweet. Won't you come in?" She took the pudding. "I'm sorry I shoved you."

Elaine waved an imaginary flag. "Good thing I have a hard head." She tapped her head with a fist. "Besides you can't help that you inherited that mean Chauvier temper."

Temper? You were coming at me with a spatula. Ofelia wanted to say but decided not to. "Please have a seat. I just made some herbal tea."

Elaine looked around the cabin. "These aren't my tastes, but you've decorated this place in a unique way, ethnic I suppose."

Ofelia didn't know if this was a compliment or not. "Would you like some tea?" Elaine nodded.

With cups in hand, the sisters sat the table. "This is nice," Ofelia said softly.

"Indeed it is." Elaine slipped into her Southern Belle accent. "Now tell me about New Orleans. I've been there only once for a short three days. We were doing 'The Glass Menagerie' and I was much too exhausted for any daytime excursions."

"Well, perhaps someday soon you can come visit me. I would love to show you all the beautiful places." Ofelia told her about the neighborhood where she and her great aunt lived. "We have festivals all year long, not just at Mardi Gras."

"That's sounds wonderful. Now you must try my masterpiece. Get a spoon and try it?" At first Ofelia thought this demand was odd but then decided her sister must be excited to be doing something special for her. She fetched two spoons, but Elaine waved hers away. "This is yours. I have some at the house." While Ofelia scooped up a spoonful, Elaine continued cheerfully, "It won a blue ribbon at state. I swear Lily Mae could live off this. I hid the batch I made for myself at the back of the fridge."

Ofelia slowly savored the flavors. "Oh my gosh, you were cheated. This is better than a blue ribbon."

Elaine smiled contentedly. "You know when I was in New York I could not for the life of me believe that those people didn't know what bread pudding was. One time after a cast party I brought two bowls of this. You know we always had lots of food and drink at those..." She stopped, noticing that Ofelia wasn't eating any more. "What's wrong, dear? You're not eating."

Ofelia shook her head. "I want to save it for dessert tonight."

"Oh well, later is better than never, as they say." Elaine shook off her disappointment. "New York was so freeing for me. I felt so alive." She went on to tell Ofelia about her acting debut and the jobs that followed. Occasionally, she would ask Ofelia a question about her singing career and appear to be interested. Ofelia imagined that a bond was forming between them. The visit lasted for almost an hour without a wrinkle. When Elaine left, the sisters hugged. "We must do this more often," Elaine lightly kissed Ofelia's cheek and left.

Do I finally have a sister? Thank you, God. Ofelia wanted to jump for joy.

Before going to sleep that night, Ofelia ate the rest of the pudding while listening to Etta James. A few hours after midnight, she awakened with severe stomach cramps. Doubled over in pain, she managed to roll out of bed and crawl to the toilet where she vomited to the point of exhaustion. If she could have spoken above a whisper, she would have called out to Rudy. She couldn't even scoot herself to the phone to call the hospital, so she lay on the cold bathroom floor and courted death. The shadows whispered, "She's poisoned you. That pudding is killing you."

She drifted off to a sleep of no dreams, just darkness. After what seemed like years, a loud pounding brought her to consciousness. *Thank God. Someone to help me.* Her whole body was sore and tender. She had pulled herself up to her hands and knees when she heard a key being forced into her door and saw the knob being twisted. That could only be one person. *Thank you, God, for giving me the good sense to change the locks when I moved in.* She sat up and willed herself to call out, "What is it?"

After a long pause, an alarmed voice asked, "Ofelia, you okay?"

Ofelia wanted to scream, *you bitch, I almost died.* She mustered all her strength and said, "Why yes, why shouldn't I be?" She wanted to add, *You're not the only damn actress in this family.*

"Oh, well it's just that it's well after noon and I hadn't seen hide nor hair of you."

"I was with Greg most of the night. Didn't get in till three." No response. She gathered more energy. "I dropped that bread pudding all over the floor." She paused, breathing deeply. "What a mess to clean up." She took several deeper breaths. "So sorry about that. I hope you'll make me some more." Still silence from behind the door.

Ofelia pulled herself up on her bed and collapsed on the pillow. She felt Elaine's loathing slithering under the door like gangly goblins. "You are supposed to be dead. You are supposed to be dead," they whispered and curled around her.

Suddenly, the good spirits of her ancestors were there overcoming and swallowing up the horrible ones. They lulled her off into a warm peaceful sleep whispering that she had won. Her sister's attempt had failed. She was still alive.

Hours later Rudy knocked on her door and waited. He pounded louder. "Ofelia, you in there?" The door opened a crack and Ofelia peeked out. "What in the hell happened to you?" he gasped. Ofelia spoke just above a whisper, "Come in and shut the door. It's too bright."

"You need to go to the doctor?" Rudy asked.

"She," Ofelia pointed a finger towards Shadow's Way, "almost killed me."

"For the love of Jesus, are you serious?" Ofelia got on her bed. Rudy propped up pillows to help her sit up. "What happened?"

Ofelia sighed, "First pour me a glass of ginger tea. It's in the fridge on the top shelf."

Ofelia drank the tea, then recounted the horror tale. "Rudy, I was at death's door. I could feel it."

Rudy looked at the patterns on the rug and shook his head. "I know she's mentally sick, but do you think she'd do something that awful? Kill her own sister? Maybe it was an accident, like using an ingredient that's gone bad."

"Come on, Rudy." Ofelia laughed. "As meticulous as she is, especially about her cooking?" She fell back. "That was no mistake." She grabbed Rudy's hand and pulled him closer, suddenly afraid that Elaine might be outside the door, listening. "Rudy don't approach her any more about selling this place and don't eat anything she cooks."

"Oh, I've already stopped having any meals over there."

"And Rudy," Ofelia pleaded, "we don't need the money from that house right now. Let's wait a few months and have the courts handle everything."

Rudy sighed deeply. "Well, I was all set to retire. Start living out my days on the beach."

"Don't be a goof. You'll have more fun promoting my singing career and helping me get your grandad's books published." Ofelia laid back on her pillows. "Now, leave. I have to rest. Be sure to lock the door when you leave."

CHAPTER FIFTEEN

Leone and his wife, Darlene, sat on their front porch and watched the lightning dance across the gulf. Darlene loved a good storm despite its potential destructiveness. Their cabin, perched high on stilts near the edge of the bayou, had been severely damaged only twice in the thirty years they had lived there. Both times they had rebuilt with stronger materials and designs better suited for the extreme weather. They had never considered moving farther inland and in fact, preferred being away from civilization. If an occasional gator happened into the yard, they were usually able to kill it before it got to their chickens. Darlene's gator gumbo was the best in the region.

She glanced over at Leone. He had been fretting all evening over a story Bastien had told him. She tried to ease his mind. "Baby, you know when he's had a drink or two, his imagination goes to workin' overtime."

Leone sighed. "He hadn't been drinkin' and it's too strange even for him. Elaine wantin' snakes and then some loose woman comin' over for the same thing." He scratched his head. "Bastien came to me for help."

Leone had been patrolling traffic at the south elementary school when he got a call from the desk clerk. "That Bastien Figurant just stormed in here wantin' to talk with you. I told him you was gone, so now he's sittin' out front in his car just starin' into space. He's probably drunk. You want me to put him in a cell?"

"Hell no! Just let him be. I'll be there in a little bit."

Thirty minutes later Leone and Bastien arrived at their usual coffee shop. Bastien desperately needed his friend's advice. "Elaine said they'll use the venom for medicine." They ordered their coffee and he continued, "But something tells me she's lying." He dumped three spoonsful of sugar into his cup. "Can you call some colleges to see if they're looking for venom?"

"Why else would she want snakes? It don't make no sense, Bastien, and I've heard they do make medicine from venom." Leone wiped his fork with his napkin. "I sure as hell don't think she wants to use 'em to scare her guests, do you?" He drank some coffee and grimaced. "Hand over that sugar."

"Mama always said I had a gift for knowin' things and I know somethin' ain't right here."

Leone knew that was true. Hadn't Bastien warned him about Julian, the white man who'd intended to kill him? "When I see him lookin' at you," Bastien had cautioned, "I feel murder in his heart." Today Leone's bones would be sunk deep in a swamp if he hadn't taken Bastien's premonition seriously. So, Leone wasn't going to dismiss his friend's concern.

"Now I'm gonna tell you somethin' that's gonna be hard to believe." Bastien continued. "I was sittin' at my table lookin' at Mama's picture and you know, talkin' to her, tellin' her I was tryin' to be good and not drink."

Bastien stopped talking while the waitress served them their hamburgers with fries. "I heard somethin' and looked out of the winder. This old Plymouth coup was coming up and I thought somone was comin' for repair. It came right up to the house and this blonde floozy gets out in a dress so short it was awful, but then she put on a big rain cape with a hood that practically covered her face. It had been sort of drizzlin' on and off all day. She comes up and knocks, then she hollered like a wild cat, 'Bastien, I'm Trixie. Your friend, Elaine sent me. I got your favorite bourbon.'"

He thought for a moment. "She talked funny like that Yankee guy at the feed store, but some different. I yelled back, 'Elaine ain't my friend.'"

She laughed real loud. 'Well, she ain't my friend, neither. Come on now, open the door and let's have a drink and get acquainted. I can give you some other pleasures too, if you like.'

"I just stood on the other side of the door, like the cat had got my tongue. Finally, she says, 'Okay then, just reach out here and get this bourbon. Elaine will give me hell if I come back with it. She'll say I drank it myself and never even came out here. You know how damn mean she is.'

"Like every other time, my weakness for liquor got the best of me. I let her in and felt a ghost walk over my grave when I caught a glimpse of her face. She looked like a carnival clown, all painted up. I know this sounds weird, but I thought to myself, *That's Elaine.* But I couldn't tell for sure cause you know in that raincoat with the hood pulled down, and it's dark in my cabin, specially on overcast days like that.

"She come in and poured us a drink and gulped hers down. I saw Mama's picture and I said, 'No, you got to go. I ain't drinkin' these days.' But she waved that bottle under my nose and danced around and opened her rain coat, jiggling her tits up and down. After a while my promise to Mama just went to hell and I started gulping down what she poured and she kept pouring. At one point I think she got another bottle. At first, I kept backing off and slapping her hands off me. But then the room started twisting around me like a tornado and I fell over my cot."

He hung his head in embarrassment and whispered. "And she tried to do stuff you know, but I kicked her hard and she landed on her bottom."

"Bastien, you don't have to tell me," Leone interrupted.

"I was so drunk," Bastien mumbled, "and it was like when I was a boy with that priest."

Leone nodded his head. "Yes, I know."

Bastien looked over at the next table afraid that someone might be listening. He lowered his voice. "But she didn't get mad. She just got up and said she should've know I was different from other men." Both men sat silently eating. Bastien swallowed the last of his hamburger and continued, "I tried to get up off the cot but fell back and passed out. Next thing I know she was shaking me saying, 'It's gettin' darker outside. We got to hurry.' She held up the doctor's kit and asked me if I'd help her get those goddamned snakes. She said, 'I don't know what the hell Elaine wants with them, but she paid me good money to come out here to gather up them little bastards. Oh, and she gave me this hundred-dollar bill to give to you too.'"

Bastien reached in his pocket and pulled out the bill. "See, here I still got it. You keep it. I don't want it." Bastien slid the money across the table and sighed in disgust. "By then, I wasn't thinkin', so I go down to the river and caught two moccasins, big ones with lots of venom. And every time I'd look at her, she'd turn and pull the hood down even lower. She snared three non poisonous ones. When I told her that, she said Elaine was so stupid she wouldn't know the difference. She turned to leave and hollered out over her shoulder and told me not to worry because she'd make Elaine pay me more. She said, "That woman has so much goddamn money, yet all she ever thinks about is getting more and more. Don't say I said this but I hate her.' Then she got in her car and drove off."

Bastien slumped down and didn't say another word and I didn't either. We sat there until the waitress came with the check. When she saw that hundred dollar bill, she yelled out, "I can't make change for that."

He shoved it in my pocket and handed her a ten. "Give that hundred to Darlene," Bastien said and then added, "Leone, I'd bet my life that it was Elaine."

Darlene swatted at a mosquito. "That Bastien is a sweet, sweet man, but I bet he just dreamed up all that while he was on one of his drunks."

"How do you explain this hundred dollar bill?" He slapped it down on the table. Darlene was silent. Leone knew his friend and he believed every word of the story no matter how strange it sounded.

Trixie had been more than ready to go back to her work. "I knew Elaine would need me again. She can't stay away from trouble." It had been a long time since she had left New York and Elaine had hardly given her a thought these past years. "Yeah, but now I'm the only one capable of doing what has to be done. Those other fluffs are worthless." After all, Trixie had been with Elaine since childhood, long before the Madame and girls came along, and like Elaine, she was evil.

That evening Elaine hummed a whimsical tune overjoyed that Trixie had gotten the snakes. After swallowing a handful of pills, she lay down on top of the comforter, more relaxed than she had been in months. Just a little over a year ago, her life had been so calm and easygoing. The occasional troublesome guest had been her only problem. She sighed deeply and spoke to the empty bedside chair, "Don't worry, we'll soon have that life again."

CHAPTER SIXTEEN

Brother Damien held the doorbell down. *I know you're in there.* Suddenly the door was flung open while his finger was still on the button.

"Stop harassing me," Elaine shouted.

Not looking directly at her, Brother Damien held out an envelope. "Since you're not answering the Archbishop's calls, he asked me to deliver this."

"What now?"

"Well, since you haven't confirmed when you're leaving, this is informing you that he'll be filing an eviction notice as soon as this storm passes." He pushed an envelope towards her.

Panic crisscrossed Elaine's face like electric currents. "And what if I've decided to stay?"

"He's already gotten someone to oversee the facility since you ignored his inquiry as to whether you'd take the job." Brother Damien waved the envelope. "The terms are covered in these documents."

Elaine took the packet as if it were a hot coal. She turned and eased down to a sitting position on the bottom stair step. Her face was drawn and pale.

"Are you alright?" He waited, but Elaine didn't respond. "Just one other thing. Mr. Jenkins, a realtor in our parish, said he'd help you to find another place for half his usual fee.

"I don't need any realtor. Tell your Archbishop I'll pay back every penny I owe for Shadow's Way."

Brother Damien cleared his throat several times. "Ms. Chauvier, he's not selling." He glanced into the parlor. "Work crews will be arriving right after the storm to begin renovations, somewhat minor, but nevertheless rendering it more suitable for confinement." The portrait of the great-grandfather caught his eye. With a wince he quickly turned away.

Elaine stood up. Poised and erect, she delivered her lines as if she were in a theater, "I shall pay back every penny that I owe. Mind you, this home shall always be in our family,"

Brother Damien was amused. "Ms. Chauvier, your family hasn't had this home for quite some time now.

Elaine's eyes blazed with fury. "You tell that lecherous man of God that I'm going to tell everyone about Madame Claudine and his women and how he used the Church's money to pay for his pleasures."

Stunned, Brother Damien stepped back. "Well, I suppose that concludes our business."

Elaine stared at her grandfather's portrait. Finally, she turned back to Brother Damien and said, "Tell Andre it'll all be gone as soon as the storm is over."

Ofelia was seated in a corner booth hidden in shadows. Within minutes Greg scooted in across from her. He reached across the table and took her hand. "Hello, darling. I'm glad you're feeling better. You're incredibly beautiful, as always."

The waiter came, and Greg ordered a Scotch and water. He nodded at Ophelia's wine glass. "I see you've already started." Breathing deeply, he said, "I've been worried. You're not pregnant, are you?" He moved the candle to the side as she shook her head with a definite no.

"Then why the urgency? Couldn't this have waited until tonight? I have another life you know." The hardness in his voice contrasted with the softness of the hand holding hers. She would miss the caresses of his soft hands. He took a paper napkin and thoroughly wiped his section of the table. The diamond on his ring finger sparkled in the dim light.

"Did that sister of yours look after you while you were ill?"

"No, she didn't, but Lanita did. She slept on my couch for two nights."

"Isn't she the Archbishop's maid?" His voice was laced with condescension.

"Yes, I'm good friends with the maid," she snapped back, emphasizing the word maid. "In fact, I feel a sister bond with the maid."

He glanced away surprised by the anger. Generally he didn't have any interest in her life away from him and was surprised to hear that she even had a friend. The waiter came with his drink. "We'll start out with the crab legs and a dozen oysters."

As always, he was taking charge without so much as asking her what she might like. It had bothered her in the past, but today she found it unbearable. "And I'd like a cup of the bisque." She looked back at Greg.

"I'm not interested in crab legs or oysters." She took a sip of wine. "But then you don't really care what I'm interested in, do you?" He began to speak, but she held up her hand and continued, "I know all about your life, your daughters, their names, where they go to school, what they like for breakfast. But you don't know one thing about me." She pulled away as he reached for her hand.

"Ofelia, what's gotten into you?" He removed a small jewelry box from his coat pocket and slid it towards her. "My dear, I understand you're upset because I didn't check on you when you were sick, but as you know I have another life. I wanted to be there with you."

"Bullshit!" She shoved the box back towards him. "Only if it had been convenient for you."

"What's going on with you today. You act like you want to end this relationship." She could see the disbelief in his face.

"You're right on target," she said with a slight laugh.

A tray slid between them. "The bisque will be out shortly."

She waited for the waiter to leave. "I'm ending this."

"There's someone else, isn't there?" He was raising his voice. "I expected as much."

"Oh, did you?" She felt her power coming back. "I suppose your wife expects as much from you too."

He yanked on his tie to loosen it and tried to undo the collar button. His breathing was labored.

"I've been so weak, haven't I?" she whispered. "So easy to manipulate."

"What? Stop mumbling." He tore open a crab leg and stabbed the white meat into the cocktail sauce.

"I feel really sad for your wife and I'm sorry I've done this to her," she spoke softly. "I've never before done that to another woman."

He looked at her with so much loathing she was thankful they were in a public place. An icy edict broke through his tight jaw. "You'll need to be looking for another job. After this weekend your gig, as you people call it, will be up."

She stood up and slung her purse over her shoulder. "Tell you what. I'm resigning as of now. Better call the club and tell them I won't be in tonight or the rest of this week. And as my people call it, 'go fuck yourself.'"

She quickly left for the door.

He called after her, "You won't get any work around here. I'll see to it."

Ofelia closed the door of her cabin, slunk down in the big chair and drew her feet up beside her. She felt alone once again, but not as alone as she did after her mother's death, or her father's abandonment, or Roderick's rejection or her Grand-mere's death. She felt about as alone as she did when she realized her only sister had tried to kill her. "I'm stronger. I won't break down."

A knock at the door startled her. *Is my bitch sister coming to finish the job?*

"Ofelia, it'll take just a minute." It was Lanita's sweet voice.

Ofelia jumped up, flung open the door and threw her arms around her.

"Oh dear, you must have told him. How did it go?" Lanita asked.

"Well, now I don't have a lover or a job. I quit him and he fired me and then I quit him again."

Lanita patted her cheek. "Oh honey, you'll get another job and you'll be fine. You've got me, a new sister, and Rudy, your foolish nephew. And oh, I forgot about your Grand-tante in New Orleans."

Lanita turned her around in the direction of the bathroom. "Now go freshen up. We're meeting Rudy at the new club in Old Town called Chez Beau. If Rudy can't talk that manager into hiring you, then no one can. I'll bet you anything you have another job before the night is out."

Feeling recharged, Ofelia headed for the bathroom. "I think I'll wear my sweltering black silk tonight."

"That's the spirit."

CHAPTER SEVENTEEN

"Elaine can't be serious?" Trixie fumed in front of the makeup mirror. She was speaking to someone in the shadows of the dimly lit underground room. "That bitch treats me like a dog until she needs me to do her dirty work." She dusted her cheeks with mounds of red rouge. "Like that stage manager in New York, the one I stuffed inside a garbage bin. No one even suspected she had a thing to do with it." She listened to the voice in the shadows and continued, "Yes, I know she's going to pay me and pay me very well."

Trixie looked down at the case holding the snakes. "But an Archbishop. I might go to hell for doing something that awful." She applied another thick layer of lipstick to her blood red lips. "Besides, this job could be dangerous. Do you really think that Archbishop will let someone like me into his bedroom?"

Trixie stood up and propped a heeled foot on the chair. She straightened the seam of her mesh hose. "Okay, Okay," she shouted impatiently. "I'll do it. But I need time to plan this. And tell Elaine to keep away from me."

When the man stepped down from the Greyhound bus, the heat caught him off guard. He staggered back a few steps. Behind him a young woman put up her hands to steady him. "You alright, Sir?"

"Oh, I'm fine. Thank you. Just been riding the bus for too many days." For months now, Josh Conroe had been following one lead after another. He prayed this would be his last stop. He was too old to be chasing phantoms and he was tired of riding buses. But he was more afraid of flying, and six months ago his driver's license had not been renewed due to a degenerative eye disease.

In the bus station Josh headed for the diner and ordered a cup of coffee. He knew better than to order food in one of these places. Once he got his land feet, he'd walk over to the hotel he'd booked. The brochure gave its restaurant a five-star review. The thought of a soaking bath followed by a ten-ounce steak and a baked potato loaded with sour cream almost brought tears to his eyes. Whether or not this was the end of his search, he was going to rest for at least a week.

Now that he was retired from the Boston Police Department, he could devote himself to a cold case that had haunted him for too many years. His youngest sibling, Eric, had been living in New York, working as a stage manager and dreaming of becoming a director. But on June 14, 1961 Eric's body was found in a garbage bin a block from his apartment. A plastic bag was tightly bound around his head and he was in his pajamas. There were no witnesses. His apartment was spotless with no clues except for one long synthetic hair from a blond wig. The New York police interviewed every neighbor and everyone working at the theater. Nevertheless, the case was quickly shuffled to a back burner and all but forgotten.

Josh had been frustrated by the outcome and knew that the NYPD had not done everything they could. Right after his retirement party, he told his wife there was one last case he still had to solve.

Leone and his partner stood sweating on the front porch of Shadow's Way. The heat and gummy humidity were hellish. Impatiently Leone rang the doorbell for the third time. The door opened a crack and Lily Mae peeped out, eyes bulging.

Hello, I'm Officer Leone Attafey and this is Officer Reggie Grant."

"Yassir, we ain't takin on any more guests."

We're not wanting a room, you dimwit, Leone wanted to shout, but instead spoke softly, "We need to talk with Elaine Chauvier. Is she here?"

Lily Mae opened the door wider. "Yassir but said to tell you she has ta pack."

"Well, you tell her the police are here to ask her some questions."

With some hesitation Lily Mae let them in. "I'll git Miss Chauvier. Ya'll jest wait."

Leone and Reggie walked into the parlor. It was the first time either had been inside this house. They had heard dozens of stories about it being one of the most haunted in the whole state. Both men felt a little creepy as the hateful-looking Confederate Colonel glared down at them. Leone picked up a magazine from a stack on the coffee table. "Would you have a look at this?" He held it up for Reggie.

A picture of Elaine in this very room was on the cover of *Modern Southern Living,* dated April 1982. She wore a flowing antebellum gown and was standing by the fireplace under the portrait.

"Oh, yes, I've seen that." Reggie said. "My wife's still got four of them magazines. Gives 'em away to relatives, friends. Makes her feel like somethin' cause she lives in same city."

Leone wanted to rip that picture into pieces. That time was filled with such cruelty and evil and should never be revered as glamorous. He remembered Bastien saying, "She thinks she still lives in slavery days."

Without a sound Elaine swept into the room with an exaggerated flourish. She was the woman on the magazine cover without the gown, but still the Southern belle, lively, gracious and charming.

"My dear policemen, so sorry to keep you waitin'. Have you come to carry me off in handcuffs?" Her high-pitched laughter rose to the ten-foot ceiling and hung there. "Do sit down, please. Can I get you somethin' to drink?" Before they could answer she pulled a rope cord in the corner. Within a few seconds Lily Mae appeared in the doorway. "Please bring some of the fresh hibiscus tea for these lovely gentlemen." She sat down on the sofa and gestured for them to sit on the chairs opposite her.

Leone began, "Miss Chauvier, some things have come up that we need to ask you about."

"Well, go right ahead. I'm an open book." She smiled at each of them. "My goodness, I hope I haven't had a most-wanted person staying here, have I?" She tilted her head flirtatiously and looked around as if afraid. "You wouldn't shoot up my beautiful home, would you?"

"It's been reported that you're gathering poisonous snakes and…"

"Snakes?" Elaine interrupted. "Why, whoever heard of such ridiculousness? What would I do with snakes? Besides, how is that a police matter anyway?"

Reggie cleared his throat. "Well ma'am, we were told you paid someone to get water moccasins for medical purposes, but when we contacted the research facilities around the state, no one knew of any such requests or needs."

Elaine's back stiffened and her eyes turned to black marbles, fixed and menacing. Both men had dealt with some very strange people but this one was especially unnerving; however, Lily Mae broke the spell upon entering with the tray of tea glasses. In a blink Elaine's face shifted back to friendly warmth. "Gentlemen, I so hope you enjoy this tea, a special blend of mine." She handed each of them a glass with a napkin.

Luckily, Leone had warned Reggie not to drink or eat anything she offered.

"Now, pray tell," Elaine tittered with a heavy coat of sarcasm, "am I involved in any other criminal activity besides helping science procure poisonous snakes?"

"What do you intend to do with them?" Leone asked. "And who was the other woman sent to get them?"

"You should be ashamed asking someone like me these questions."

Reggie had to look out the window. Her arrogance was hard to take. "Who filled your heads with such nonsense? I have a right to know my accuser?" Before they could answer, she jumped up and clapped her hands with excitement. "Oh, I bet I know. It was that horrible Bastien Figurant, wasn't it? How could you possibly listen to someone like him, a hopeless drunk? And believe him?"

She took a drink of tea and exhaled. "I really thought the police department had better things to do than listen to some sot." She wagged a finger at them. "Rest assured, I'll be contacting the police chief, a dear friend. I know he won't take kindly to this sort of persecution."

Leone and Reggie glanced at one another. That very morning the chief had said, "I don't know Elaine Chauvier, but I know of her. Her half-sister recently filed a report about an attempted poisoning." The chief read from Ofelia's statement. "I believe Elaine Chauvier gave me bread pudding containing poison on the 3rd of September." The chief looked over his reading glasses. "Here, you can read the whole thing." He slid the report towards them. "I told Miss Ofelia to bring in the bowl even though she had already washed it. There could still be traces of poison there."

After taking some moments to think, the chief nodded his head. "Yes, go ahead and investigate this snake story. And ask her about the pudding accusation, too. I want to know how she reacts."

Leone studied Elaine before deciding the direction his questioning should go. "I've been wonderin' ma'am, why do you think Bastien would makeup somethin' like this?"

Elaine crossed and uncrossed her legs several times in quick spasmatic movements. She had betrayed herself by naming Bastien. "He's always causing trouble for his brother the Archbishop, and he's jealous of the friendship the two of us have. God knows he's had a crush on me since we were kids. Perhaps he feels scorned because I've always rejected his drunken advances."

She got up and took a few steps towards the foyer. "Now, gentlemen, I have important business to attend to. Thank you for coming by." She laughed dryly. "And I do hope you find that floozy with those awful snakes."

"Who said anything about a floozy?"

Elaine froze. *Another slip.*

"Just one or two more question, Ms. Chauvier. The police chief wants to know about the bread pudding you gave your sister."

"Half-sister," Elaine cried out louder than she intended. She swallowed several times and continued in a civil tone, "I have never in my life made bread pudding. Why would I when I can get the best in the world from Evangeline's bakery?" She adjusted a pillow on the sofa and spoke as if to herself, "It's so sad. You know her mother was a whore and to this day she is eaten up with jealousy. She wants to get this place all to herself when she has no legal right to it." To keep her hands from shaking she rearranged the flowers sitting on the coffee table. "Lily Mae," she called out, "show these gentlemen to the door."

"That's alright, we'll can leave on our own. You'll hear from us as soon as we've had the pudding bowl tested." Elaine acted as if she hadn't heard this but once the door closed, she hurried to her apartment, fastened all the locks, double-checked them and went into her closet. A lavender Princess phone sat on a tiny table in the far corner, behind the winter coats. She dialed a number.

"Madame Claudine, Tell Trixie she has to stay out of sight."

Elaine paused, listening, "She's to stay down there till everything is done. There's also a problem with Ofelia." Another pause. "Forget that. I'll take care of her once this other business is finished." She put the receiver back and removed a pill bottle from the drawer. Dumping out a handful, she turned towards the corner and screamed, "But I have to have something until all this mess is cleaned up, so don't start chastising me."

CHAPTER EIGHTEEN

Rudy walked into the crowded diner, the best one for Creole food. At least a dozen people were waiting to be seated. Too hungry to wait, he was about to leave when he saw an outstretched arm waving him over. Bastien was sitting opposite a police officer. Rudy wasn't in the mood for Bastien, much less an officer of the law. His cramped stomach reminded him he hadn't eaten since last evening when Lanita had prepared an island meal for him and Ofelia in her tiny yellow and orange kitchen. It was now two in the afternoon.

On second thought, he decided he'd rather eat with distasteful company than try to find another place. Bastien stood up as Rudy approached the table. "Rudy, my man, I would like to make your acquaintance with my friend since when I was a kid. This is Leone Attafey."

After handshakes and customary greetings, Bastien scooted over. "Come on, have a sit. It could be a long wait. Popular place it is. Best food in town."

Rudy sat down. He had planned on a quiet meal alone, needing time to think about the fling that was turning into a full-blown affair. Never had he gone from casual fling to over-his-head in love. Last night he had almost whispered, "Lanita, I want to spend the rest of my life with you." Was she destined to be his Monique? Would he marry a black woman as his grandfather had? He had already postponed his trip to England for another two weeks. Also, there were the financial possibilities tying him here. The appraiser's quote for Shadow's Way had been well beyond what he had imagined. On top of that, there was the possibility of a hidden treasure and more money.

He had made his case to Ofelia again that morning, "The two of us own more than half, so we can sell out from under her." But Ofelia had shaken her head. "We've already been over this. We're dealing with a very unstable person, a possible murderer."

"That number three on the specials is the best," Bastien suggested.

Rudy came back to the menu. He was uneasy. Why was Bastien being so friendly? For too many nights now, he'd been with the woman Bastien had wanted. *Maybe he's going to have this cop run me out of town.* He sighed and read the number three.

"Well Rudy, how do you like it here below the Mason-Dixon?" Leone asked as he tapped a straw on the table. Rudy shook his head and said softly, "The sweltering heat is like nothing I've ever experienced. And the people, well they're different, hard to figure out."

Leone and Bastien were silent. Rudy shuffled in his seat. "I guess us Yankees just aren't as nice, and I'm not used to that," he said, hoping to iron out any wrinkle he may have created.

Leone laughed out loud. "That be true, sure enough. Never can tell when someone's lying down here 'cause that's about all we do." Both men laughed and after a moment, Rudy joined them. *They must be setting me up for something. Just keep your mouth shut.*

The waitress brought Leone and Bastien their plates. When she saw another face at the table she barked out, "Where d'ya pop up from?"

"Oh now, Nelda, go easy, he's a hungry child from a far-off land," Leone teased.

With hands on her hips, she watched Rudy as he fumbled around, turning the menu from one section to another until Bastien took charge. "Bring 'im the number three."

The talk immediately turned to the brewing hurricane in the Gulf. "It's gonna be a big one alright. The critters are as edgy as all get out and the birds are flying away. Andre wants me to come to his palace and I might just do that. I damn near drowned in '76. Had to climb a tree." Sadness covered his face. "Lost two sick dogs locked in their pens in that one."

Leone consoled him, "It come up fast and you had no radio then." He turned towards Rudy and said, "That explain the steamin' weather and the..."

"No, Leone," Bastien interrupted. "I was drunk. I know the signs. I don't need no radio."

Leone repeated, "Yes, sir, that explain the humidity."

"This time Andre is tellin' me he'll pay for my animals to stay at the vet's place. He's always good to me and I treat him so bad." He looked at Leone, "Will you help me get 'em over there?"

The waitress slammed Rudy's plate down in front of him and started off. Rudy cleared his throat, "Excuse me, could I have a large glass of your sweetened ice tea?" Pursing her lips, she turned away without a word.

"Don't mind her," Leone said. "She be a swamp woman and they gets all skittish like the critters when a storm's comin.'"

Rudy just nodded. He didn't really give a damn. He began eating. Once again, he was amazed. The Southern food was so very good, every place he went. *The North may have won the War, but it sure as hell wouldn't win any culinary war.*

"I called you over," Bastien started out, "to tell you I ain't got no hard feelin's 'bout you bein' with Lanita." He took a deep breath and continued, "But I do want you to get her out of that house when the storm comes. It be in too low a plane."

Rudy looked up at him and smiled. "That's very kind of you, Bastien. I'll do that."

Bastien beamed. "Leone got me goin' to AA, two meetin's a day. I haven't had a drink in over a week now. Never since I was in prison have I done that."

"That's wonderful, Bastien. Congratulations," Rudy said, genuinely moved. The swamp woman slammed the glass of iced tea down on the table. He shook his head. *Lots of strange, scary people down here. Maybe there is a hell, and this is it.*

Early the next day, Ofelia sat on the edge of her bed and again read the note that had been slipped under her door. *You've been here for months and haven't contributed to the welfare of Shadow's Way. I need your cottage for Paying customers. I expect you out by the weekend. Elaine Chauvier*

"This is as much mine as it is yours, you fiend," Ofelia screamed as loud as she could. Furious, she tore the note into teeny tiny pieces and threw them out the front door, praying Elaine would see her littering. *That'll freak her out.*

Ofelia had no more doubts. She knew what she was going to do. She headed for the bathroom to get ready. As she moved from showering to brushing her teeth to putting on clothes to applying makeup, her anger grew until it was a prairie fire of rage. "Okay, Rudy, I'm ready to sell this damn place now." She saw a determined person looking back at her from the mirror.

She grabbed her purse, then set it down to write a note, *I'll see you in court and then in hell, Sister dear.* She folded the paper, paused and tore it up, dropping the pieces in the trash can. *I don't want to give her any warning. Let the lawyers deliver the news.*

From beneath her bed she pulled out a suitcase containing all the papers she needed: a copy of her father's last will and a document proving that she, Ofelia, owned all the rights to his artistic estate, which included his trilogy of novels. Stuffing these papers into her shoulder bag, she headed out the door.

She glanced over at Rudy's cottage and saw a similar piece of paper sticking out from the bottom of his door. She quickly retrieved it and read, *I do believe you've overstayed your welcome and since you never bother to see me, I demand that you to go back to your own home. Aunt Elaine*

Ofelia put it in her bag. Now to find Rudy. She decided to knock on his door before leaving. After the third tap, he peeped out squinting into the daylight. "Lord, I figured you'd be in some dusty basement going over treasure maps."

"Christ, Ofelia, what time is it?"

Ofelia thrust the note at him. "I got a similar one."

He read and then laughed, "Homeless again."

"Come on, we're going to a lawyer. She can't evict us from our own home. Now get dressed."

After a few minutes, Rudy came out looking about as unkept as he had before. "The news had just announced that they've named this new hurricane 'Elaine.' Isn't that appropriate?"

"I wonder if it's as evil as the one we know." Ofelia trembled remembering the night she almost died.

"It's stalled in the Gulf," Rudy said enthusiastically, "gaining power and momentum. It's sort of exciting, don't you think?"

Ofelia looked at him in disbelief. "You've never been through one, have you?"

CHAPTER NINETEEN

Even though it was still early afternoon, Josh nursed a Scotch and soda at the hotel bar. He wore the same suit, a drab brown, baggy and wrinkled. His clean shirt had been the last in his suitcase. Outside his door in the hallway, he had left two bundles, one marked *laundry* and the other *cleaners*. The young man at the main desk had assured him he'd have clean clothes by that evening. He rubbed a hand over his bald crown and the bristly gray and black growth around it. A visit to the barber shop was on his to-do list for the afternoon.

A handsome young couple were engaged in a heated discussion farther down the mahogany bar. "Alright then, you go," she cried out. "I'll be up in the room." Josh watched her stomp off and smiled. In the early years of his marriage, he and Cheryl had argued almost daily. He was thankful those stormy times were in the past; however, just this morning during their daily phone call, she got angry when he told her he was going to stay through the storm. "This old hotel has gone through countless storms, Cheryl. I'll be safer here than on a bus."

Since arriving yesterday morning, he had spent most of the time in bed, sleeping and watching the weather channel. "She's just sitting out there in the Gulf building up steam," the Channel Four broadcaster said and then added grimly, "Elaine is too nice a name for this one."

A slight shiver passed over Josh. *Elaine. Is this a warning?* He shook off the premonition. Throughout the past year as he investigated his brother's death, the name Elaine came up over and over. He opened his notebook and flipped through the pages.

Elaine was the most egotistical actress I ever worked with.

No one could get along with Elaine.

Oh, Elaine was good alright, one of the best. But everyone paid a price for her brilliance.

Elaine treated your brother Eric like, I imagine, her ancestors treated their slaves.

Elaine had a charm that fooled most men, but we women saw right though her, and so did your brother.

Eric never once treated Elaine like she was any better than the rest of us and that really made her angry.

One time, Eric told Elaine in front of the entire cast that she wasn't nearly as good as she thought she was and to get over herself. We all laughed. From then on, she really had it in for him.

"Excuse me honey, would you like another drink?" Josh looked up at the petite blonde with the waitress-out-to-get-a-good-tip smile. He realized he was now in a place where it was considered acceptable to call anyone over a certain age "honey."

He smiled good naturedly, "No thank you, honey. What I'd like is one of those delicious hamburgers with a salad and a large tonic water with lime."

"It comes with fries."

"No more fries. I have to watch my figure, not to mention my cholesterol."

"Okay, sweetie, I'll have that right out." She put the pencil behind her ear and darted towards the kitchen.

Josh opened his folder of police reports. He had arrived on the scene from Boston within two hours of being notified of his brother's murder. He had asked that nothing be moved, but Eric's body had already been taken to the morgue.

The autopsy confused him. His brother had been heavily sedated with a barbiturate and Josh had never known him to take an aspirin, much less sleeping pills. On top of that, no prescription bottle was ever found. The state of the apartment also bothered him. The bed was perfectly made, and the entire apartment was as neat as a pin.

"This looks like something a woman would leave behind, a very meticulous woman," Josh's partner, Ginger, had insisted. Josh had to agree. He remembered as a boy his brother never made up his bed or picked up his room except after serious threats of groundings and allowance suspensions.

It angered Josh to realize that the case had never been given the consideration it deserved because Eric was homosexual. While at the crime scene, Josh overheard an NYPD officer joke, "It was probably a rejected lover. Those homos don't take too well to being double-crossed."

Josh had stood face to face with this officer and copied his name and number off his badge. "I'll report your insightful conclusion to downtown. Now get the hell out of here." He had filed a report on the officer's conduct, but never received a reply that any reprimand had taken place.

"Here you are, darlin.' The waitress set the plate in front of him. Fries toppled off the edges. Josh inhaled and blew the air out through pursed lips. He looked up at Miss Blondie. "My name is Mr. Conroe. I'm not a honey, a sweetie or a darlin.' I'm either Mr. Conroe or Sir to you. What did you scribble on that pad? I specifically said, 'No Fries.'" He raised his voice as if interrogating a suspect. "And where is the salad?"

The man at the bar turned to look. The waitress backed away. "Oh, I'm sorry, dear, I mean Mr. Conroe. I'll get your salad. You can just keep the fries at no charge."

Josh angrily scrapped all the fries off his plate scattering them in all directions over the table top. He picked up his hamburger and said a prayer for a speedy delivery from this God-awful country.

At two-thirty he walked into the police precinct station. The place seemed deserted. A lone officer behind the desk was on the phone. "Yes, Miz Harold. I've already radioed someone to go see about Fred. Yes, Ma'am. Thank you, Ma'am. You have a good day too, Miz Harold." He hung up and noticed Josh.

"Yes, sir, what can I do for ya?" He got up and came to the counter.

Josh took out his badge. "Hello, I'm retired Detective Josh Conroe from the Boston Police Department."

Josh held out his hand for a shake. "Well hello, Detective Conroe. I'm Officer Leone Attafey." Leone shook his hand and could tell that this man was on a mission. "How can I help you?"

"I'm here investigating a New York City cold case from 1969." He looked around. "Where is everybody?"

"They're out trying to get people to move out of the lowlands and helping 'em if they'll go. They can be pretty stubborn, even with a big storm like this one comin.'"

"Oh yes, that's all I've been hearing on the news this morning." He took out his handkerchief and wiped his forehead. "I wanted to let your department know that I'll be questioning Elaine Chauvier."

"You don't say?" Josh saw that Leone was immediately interested. "I think this is something the chief might need to hear. His office is at the end of the hall. Wait up just a moment. I'll get the file clerk to answer the phone out here."

Over an ice-cold RC Cola Josh told the two men about his brother's death and the circumstantial evidence he'd gathered over the years. "All leads," he concluded, "seem to come back to this particular person."

The chief leaned back in his chair. "Well, her name's been comin' up here quite a bit lately. Her half sister believes she tried to poison her and then there's a bizarre report about her rounding up water moccasins."

Josh fumbled in his pocket and then remembered. He had quit smoking to please both Cheryl and his doctor. He felt his thinking was sharper with a cigarette in his hand, no matter what they said about clogged arteries. "Snakes? Well, you know she once played Cleopatra on the stage and, according to accounts, became quite comfortable at handling them." Josh took another swallow of his drink, relishing the coldness. "There's another unsolved case in New York. An actress died or was killed just weeks after she got a part that Elaine had wanted. The actress's mother had accused Elaine but there were no concrete leads and in the end, it was ruled a suicide. She had been heavily sedated with over-the counter cold medicine and all the gas burners on the stove had been turned on."

Josh studied the RC bottle in his hand. "But that never set right with me. Everyone said she was thrilled over her new role and there was no note. Elaine got the part and ended up with a Toni for best actress." He laughed. "How's that for justice?"

"Maybe it's about to catch up with her." The chief said as he stood up. "But now you'll have to excuse me, I've got a hurricane breathing down my neck."

"Just so you know. I'll be posing as George Cummings, a writer working on a book about the Old South. I'm hoping she'll slip up during the interviews."

"I've heard she's narcissistic as hell and also very clever. Leone here is a fine cop and will assist you with anything you need." When Josh and Leone got to the front counter, Leone pushed a plate of Darlene's left over chocolate cake towards him. "Like a piece? Ordinarily, there wouldn't be a crumb left, but so many are out today."

Josh waved his hand, "No, no, thank you."

Leone began to cut a big slice. "My wife's feelin's 'ill be hurt if I bring any back home."

"Well okay. Wrap it up for later." Josh took out his wallet and handed Leone a card. "Here's my number at the hotel. I'll check in with you from time to time."

Once Josh stepped outside he decided to scope out Shadow's Way before going back to the hotel. He had the cab driver drop him off a block away. As he headed down the tree-lined street of old two-story homes on either side he got a little spooked. Several times he looked up at a second-floor window expecting some phantom to be gazing down at him. The air was still and thick. Nothing was moving, not a leaf or a bug. The overcast sky had a foreboding greenish hue.

He came to the Cathedral complex and looked across the boulevard at Shadow's Way. It was imposing alright, and eerie. He spotted a tall woman in a wide brimmed sun hat, wearing an apron over jeans and down-in-the-heels tennis shoes. She was barking directions at a black man who was nailing plywood sheets over the windows.

That must be Elaine Chauvier. Even at this distance he could see that she was a remarkable-looking woman. He had spent hours watching her movies and the reels from her plays. He had studied her telegraphing facial expressions and the myriad subtleties of every personality she assumed. She had been an outstanding actress, no question about that.

He crossed the street and walked through the gate and wondered if he were about to meet his brother's killer. His hand shook as he put on a pair of glasses with thin metal frames. He felt his unkept appearance in the wrinkled suit added to the character he was playing.

He picked up his stride, "Excuse me, excuse me, are you by any chance the lovely Elaine Chauvier of this glorious antebellum home?" From his coat pocket, he pulled out the folded copy of *Modern Southern Living* and held it up for her to see. She studied him for a moment, then purred in a soft gracious drawl, "I'm so flattered that you are able to recognize me, dressed as I am in this terrible attire."

Oh yes, the narcissist. Just feed her vanity.

"Ms. Chauvier forgive me for being forward, but that beauty of yours can't be hidden by a straw hat." He adjusted his glasses, awkwardly shuffled his feet and looked down. *Must make the murdering bitch think I feel inferior.* Keeping his eyes on the ground, he slowly put out his hand. "I'm…I'm George Cummings."

She didn't move an inch. He waited a second and quickly shoved his hand in his pocket and ducked his head even more.

"Well, what can I do for you?" she demanded impatiently.

He cleared his throat a couple of times and began in a halting voice. "I was hoping you might grant me an interview if it wouldn't be too much trouble. You see I'm working on a book about the Old South and the descendants of plantation owners. I've saved the best for last." He laughed nervously and looked up. She held him in a steady gaze. "You're from Yankee Land. Sounds like Boston."

He continued, "Now I hope you won't hold it against me but yes, I'm from that part of the country."

"And why should I hold that against you, for pity's sake? The War's over, if I'm not mistaken."

He ducked his head once again. "Just joking, of course." She was a tough one alright.

"You see," he began again, "I met a couple who went on and on about you and your beautiful home and wonderful cooking. They said you were the real thing, a direct descendant still living in the same plantation home."

The lines on her face began to soften. *I'm starting to reel her in. One small victory.*

She took off her hat and shook her head a couple of times allowing her hair to fall over her shoulders. Then she tilted her head ever so slightly and fanned herself with the floppy straw hat, transforming herself into a Southern coquette. "You're sort of cute for an old Yankee."

Is she trying to seduce me? Josh recalled one interview. *She'd have sex with any man she found to be weak, a genuine dominatrix.*

Her drawl became more pronounced and charming. "What an honorable project you've taken upon yourself, writing about the only enchanted and sophisticated bygone period this country has ever…for God's sake, Tobias," she clapped her hands and angrily shouted at the handyman. "That one goes over the dining room window. For heaven's sake, can't you see that the size is different?"

She turned back to him, "Forgive me," once again soft-spoken. "I swear I don't know how they can be so stupid. His wife is my maid and he tends the yard, and between the two of them they don't have the sense of a donkey. If it weren't for me, I'd hate…but I digress."

Josh's blood pressure was rising. *Will I be able to endure this sense of superiority?* In that moment, he knew she was the murderer, but he would have to get proof. Elaine flicked her hand through her hair, fluffing out her curls, and licked her lips. *She goes from ice queen to flirt to cruel boss to seductress with the greatest of ease.*

"As you've heard, this dreadful hurricane is upon us, although it's taking its merry time to get here," she drawled. "If it isn't here by tomorrow, you are more than welcome to drop by. I could prepare a humble lunch for you." The stories of poisoning and drugging came to mind. In the stillness and murkiness, the house seemed to be whispering, *she will suck you up.* He took a few steps back to regain his equilibrium.

"Why, Mr. Cummings, you look ill. Should I get Tobias to fetch you a glass of water?"

"No, no, it's just this humidity and a murkiness. I'm not used to it."

"So, shall we say one tomorrow? I have a new crepe recipe that I've been dying to try out. You can be my guinea pig." Her light laughter bounced off the heavy air.

"I'm really sorry, but I have a conference call with my editor tomorrow afternoon. Could we possibly make it tomorrow morning?"

Angry quills seemed to shoot from her eyes. His impulse was to duck to avoid getting pricked. *She likes to have it her way.*

"Very well, then, be here at ten sharp." Without a nod or a goodbye, she turned back to overseeing Tobias.

Josh hurried down the street. He felt desperate to get back to his room and take a shower. His chest felt weighed down. He decided he'd go to Mass in the morning before the meeting. His intuition and premonitions were hardly ever wrong. *She killed my brother and she wouldn't hesitate to kill me.*

CHAPTER TWENTY

Monsignor Rodin knelt on his prayer stool before a crucifix extending to the ceiling and gazed at the face twisted in agony. Ironically, the sight of this suffering comforted the priest. If Jesus could endure so much and give up his life, then surely he could carry out his mission to protect His Church from a malicious Archbishop. Monsignor Rodin imagined he was also suspended on a cross. He had been given orders, orders veiled in ambiguity, but nevertheless clearly understood. His Cardinal, one of the Church's highest-ranking ecclesiastic officials next to the Pope, had chosen him for a mission that would save Holy Mother Church.

Over a week before, Monsignor Rodin had boarded a plane to meet his Cardinal, the lofty protector of the Faith and one never to be questioned. "Don't bring your cassock or collar," had been the last order, so he wore stiff new jeans and a soft flannel shirt. With hands jammed in tight pockets he strolled into the municipal park, miles away from the Cardinal's residence. He walked along a path next to the lake, failing to look closely at the elderly man in a grey turtleneck and corduroy pants standing by a water fountain. He strolled right passed him.

"Monsignor Rodin, where are you going?" The commanding voice startled him. He turned and met the impatient eyes of his superior.

"Oh your Grace, I'm so sorry. Didn't…notice… you," he faltered.

The Cardinal turned towards the water. "Nice day but somewhat chilly." They made a few insipid observations about the swans gracefully gliding by. Then the leader stood up and got to the point. "Archbishop Figurant must be stopped." Red spots peppered his face.

"I've ordered him to quit this nonsense about pedophile priests, but he continues to defy me. Did you hear, he's defied me?" Rodin took a step back and nodded his head. Words wouldn't come. The Cardinal continued a little louder. "He's refused to move them to other parishes which is how we've always taken care of these problems." He raised his hand in a fist. "Then he threatened me. He said he'd go to the secular authorities if I got in his way. He'll have those priests thrown in prison."

The Cardinal choked with rage. "No one, especially a subordinate, has ever dared to speak to me with such irreverence." Out of breath, he dropped down on the nearest bench. He had to calm his racing heart. Monsignor Rodin remained standing. Protocol didn't allow him to sit beside this man unless he was given permission. He pulled his hands out of his pockets and blew on them. He was cold, and he felt like a bumpkin not knowing what to say.

Yards away kids break danced to music blaring from boom boxs. The Cardinal shook his head and pointed. "And there's the devil's disciples!" This indignation seemed to renew his energy. He stood up briskly. "And when I threatened Archbishop Figurant with excommunication, he said, 'You must do as you see fit.'"

The Cardinal paced in front of the Monsignor. "We'll have to resort to," he paused and looked directly at the Monsignor, "austere measures. That's God's will. Do whatever it takes. It's God's will, you understand?"

The Cardinal came close to him and whispered in his ear, "You are the only one I can trust. He must be stopped."

Monsignor Rodin felt his knees sag with weakness. *Is he saying what I think he is?* This wasn't the first time he'd been ordered to engage in questionable actions, but this was different. *Austere measures? Whatever it takes?* The Cardinal grasped Rodin's hand and held it tightly. "You'll be the next Archbishop. You have my word." Then he smiled kindly and took Rodin's elbow to escort him along. "Come, I'll treat you to a beer. We deserve one."

Now nine days later Monsignor Rodin still hadn't formulated a plan. Perhaps the hurricane would help him create an accident. *I can't do this myself.* He had already searched for the sort of person who would possibly carry out this heinous crime but had not been successful. However, he still hadn't approached the ex con who was helping with renovating the Senior Center. He looked up at the suffering face of Jesus and prayed for the strength to do what God wanted. He must act quickly. That morning a telegram had arrived. "No action so far. Why the delay?"

Andre knelt in an isolated side chapel of the Cathedral. It was dark except for the dozens of vigil lights that shone on the statue of Mary, the Mother of Jesus. Andre looked at her face and saw kindness and forgiveness. He felt the way he did as a boy resting in his mother's lap.

Silently he spoke to her, "*As a mother, please help me save the young children from these predators. I allowed my own brother to suffer. I didn't have the nerve then, but I do now. I've been a disgrace to my calling.*"

He bowed his head and was consumed with fear. *You're in great danger,* the shadows whispered. He softly addressed the statue, "I'm ready." As soon as he said that, a profound peace overpowered the fear.

When he got to his office he removed a folder from his desk drawer and handed it to Damien. "Here's the list and orders for the first priests who are to report to Shadow's Way. Wait until after the storm to mail them. I don't want them getting lost."

"Yes, your Grace." Brother Damien began to leave and then turned back. "I almost forgot. Brother Paul, the therapist, may be delayed by a few days. His abbot wants him to complete a retreat before beginning the assignment at Shadow's Way."

"That's fine, Brother Damien."

Andre stood at his desk, picked up the phone and dialed. "Hello, Elaine. The first priests will be arriving as soon as the storm is over." He listened and sighed, "We've already been over this. I have nothing more to say to you. Just be out the day after the storm." Pause. "Yes, Lily Mae and Tobias have agreed to stay on." He sat down and leaned his head back on the rest. "And remember you are to take only the furniture in your bedroom, nothing else." There was a loud click. He replaced the receiver.

I suppose this is a little like a divorce. A knock on his door interrupted the thought. "Yes, come in."

Lanita opened the door and peeked in. "Your Excellency, Ofelia and Rudy would like to see you."

"What now?" He sighed. "Well, show them into the parlor and bring some sandwiches. I'll have lunch there." He looked out the window and watched the pigeons eating the grains he had thrown out earlier.

Ofelia sat in one of the oversized parlor chairs and nervously tapped the folder resting on her lap. Rudy stood by the window, looking over at Shadow's Way. "I'll be damn. I still can't believe it."

"I'm not up for a long-drawn-out court battle." Ofelia spat out the words. "I have my dad's trilogy, and hopefully I'll have a singing career. It may be best to forget all about that cursed place."

"Well, I want my mother's share," Rudy said angrily. "It's mine just as the lawyer said."

They stopped talking as soon as the Archbishop entered. Lanita followed, carrying a tray with coffee, ham sandwiches and a fruit salad. "Put them on the side table," Andre directed. He looked at his visitors. He could see that they weren't here for a friendly visit. "Please join me for a light lunch." He motioned with his hand.

Ofelia sat up straight. "No, thank you."

Andre began to fill a plate with the food. "I see you're upset. What can I do?

"We found out that you hold the deed to Shadow's Way," Rudy blurted out.

Andre nodded, "That's right."

"Are you aware of a later will?" Rudy waited, but Andre remained quiet. Rudy continued, speaking louder, "The original one was written before Ofelia was born and named Elaine and my mother as the sole heirs. It stipulated that if one died, everything went to the other. But that document became null and void on this date." Rudy held the paper for him to read. "The second one lists all three daughters, Elaine, Gabrielle, and Ofelia, and says in case of death, their offspring are to receive their share."

Ofelia then spoke up, "The first will was already invalid when Elaine signed the deed over to you, and the previous lawyer either didn't know about a second will, which is unlikely, or he was afraid of going against Elaine." Ofelia began opening the envelope on her lap. "My mother had given Grand-mere the original draft of the second will long before she died." She handed the document to Andre. "How Elaine was able to sign the deed over to you without any of us being informed is a mystery."

Andre smiled as he poured a cup of coffee. "Knowing Elaine, I'm sure she was able to sway that old lawyer, crooked to the core, to ignore a second will." He sat down on the couch. "I was totally unaware of this, but rest assured, we'll settle this without any battles." Ofelia and Rudy sat back in disbelief. They had anticipated an ugly conflict.

Josh turned off the TV. "Elaine," he said. "You confuse even the weather experts." The official Hurricane Elaine was headed for this coast, then had stalled for four hours and seemed to be changing course and heading towards Florida but was once again coming their way. Heavy rains were drenching Florida, but so far only a light mist was falling outside his hotel window, nothing like hurricane rains.

Although his morning session with the human being Elaine had lasted for several hours, Josh came away with virtually nothing connected to the case. She rigidly adhered to the history of Shadow's Way and never once drifted onto anything personal. She never mentioned being away in New York. It was as if she had been an occupant of Shadow's Way since the days of slavery. Josh realized that if she were a psychopath, as he suspected, she was one of the cleverest he had encountered. "You were quite the actress in New York," he casually noted at the end of the interview. "Did you get your inspiration from your roots?"

"I thought you were here to find out about Shadow's Way and the Old South." She straightened her back and glared at him.

He looked at the floor. "Of course, but I would also like to write about any of the descendants who are still around. Get a human-interest side."

She smiled at the portrait over the mantel. "I was encouraged to leave this beloved home due to circumstances beyond my control," she said softly. "But then when the time was right, I was led to leave the spotlight behind me and come back to my beloved haven."

"Now how about some homemade lemonade?" The voice had changed to that of a little girl. An eerie chill settled in Josh's stomach. Elaine then hopped up from the couch and took a couple of skips to the doorway. "Lily Mae, we are parched. Please do bring us some of your delicious lemonade. Pleeease." She glanced back at him, smiled sweetly and twisted a loose strand of hair, rocking back and forth on her heels. *She's acting like a six-year old. She may have a multiple personality? A criminal psychiatrist is what I need.*

"I must get going, but thanks anyway," he firmly announced stuffing the tablet inside his briefcase. He was already nervous over an earlier incident and wasn't about to take a chance on swallowing anything she offered.

They had been in the Robert E. Lee room where she was showing him an armoire. "This has belonged to the Chauvier family for well over a hundred years. My great granddaddy made a special trip to France…" She stopped abruptly. "Who was the Boston couple who referred you here?"

Josh paused and said a prayer of thanksgiving that he had not lied about that. "It was the McCrethers." He didn't elaborate, less is better.

"Oh, really?" The skepticism and raised eyebrows made him want to run. *Is she on to me?*

Nevertheless, he decided to book one more session. He must try to get something concrete. Instinctively knowing that she was his brother's killer wouldn't hold up in court. If the next session was as unsuccessful as this one, he would go back home. He'd let God take care of her. Being with her and in that house was downright scary. Plus, it was damn boring to hear her go on about those goddamn wonderful antebellum days.

Another thing he had noted on the tour was that certain pieces of furniture seemed to be missing and he saw marks on the wall paper which indicated that a picture frame had been there. When he mentioned this to her, she batted her eyes at him laughing, "My, you are so observant. Yes, I have stored some of the more valuable things because one never knows what might happen when a big storm is coming our way."

On his ride back to the hotel, he recalled Nora McCrether sitting at their kitchen table. "Oh it was a wonderful vacation, but there was something about Miss Chauvier that gave me and Joe the willies." She stopped to get a fork full of Cheryl's rhubarb pie. Josh pressed for more. "Why was that?"

"Well, I'll tell ya," she said while chewing. "I woke up the first night around one and couldn't get back to sleep, so I decided to go downstairs and sit in the sunroom. About half way down the stairs, I saw a lady in a long old-fashioned dress like in the 1800's rush through the foyer and disappear. A foyer night lamp plus an outside streetlight provided enough visibility for me to realize it was Miss Chauvier. But it scared me so much I ran back to bed."

"Then the next morning after breakfast I said, 'I believe I saw you last night in the foyer.' She looked terrified and then matter-of-factly said, "Oh dear, was my great-grandmother roaming around again last night? You're not the first to have seen her. I do resemble her quite a bit."

After sharing lunch and conversation with Andre, Ofelia and Rudy were delighted that they would be dealing with him rather than Elaine over the sale of Shadow's Way. Andre was disturbed over what had happened. "I know that Elaine is a manipulator and a con-artist, but I never for one moment suspected something like this."

Ofelia exhaled with a sigh. "Well, all I know for sure is that she's known about this second will since I arrived. She turned pale and had to sit down when I showed it to her." Ofelia shook her head. "But perhaps she was shocked because I had the original and had already told Rudy about it. It seemed strange but she laughed when I told her that I hadn't know it existed until my grand-mere was dying."

"How is it you got the deed?" Rudy asked.

Andre's shame kept him from explaining the full extent of their arrangement. "She offered to sign the deed over to me if I kept Shadow's Way from being repossessed. I paid the overdue taxes and fees and helped her establish the bed and breakfast business. We agreed that she could keep the profits without paying anything back. She also asked that in the event of my death, the deed would be returned to her."

"Wow," Rudy exclaimed, "it sounds like you were her sugar daddy." Ofelia shot a look of reprimand at Rudy but Andre didn't seem to be offended.

Andre didn't have the nerve to admit the whole truth to them. "I never agreed verbally or in writing to leaving the place to her in the event of my death. That's something she came to believe. Bastien is named in my will as the benefactor."

"I really appreciate that you saved the place." Ofelia said.

"Me too," Rudy added. "If you hadn't, there wouldn't be anything for us to divide."

Andre poured himself another cup of coffee. "I'd been planning to turn the home into a treatment center for pedophile priests." He sighed deeply. "But that won't be possible with this new development." Ofelia and Rudy were stunned and confused.

"I guess that's for the best," Andre continued. "I spoke with a well-known psychiatrist just last evening.

He told me that the likelihood of rehabilitating a pedophile is rather bleak. No cure, so to speak."

Andre bowed his head and reflected. He had the wealth to buy out these two, but he realized he no longer wanted to deal with the scandal or the church's authorities. The surfacing of this latest will was actually a blessing. He would turn these priests over to the legal authorities and be done with it. His days in the Church were ending and for that he felt nothing but relief.

"I thought you would fight this," Ofelia said softly. "Elaine told me you were completely devoted to her." Andre gazed across the room. *Devoted? No, a more correct word would be possessed.* Like his brother he too had had an addiction, an appalling addiction.

Josh rang the doorbell for the third time and then checked his watch. He was right on time. The intercom clicked on and the soft sweet voice of a Scarlet O'Hara wafted out, "Come on in. The door is unlocked. Make yourself comfortable. I'll be down in a moment." Josh felt an impulse to turn and run, but his detective's curiosity crushed his premonitions. He straightened his shoulders and firmly grasped the knob.

The door opened to blackness. Unlike yesterday's visit no lamps or chandeliers had been turned on to offset the darkness from the boarded-up windows. His eyes adjusted enough so that he could make his way into the living room. He switched on the table lamp, but nothing happened. On examining the socket, he saw that the bulb had been removed.

"So, Detective Josh Conroe, you think you can trap Elaine, do you?"

Josh spun around, alarmed by the shrill Boston accent behind him. A woman holding a candle stood in the doorway. Her opulent breasts drooped over a lacy red bustier. A short black skirt, fish net hose and stiletto heels completed her ensemble. But the overall effect was terrifying rather than sexy. Heavy white makeup caked her face and her lips were large, red and mis-shapen. Heavy mascara and black liner encircled feral eyes. Tendrils from a long blond wig jutted out in all directions. Josh remembered that a strand from that wig sat in his brother's case file. He had his proof.

"Joe and Nora McCrether don't know a George Cummings," the grotesque figure said. "However, Nora, the dumb cow, told Elaine that her next-door neighbor isn't George Cummings. He's Josh Conroe. "I must've gotten the names mixed up," Elaine had said to her, real smooth. Elaine made a few more calls and what do you know? Josh Conroe was a Boston detective whose queer brother got killed in New York."

Trixie threw her head back and cackled like one of Macbeth's witches. "You know Elaine's smart, much smarter than any detective. Well, that's what she claims. She's really a conniving cunt. I'm the smart one."

Josh's breakfast of steak and egg began to churn. He swallowed several times while hearing Cheryl's reprimand, "You're getting too old for this job." No question, he had been careless.

Trixie continued in a loud grating voice, "I hate Elaine, but I have to hand it to her, she's got everyone fooled except that lecherous Archbishop. Some man of God he is."

Josh willed his voice to be strong. "Elaine, Elaine, I know that's you."

"I'm Trixie, you son-of-bitch. You think someone of Elaine's importance would associate with a murdering whore like me?"

"Trixie, you are Elaine." He raised his voice to a shout. "Elaine, you killed my brother."

He caught his breath and continued shouting, "You are Elaine Chauvier. You killed my brother!"

An eerie screeching pierced Josh's ears as she lunged at him. In a flash he saw the hypodermic needle pointed at his neck and grabbed her wrist and twisted it as hard as he could. Then a stiletto heel jabbed into his shin, collapsing him to his knee. The needle plunged into his thigh and numbing liquid raced through his veins.

CHAPTER TWENTY-ONE

Lanita slowly folded a freshly ironed blouse and placed it on top of a pair of jeans in the suitcase on her bed. Jangles sat on the pillows watching her every move. He felt the immensity of what sat churning in the Gulf. Since Hurricane Elaine had first begun to form, he wouldn't let her out of his sight. When she left for work, he would jump onto the window sill and caterwaul until he could no longer see her. Then he'd crawl under the sofa and stayed there all day, impervious to the needs for water, food or the litter box.

As Lanita prepared to leave her beloved home she felt like a weight was pulling her soul. Tears began to well up. *I can't do this.* But last evening the Archbishop had insisted, "You're in the lowlands which means you'll wash away at the first gale. The room off the kitchen is there for you."

Since the previous housekeeper had left, the room had sat empty except for the month a destitute mother and her two children had lived there. Even if Lanita hadn't been given this place, she wouldn't have lived at the mansion. She had always needed privacy and distance from her place of work. She stuffed several pairs of panties in a side pouch and recalled how upset Rudy had gotten. "You're not serious, are you? The Elysian will be just as safe as that place."

"The Elysian doesn't allow pets and I'm not boarding Jangles even if you do pay for it."

"So, that cat's more important than me? Is that it?"

She walked out onto her front porch wanting to scream *sometimes you can be such a spoiled brat.*

Lanita dropped a folded nightgown on top of the other clothes. "Jangles, I'm ready for this thing with Rudy to be over. We're too different. We've had our fun and now it's time to move on." Jangles mewed softly several times.

"Yes, it's partly my fault, but I thought he'd be leaving in two or three weeks and now they've dragged out to five." She placed her cosmetic bag in the case and zipped it up. Jangles jumped on the lid and rubbed his midsection across her arm purring.

"I love you too." She picked him up and carried him through the three rooms of their home. "Jangles, I never dreamed I'd have a home of my very own. Tilly Marie gave me this home and then sent you to me. Remember how you showed up on that front porch, half starved?" Jangles continued to purr in acknowledgement.

Lanita removed a picture from a shelf and showed it to Jangles. "That's Tilly Marie at ninety-four just before she died." The portrait showed a tiny woman whose white skin was wrinkled and leathery brown, weathered by years of field work. "She was ninety-five pounds of pure, packed-down love."

Lanita had cleaned Tilly Marie's room every day at the charity nursing home, the only place that would hire her when she first arrived. Soon a mother-daughter bond began to form between the women. Tilly Marie had no family, no one to care for her. She was withering away in the home. One wintery afternoon as Lanita swept her floor, Tilly Marie grabbed the broom. "I want to go my home, but I ain't got no one to look after me." She began to cry.

"I'll take care of you." Lanita took her in her arms.

"All I got is a little pension. I can't pay you a thing."

The next morning Tilly Marie's eyes were aglow when Lanita came into the room. "Darlin' all I own in this world is my little house which I've refused to sell and now I know why. It will be yours if you'll take it as payment for my care. You'll have a place to stay and my pension will keep food on the table."

So Lanita took Tilly Mae home and cared for her with all the love she had in her. Weeks later, she returned from grocery shopping one morning to find Tilly Marie putting papers in a large envelope. "This place now belongs to you, my darlin' girl. The Archbishop took care of everything." She handed her the envelope. "Now put these in a safe place, you hear?"

Ten months later, Lanita held Tilly Marie's hand and massaged her forehead with a damp cloth. The local priest had just given her the last Sacraments. "I promise I won't let go of your hand until you cross over," Lanita whispered in her ear.

Around two o'clock in the morning exhaustion overtook Lanita. Her head dropped down on the pillow next to her friend's face. She fell into a deep sleep, clasping Tilly's little birdlike hand. At dawn Lanita bolted upright. She felt an armless embrace around her. Then with a puff all was gone. After the funeral the Archbishop offered her the housekeeping job. A week later Jangles showed up at her front door. "Tilly Marie got me a home, a job and then sent you to be my friend."

A sudden loud knock on the front door caused her to jump and sent Jangles leaping from her arms and darting under the bed. Bastien stood behind the screen door. Beyond her fence, she saw his pickup loaded with plywood.

"Hello, Lanita, I…" he hesitated, but then seemed to gain confidence. "I thought I'd board up your house just in case the wind don't tear it down and then Andre asked me to bring you over there today. It's comin' on shore tonight." He stepped back a couple of feet.

Rudy hadn't offered to help with anything once she refused to go to the Elysian. "Bastien, that is so kind of you. I thought I'd have to call a cab."

Touched by her words and not wanting to show it, he quickly stepped off the porch and through the tiny yard. At the gate, he turned back. "I done brought you a crate for Jangles. Put his favorite blanket or pillow in there and then I'll cover it up so's he won't get too skittish."

"Jangles, he cares about you too." Jangles stuck his head out from underneath the bed and some of her inner heaviness began to lift. She stepped out on the porch and studied the sky. It was an scary greenish yellow. Black clouds churned in the distance, moving towards them. For some reason Shadow's Way popped into her mind. She shuddered. Like the sky it projected malevolence. Not anything like this sweet home that would probably be destroyed by the evil energy.

The pictures on the walls shook with each stroke of Bastien's hammer. Lanita tried to focus on which little treasures she wanted to take. Tilly Marie's picture was the first to go into the box. Then the little statue of New Orleans minstrels that Ofelia had given her. "Now, Jangles, should I take this ceramic cat I won at the carnival or this blue bottle we found on the beach?" Jangles twisted his head from side to side. "Okay." She wrapped both and then chose a set of salt and pepper shakers from her island, Jangles' toys and several jars of seeds for next spring's planting. "Maybe the Archbishop will let me have a little garden plot by the mansion."

She cleared both the front and back porches of pot plants, chimes, bird feeders and chairs. She carried a basket of vegetables from her garden to the back of the pickup. On her way back, she paused to watch Bastien hammer in the last nail. Her throat tightened as she viewed her home for the last time. It was no longer happy, all naked and boarded up.

"Jangles crawled back under the bed," Lanita called to Bastien.

He came inside, dropped to his hands and knees and looked under the bed. "Oh, pretty boy," he said in a soothing tone. "I understand how afraid you are, but I'm gonna take you to a safer place." Finally, Jangles came out and allowed Bastien to pick him up. He held the cat close to his chest.

"That's amazing, Bastien. Animals trust you, don't they?"

"Seems that way," he said softly and carried Jangles outside.

Lanita had one last task. She picked up the vial of holy water from her dresser. "Please Angels, Mother Mary and Tilly Marie, protect my little home." She sprinkled drops in every room and onto both porches. She said, "goodbye" and turned to leave. When she climbed into the pickup, she saw her bicycle loaded in the back. "Oh, thanks so much. I had wanted to bring it."

"I figured so." The motor was already running, and Jangles' cage sat between them. A frightened mewing filled the cabin. Bastien lifted the cover. "It's okay, little friend, your mama's here. We'll take care of you."

He put the truck in gear and started off. "I'm staying in the room just down from my brother's. Never slept in such a nice bed. He finally talked me into it. I'm glad you took up his offer too."

Tears fell on Lanita's folded hands as big rain drops began to splatter the windshield. *It's taken all this for me to see the goodness in this man.* Bastien noticed. "Your home will be just fine, don't fret." He spoke as gently to her as he had to Jangles. For the first time since her mother's death, Lanita felt safe.

Ofelia wheeled her suitcase out of the cabin; a stuffed briefcase rode on top. She looked around and shook her head. The main house, the honeymoon suite, the work shed, even the garage windows and doors were boarded up. Everything had been secured except for her and Rudy's cabins. *She must think we'd be stupid enough to stay and get blown to Oz.*

Yesterday Rudy said he had reserved a room for her at the Elysian. "But Lanita's invited me to stay with her at the Archbishop's."

"That place is going to be jammed with people," he said impatiently.

"Only Bastien and two families. The maid's room is large, with twin beds."

Now she stood on the sidewalk, confused. Should she be with her nephew or with her friend? She didn't want to upset Rudy, but she didn't particularly want to be around him, either. All he talked about was the money they would be getting from Shadow's Way and the hidden treasure underneath.

She made up her mind and crossed the street. *I'll be safer in a brick and mortar house. The Elysian is all wood, like Shadow's Way."* Suddenly she recalled a childhood memory of Grand-mere acting out the story of The Three Little Pigs and spontaneously laughed out loud.

Earlier Rudy had marched decisively up the front steps of Shadow's Way but before he reached the door, Leone was parking his squad car in front. "Good afternoon, Mr. Rudy," he cried out as he started up the sidewalk.

Rudy sighed. *Had pesky Ofelia sent him to intercede?* "If you've come to stop me, you might just as well go back to your station."

Leone looked puzzled. "What are you talking about?"

"Sorry, don't mind me." Rudy rang the doorbell.

The intercom clicked and Elaine's soft sweet drawl floated across the porch, "I'm so sorry, but I'm not taking any guests at this time."

Rudy pushed the reply button. "Aunt Elaine, we're not guests. Open the door. We have business to discuss."

There was no reply.

Leone pushed the button. "Miss Chauvier, this is Officer Leone Attafay. I have some questions for you regarding Josh Conroe."

"Who's Josh Conroe? I don't know any such person." The reply was immediate and the tone was sharp.

He took a deep breath. "You knew him as George Cummings."

The deadbolt turned and the door opened a crack, but they saw no one standing there. It was pitch black inside. Leone swung the door wide open. Neither man moved forward. Leone unlocked his holster.

"Aunt Elaine," Rudy finally leaned inside and shouted. "Just wanted to confirm with you that Andre, Ofelia, and I plan to put this place on the market right after the storm." There was only silence. "Okay then, I'll leave copies of all the papers inside here. There's a court order here for you to leave the premises." He placed a large white envelope on the floor and slid it towards the staircase, then turned to leave. "Leone, you might as well come too. She's not going to show her face."

The men were half way down the steps when they heard a sweet chuckle. Both men whirled around. A nun was standing in the doorway. "For God's sake," Rudy gasped. "Aunt Elaine?" She spoke with an Irish brogue,

"Oh, I'm rehearsing for a part in a New York play. My home is being taken by shysters." She bowed her head and grabbed the long rosary hanging from her skirt. She began moving her lips in silent prayer.

"Miss Chauvier," Leone was direct, "Detective Josh Conroe was on his way over here when his wife last talked to him. He hasn't been heard from since, and he hasn't checked out of the hotel.

"All right, Officer." The Irish inflection was gone. "I'll drop the Sister role and let Elaine answer. A detective never came here. A writer by the name of George Cummings had an appointment day before yesterday, but he called and cancelled without so much as an apology." She sighed. "You know those Yankee people just don't have any manners whatsoever. And for someone with our breeding, well, that's hard to take."

"So, you never met with a George Cummings or a Josh Conroe?"

"Isn't that what I just said? Doesn't anyone understand the King's English these days?"

"I would like to have a look around."

Elaine swung the end of her rosary in a circle. "Well, you might like to, but you're not goin' to. It's all boarded up and I've switched off the electricity, so you can't see anything anyway."

Leone sighed. "Okay, then, I'll get a warrant." He turned to leave. "Come on, Rudy. Let's go."

Back on the sidewalk, Rudy turned and saw Elaine standing in the doorway. "Hey, I meant to tell you. I saw a pretty little one bedroom over on Redbud Street that you might like to..." He stopped abruptly. A dark creature stared out from the nun's habit. *She's now someone else. How many are there?*

Hurrying to get away, he called out, "Leone, I'll be at the Elysian if you need to reach me." The rain began to pound. Leone ran to his car and Rudy dashed through the yard. Inside his cottage, he stuffed his clothes into a suitcase and duffle bag. "That damn Jangles." He kicked the trash can across the floor, scattering empty McDonald's cups and sacks across the room.

"If it weren't for that damn cat, we could have had so much fun going through the storm."

He went to the bathroom and pushed his toiletries into a shaving kit. *I'm more than ready to leave this hell hole.* A bottle of hair tonic broke. "Oh shit." He began to sop up the mess with a towel. "What the hell am I doing?" He threw the towel on the floor. "I'm never coming back here."

He took a beer from his cooler, plopped down on the bed and popped the tab. The small dining table was covered with blueprints. He felt one hundred percent sure that a treasure was buried somewhere under that property. He looked through the window at Shadow's Way, boarded up against the backdrop of greenish black clouds as if draped in a cobweb of wickedness. An electrifying shiver ran down his spine. *I'll wait till after the storm.*

However, after the third beer, Rudy could no longer control his curiosity and impatience. *Damnit, why not find out before going to the Elysian? There's still time, just rain, no winds yet.* He grabbed the blueprints off the table and put them in his briefcase. *There's got to be a way to get to those tunnels from that house, and I bet Elaine knows more than she lets on.*

He put on his rain cape, slung the duffle bag over his shoulder and picked up his briefcase and suitcase. Outside he threw the duffle bag and suitcase in the back of his car parked next to the cabin and headed across the yard.

CHAPTER TWENTY-TWO

Seated at his desk, Andre talked on the phone, consoling one of his flock. "Yes, Freddy, don't worry. Brother Damien will make sure a bus gets over there to pick up you and your family…to the St. Thomas Center…yes, they'll have baby food there…I know it's starting to rain, but don't worry. You'll get there in plenty of time...okay, then…thank you and God bless you too."

He hung up the phone and glanced at the architectural drawings covering his desk. Sketches he had spent weeks working on in an effort to transform Shadow's Way into a rehabilitation center. He had ardently felt it was his mission to protect the children as well as help the priests in his diocese. His entire adult life had been haunted by the memory of the little boy clutching a new pair of shiny shoes. *This will be the one heroic thing I'll do in my life* had been his governing thought.

But all that had changed once he discovered he was not the sole owner. Ironically he had already been having some misgivings about this undertaking after he had conferred with several psychiatrists. "The best thing is for pedophiles to be removed from society. If that can't get done, then warn the parents and publish lists of the offenders." Andre took out a handkerchief, wiped his brow and began feeding the designs into a paper shredder.

He heard footsteps approaching from behind and assumed it was Brother Damien. Labored wheezing triggered him to swivel his chair around. The first thing he saw was the gun pointed directed at his forehead.

Then he noticed the shaking hand belonging to Monsignor Rodin.

"You're not going to bring down Mother Church," Rodin's speech was slurred, his eyes bloodshot and his cassock wrinkled as if it had been crammed in a suitcase for days. A wine-splotched Roman collar dangled from his neck. "No scandal will ever violate her sanctity." He raised his voice. "I'm the defender." The corner altar with the vigil lights and the statue of Mary distracted him for a moment. He made a cursory sign of the cross with the gun.

Andre stood up slowly while his hand inched a letter opener inside his cassock sleeve. He faced his attacker squarely. "My dear Monsignor, what kind of deal with the devil have you made?"

The Monsignor flinched and gazed to the side with vacant eyes.

Andre continued in a soothing voice. "You are better than this."

"No, no, no." Rodin shook his head several times. "Shut up and get over there to your altar and ask God to forgive you for your sins."

Andre remembered Hamlet. He had wanted to kill his Uncle Claudius before prayers, thus ensuring that he would go straight to hell. "Alas, my dear Monsignor," he spoke with the eloquence of a Shakespearean actor, "you are far kinder than the fair prince of Denmark."

He took a few steps towards the altar, then stopped. "You don't have to do this."

"Move," Rodin ordered.

Andre looked at him. "You sound tired."

A knock at the door startled both men. "Archbishop, this door seems to be locked." Brother Damien's voice was muffled.

"I'm at prayers. Can it wait?"

"Not really. Mrs. Donavan is in the driveway. She wants you to bless her car before she leaves town."

"Tell her I'll be right there. Oh, and tell Bastien not to worry about the animals."

Like many twins, as boys Andre and Bastien had shared code words as secret ways of communicating. "Worry" meant that something was very wrong. Andre prayed that Bastien would remember this code and come.

Brother Damien softly said, "Well, okay."

Rodin pressed the gun into Andre's back and shoved him towards the prayer stool. Andre swung around and looked down at Rodin who was six inches shorter. "No, you little swine, you're not going to shoot me in the back. You'll kill me while I'm looking at you."

Rodin sneered and pulled the trigger. There was a click. Nothing more. "Holy Mother of God," Andre cried out.

Rodin looked down at the gun, and when he did, Andre quickly and forcefully thrust the blade of the letter opener into his shoulder. Rodin dropped the gun which fired as it hit the floor, wounding him in the calf. He screamed and fell over grabbing his leg. Andre kicked the gun over to a far corner of the room, then unlocked and opened the door. Bastien was running down the hall with Brother Damien right behind him.

"You okay?" Bastien yelled.

Both men entered. "Don't touch anything. The Monsignor just tried to kill me." He knelt and examined Rodin's leg. "Bastien, call Leone to come and Brother Damien, go down and bless Mrs. Donavan's car. Tell her," he paused to think, "tell her there's a man in my office who needs help."

Brother Damien took the bottle of holy water from Andre's altar and hurried out. He encountered Lanita and Ofelia running up the stairway. Lanita was terrified. "We thought," she said between breaths, "we heard something like a gun shot from up here."

Brother Damien patted her shoulder. "Don't worry. Everything is under control. But I need you to go to the main parlor and let Officer Leone in when he comes. Bring him to the Archbishop's office. Everything will be explained." He rushed past them.

Bastien picked up the phone receiver, glanced at Rodin writhing on the floor and put it back. He walked over and kicked him solidly in the gut. "You son-of-a bitch, you try to kill my brother?" Rodin doubled in pain, coughed several times and threw up on the floor.

"Stop that Bastien," Andre commanded. "Leave him alone." He pointed at the desk. "Now call Leone. The legal system will take care of this."

"The damn church will protect him," Bastien roared.

"I'm a part of that church and I will press charges."

"How the hell did he get in?"

"He must have persuaded one of the custodians to give him a key. Since he's a Monsignor, they wouldn't have given it a second thought."

"You're gonna have to change all the locks." Andre nodded in agreement.

An hour later, Andre stood at the window and watched the patrol car pull away with the Monsignor handcuffed and bent over in the back seat. Bastien sat in the swivel chair drinking a cola. "God, it's so tempting to pour me a glass of your fine bourbon." Andre patted his shoulder. "I admire your strength, Bastien. I know it's not easy."

Outside, pitch black clouds were turning the day into a dark night. By now the winds were beginning to churn the tree limbs like egg beaters. Andre pushed a button next to the window. Exterior metal blinds descended slowly, turning the house into a fortress. "Are all the others down?"

Bastien didn't respond. He was thinking of Lanita. Earlier she had invited him to lunch. He had been so disappointed when he got to the kitchen and saw that Ofelia was also there. He didn't say two words during the whole meal.

"Bastien, have you closed all the shutters?" Andre asked again.

Bastien nodded, "Yes, right before I heard the shot. Why was he tryin' to kill you?" Bastien sensed it had something to do with him. He and his brother had been psychically connected since birth. Andre walked over to the bar and started to pour bourbon into a tumbler, but on second thought got a can of cola from the chest refrigerator. He came back to the front of his desk. "Please move over so I can get to this drawer." Bastien rolled his chair out of the way.

Andre removed a stack of letters secured by a wide rubber band and handed them to Bastien. "I want you to mail these if I don't get the chance." Andre sat down in the chair opposite the desk. "I want to make up for what happened to you. That crime and others have gone unpunished for much too long." Bastien shuffled uncomfortably in his chair. They had never really talked about his abuse. "I had intended to put a stop to these priests who abuse children." He popped the can of soda and took a drink.

Bastien rubbed his hand back and forth over his forehead. "And that's why that sorry bastard tried to kill you?"

"Yes, it is. My life's in danger. I'm going against a very powerful institution."

Bastien's lower lip quivered. "You don't have to do this for me."

"I'm doing it for you and all the powerless innocents out there. And I'm doing it for myself. I'm tired of being a coward."

Bastien fanned through the stack of letters. "These're all to newspapers."

"Some are going to police departments. I want to send them once the storm passes. If something should happen…please mail them for me."

Bastien nodded. "I will, but don't talk like that." Bastien felt weak realizing how lost and alone he'd be if anything were to happen to Andre.

"It's just a precaution, Bastien. After what just happened, I don't want to take any chances. These letters must be delivered."

Something powerful crashed into the metal blind on the window. Both men jumped up, half-expecting a boulder to come flying through. The metal blind was dented, but the windows were still intact.

"That's a powerful wind out there," Bastien said and put an arm over his brother's shoulder.

Consciousness was returning to Rudy. He was lying face down on cold concrete. Pain ran through every cell of his body and his head felt like a ripe melon about to burst. Slowly he pried his eyes open. Nothing but blackness. He turned his head ever so slightly and saw a pin prick of light at the far end of a tunnel. He panicked. *Where am I? What has happened?*

With a painful effort, he moved his arm to the side. There was a small puddle of water next to him. Even though he could hear the rains outside, he was puzzled, *is it leaking?* He reached over the puddle and touched something cold and stiff just as a flash of lightening streaked thought a ground level window. The eyes of an older man were fixed on him in a death stare. Horrified, Rudy jerked his arm away screaming as loud as he could, but the thrashing winds and pounding rains coming from all directions outside the basement absorbed the sounds. He then remembered Leone asking Elaine about a Josh Conroe.

The terror shocked him to full awareness. *Which day was it? How long have I been here?* Some memories began to emerge. He was standing in the rain and pounding on the back door of Shadow's Way. Finally, Elaine peeked out. "My dear Rudy do come in and get out of that nasty weather. It's really starting to come down." She held the screen door open for him and glanced up at the sky. "Hurry in. I hate to think what lies ahead of us."

Rudy entered the kitchen, dimly lit by a dozen candles. "I was praying you'd come and stay with me for the duration of this storm? You might be in danger if you stay in that cabin especially since I didn't board up those windows. I know it was a bit mean, but I did that hoping against all hope that you and Ofelia would forget our differences and stay with me." She ended with a frenzied cackle.

"No, no, I'm staying at the Elysian. I just came over to..." He felt dizzy. *How stupid drinking those beers on an empty stomach.* He confronted Elaine. "You never once mentioned to either one of us about staying here through the storm."

She ignored him and got two cups from the cabinet and filled them with coffee. "Lily Mae and Tobias insisted they were going to her sisters who live up the state from here." She motioned for him to sit down at the table and removed a platter of croissants from bread cabinet. She put several into the toaster oven. "I made these just yesterday, once again hoping that you and Ofelia might come over."

Rudy's hand trembled slightly as he took the cup. *Ofelia said not to eat or drink anything from her.* However, he couldn't resist the steaming liquid and after several sips began to feel the alcohol effects ebbing away.

Elaine chattered wildly, "Goodness, haven't we been having a lot of activity around here lately?" She switched to her little girl's voice listing the events in sing-song, "Interviews with a researcher, questions about snakes and missing writers, bogus papers being left in my foyer," she stopped and clapped her hands, "and now this storm named after me. Isn't it all so perfect?" She winked at him, so pleased with herself. An oven ping sounded and she removed the plate of croissants and placed it before him.

Not able to resist, Rudy took a big bite of the warm croissant, reasoning that Ofelia had no proof that her pudding contained poison. The pastry melted in his mouth and left an aftertaste of anisette which he loved. "These rolls are delicious. But listen, those papers aren't bogus."

A cold silence followed. Rudy finished the croissant. Elaine pushed the plate closer to him. "Please have another and then another and let me refill your coffee. I can tell you're hungry." He quickly ate two more.

She chattered away about waiting out the storm and then with hammering staccatos, shouted, "As…Soon…As…The Archbishop…Dies, I Get…It… ALL." Rudy jerked back nearly tilting his chair over.

Once again cackling, she cried out, "Oh, be careful, you'll topple down, down, down."

I've got to get out of here, but first… "I'm convinced there's a fortune under this house." He stomped on the floor. "I'm sure of it." He pulled out the crumpled blueprints. "Just look at these. I promise I'll demand that you get a share, then you won't care what happens to this house. All I ask is that you study all these papers and consider." Elaine hopped up and disappeared into the broom closet.

Rudy tried to get up. "I'll come back as soon as this blows over." He dropped back down feeling weak. "I need a glass of water." He went to the sink and filled a glass, drank it down and refilled it. Just as he finished his second glass, he saw Elaine standing in the doorway holding a large flashlight. "You want to look down in those tunnels?"

"You know how to get to them?" He couldn't believe it. "I've been wondering if you had any idea how to do that."

"Certainly I do, silly boy. Come along."

The floor seemed to wave beneath his feet. He staggered to one side.

"Are you okay?" Elaine asked with concern.

"Just feel a little weird, that's all." He steadied himself. "Have you been down there before?"

"Oh my yes, hundreds of times." Elaine lowered her voice to an audible whisper. "That's how the girls get to Andre's. They go through my basement over to his quarters. Avoids scandal, you know."

"What the hell are you talking about?" Rudy knew he should be heading out that back door and over to the Elysian, but his powerful curiosity was in control.

"Be patient, sweet nephew." She unlocked her bedroom door, walked to the middle of the room and removed a throw rug. Rudy saw a bolted trap door. Elaine undid the bolt and opened the door. She began to descend the stairs and motioned for him to follow. Rudy took several steps down and grabbed the railing for support. *It must be the sweet bread on top of the beer making me feel this way.*

"Careful now. You don't want to fall. These steps are steep." Her voice was full of concern. At the foot of the stairs, she switched on a light. They were in a small area and beyond a wide archway, he could see a large room. The walls of the rooms appeared to be railroad ties bonded by concrete. Large pillars strategically placed supported the ceiling. "Pirates constructed this?" Rudy whispered in disbelief.

As they entered the room, Rudy gasped, "My God, what is this?" He was reminded of his fraternity talent shows. Once he'd gotten first place as a drag queen. "I guess you've inherited something from your Aunt Elaine," his mother had teased. Once again he was in a theater dressing room. Situated along one wall were five makeup stations, each with its own makeup kit and wigged mannequin head. Next to each station a small open wardrobe contained an outfit. A nun's habit was in one.

"Whichever girl the Archbishop requests for his amusement comes down here, gets dressed and goes off in that direction." She beamed the flashlight to her left. "The path forks off to the left, then up some stairs and into the Archbishop's study next to his bedroom."

Rudy sat down at one of the dressing tables. "Girls? Archbishop? What are you…?" His body felt like it was inwardly collapsing.

"He's a sinful lecherous man," she spat out. "And now he wants to turn this diamond of a home over to men who play with little boys. All these years these poor girls have done whatever he's wanted, just so I could live here." Startled, she clasped her hand over her mouth. In the next instant she spoke in a little girl's voice. "My G-G-Daddy worked out all the details."

Am I hallucinating. Rudy held his head, but Elaine's babbling continued, "The nun worked just like the others, except she'd always pray first. And then Trixie…" she picked up the long blond wig from one of the station, "she never went to him. He didn't like whores."

"You are insane," Rudy mumbled. "Totally insane."

Elaine wasn't listening. She was having fun, flashing the light in all directions as if she were conducting a tour. "As you can see, there are myriad tunnels down here, some of them I've hardly been in. You might be right. Pirates' loot could be down here."

Rudy was going to have to lie down. He could hardly focus. Elaine continued prattling, "It would be easy to get lost. I had to make signs, so the girls could find their way to Andre's room. His women are not very bright, you know."

"Aunt Elaine, I'm not feeling well. Can we go back up?"

"My dear boy, don't you know by now?" She stood within inches of him, face to face. "You're never going back up. Thanks to the croissants."

"You've poisoned me!" He shrieked and stuck his finger down his throat, trying to vomit. He fell onto the floor unable to bring up anything. His aunt's mouth pressed on his ear. "It won't be long now before G-G Daddy and I will be living in peace forever."

Rudy was drifting away. He had to hold on somehow. He heard her going up the steps and closing the trap door. He rolled over onto his stomach and managed to heave up some of the poison. But he was sinking into darkness and realized it was too little, too late.

CHAPTER TWENTY-THREE

In pajamas and night robes, Lanita and Ofelia sat on separate twin beds and faced each other. Between them, a small table held a chess board with a game in progress. Jangles slept soundly on Lanita's pillow. The mansion's thick walls muffled some of the outside's raging winds. A kerosene lantern flickered on a nightstand. The electricity had been out for hours.

"Are you going to move before this storm is over or not?" Ofelia teased.

For weeks now, a sister-like bond had been forming between them. They had similar stories and secrets. As little children both had been deeply loved by their mothers as well as their fathers. In their middle childhood years, both their mothers died leaving husbands who were unable to cope. Lanita's father, weakened and overwrought, married the first woman who came along and Ofelia's became a hermit, wallowing in his grief. As a result, both women had suffered from depression; both felt alienated and alone, not only because they were orphans but also because they were mixed with white fathers and black mothers.

Ofelia threw a paper wad at Lanita who was intently studying the board. "Did you hear me?"

"Be patient," Lanita said, "I'm not as smart as you."

"Silly girl. What gave you that idea?"

Lanita sat straight up. "Did you hear that?"

Ofelia gave her a blank look.

"It sounded like a scream. A man's scream."

Ofelia grabbed her pillow for protection. "Do you think someone else is trying to kill the Archbishop?"

"Shhh," Lanita listened. "It seemed to come from somewhere under the floor."

"Oh, my God, maybe there are ghosts here too," Ofelia whispered, "like at Shadow's Way."

Lanita jumped off the bed. "Let's have a drink?"

"Good idea." Carrying the lantern Ofelia followed closely behind her into the kitchen.

"Let's see." Lanita began. "There's sherry, crème de menthe, white wine and crème de cacao, all for cooking. But tonight, they're for drinking." She took down two glasses. "Name your…" Another muffled scream caused Lanita to drop a glass onto the counter-top.

"Lanita, I heard that," Ofelia whispered.

A loud crash hit the back door. Lanita screamed. "What was that?"

"Something flying around. Come on." Ofelia picked up the lantern and Lanita grabbed another glass and the sherry bottle. They hurried to their room.

"Should we try to see what's going on?" Lanita asked.

"That's a bad idea. Let's just make sure we're safe." Ofelia shoved the dresser in front of their bedroom door. "You said a couple of families were staying here and we don't know a thing about them, so I'm not about to go creeping down the halls of this giant house"

Lanita sighed, "I wish Bastien wasn't so far away."

Ofelia poured the drinks. "We'll be okay."

"You're right. With the attempted murder, it's natural to be edgy." Lanita made the sign of the cross. "Let's drink and play our game. The sherry will chase the spooks away."

"You're right." Ofelia handed her a glass and held hers up, "To the scary storm."

"To the scary storm."

As the night progressed, they heard more sounds that could have been construed as screams, but they tried not to notice. Once Jangles raised his head, stared intently, flicked his tail and walked around the room smelling at the baseboards. After a while, he settled back down on Lanita's pillow.

Once Rudy fully remembered all that had happened, he felt very lucky to still be alive. Perhaps the large glasses of water had diluted the poison. Perhaps he had thrown up the final lethal dose. Or perhaps he had one hell of a guardian angel. He sat up and leaned on the wall. He wasn't in the same place he'd been before the poison overtook him. There was no puddle of water or dead body next to him. He shivered and felt weaker than he'd ever felt in his life. His legs seemed like they'd been severed. He tried to stand but couldn't. "I refuse to join the other dead man down here," he declared out loud.

A streak of lightening blazed through a basement window. The flash seemed to further clear his memory as all the recent horrors leapt to the surface. "Let's put his body in one of these other tunnels," Elaine had said to someone. He was then dragged by his bare feet. Where were his shoes? His head bounced on the uneven concrete floor. His eyes wouldn't open, no matter how hard he tried. He moaned and the dragging stopped. His feet hit the ground.

"Elaine, you said he was dead. Dead men don't moan." The voice was nasal with a Boston accent. "For pity's sake, can't you do one thing right?"

"Trixie, he ate three croissants and each one had more poison than Ofelia's pudding." Elaine's voice quivered with fear. *Trixie, that's the whore.* Rudy recalled Elaine using that name when she held up the long blonde wig.

"You goddamn fool!" Trixie screamed. "He weighs at least a hundred pounds more than she does. Just look at his big frame and those muscles. Ofelia is skinnier than you."

"I'm sorry," Elaine mewed.

"As usual, I'll have to do this for you." Trixie's voice was going away. "God, I don't know why I don't just go ahead and kill you too."

"What do you think you're going to do with that log?" Elaine exclaimed, more frightened.

"I'm finishing what you started." Trixie was next to him.

The log smashed his lower left leg. He heard cracking sounds. His screams were deafening. Yet despite the horrendous pain, somewhere in his mind, he registered that the winds seemed to be shifting. *Is the eye about to go over?*

Trixie was walking around him and slammed the log squarely down on his right leg. Rudy shrieked even louder, praying that someone would hear. Trixie laughed and walked behind his head. "This should finish him off for sure."

"No Trixie, not his head," Elaine shouted. "Let him lie here and die a slow death. I wish that his goody-goody mother could be here to see this." Elaine's voice came from the same spot as Trixie's.

"Trixie, Elaine, they are one and the same person. All the girls, the same." He then went into the darkness once again.

Sometime later he leaned against the wall, more grateful than ever to still be alive. *I've got to get out of here or I will die. Which tunnel leads to the Archbishop's quarters?* He tried to remember what Elaine had told him. His eyes were adjusting to the darkness and the frequent lightning helped him to get his bearings. He began dragging himself along on his elbows. The pain in his useless legs was unbearable. *Fuck the pain. I'm going to get out of here.*

Rudy inched his way forward with his upper body, grateful for his years of high school and college swimming, and his coaches' insistence on the long hours of weight lifting. *When I get out of this, I'm going to build an altar for all those blue ribbons and trophies now gathering dust in my dad's attic.*

Every fifteen seconds or so the lightning came through various ground-level windows providing some visibility. The faint sound of voices came from just ahead. The Boston demon was speaking, "Of course, you can. He's just an Archbishop, not Jesus Christ. If he wakes up, which he might do, then fuck him. Once he's asleep, drop the snakes in the bed."

A soft sweet voice with a Spanish accent said, "I just can't. That would be a sin."

Hardly breathing, Rudy slowly scooted closer to the wall and peeked into the same dressing room as before but from a different direction. In the dim candle light, he could see his aunt scramble from one dressing table to the next. She put on a long straw-colored wig and spoke with the nasal tone. *Now she's Trixie.*

"Of course, you can." Trixie shrilled. "You just won't because you're a coward."

She flung off that wig, ran to another station, put on a cropped black wig and spoke with a French inflection, "Just because he's reformed and no longer wants any of us, we still love him deeply."

Elaine walked over to Trixie's station, put on the yellow wig and looked in the mirror. "You are all cheap whores. Like all the other times, I'll have to be the one to make things right. The rest of you can just go to hell."

Elaine walked from station to station, throwing wigs, makeup kits, jewelry and clothes into a large cotton sack. She cleared every station except Trixie's. Nothing was left, not a cotton ball, not a tissue. "You're all dead, you hear me. All dead," she shouted. "I just wish I could kill that bitch Elaine, too, but then..." A little girl's voice whimpered, "My G-G-Daddy would be so sad if you killed his little girl."

She tied the bag securely several times, threw it in the corner, sat down at Trixie's station and began applying latex to her face.

Rudy felt his chest and throat tighten. A panic attack was coming on. He had begun having them after his mother's death. If the Trixie monster heard him gasping for air, he wouldn't survive another assault. Rudy put his head on the cool damp ground. *I'm helpless. From the waist down, only dead weight.* He clenched his teeth to keep from sobbing.

Suddenly he sensed his mother at his side. He'd heard people talk of miracles, but he never believed in them. A calmness began to settle over him. His mother whispered, "My sweet Rudy, you're going to make it. Turn around and follow this wall and pretend you're swimming laps. Count each overhang as a lap."

With a new tenacity, he turned and began pulling himself along the edge of the wall. He saw one of the signs Elaine had put up for the girls pointing towards the Archbishop's. Rudy felt joy despite his bleeding hands and elbows. From time to time he'd glance back to see if any light was coming his way. He felt the wall fork to the left and attempted to pull himself even faster. He had to get to the Archbishop before that thing did. Ahead he could make out overhang number three. *Lap number three.*

The movie *The Three Faces of Eve* popped into his head. He remembered watching it with his mom years ago. At the time he thought it was just a made-up story. "Mom," he whispered, "your sister has outdone Eve." He thought he heard his mother's soft sweet laughter.

He heard something and stopped to listen. To his horror the sound was faint click-click of stiletto heels coming his way. Then he heard glass shattering as a limb smashed a distant window. "Son-of-a-bitch, that almost cut me," the creature yelled.

Rudy hurried, pulling forward with all his strength. He reached an overhang, rolled under and scooted as far inward as he could. He turned his head and saw a flashlight beam dancing on the opposite wall only yards away. He scrunched down tighter under the shelf of railroad ties and prayed, *please don't let this be the home of any creatures.* He flattened himself and held his breath.

He heard the nasal gibbering before he saw her. "They're all motherless children so no one will cry. Elaine's mother was worthless, Rudy's mother was spineless and Ofelia's mother was a whore."

A sharp heel landed within inches of his nose. The light swerved around the nearby corner and she was out of sight. He heard a metal key twisting in a lock, next a door opened and then the tapping of heels going up steps.

I'm already under the Archbishop's mansion. A shot of adrenalin strengthened his body and spirit. *Pull forward, forward, forward, one, two, three, four.* He thought he was going to black out a couple of times. *Bear up now, you don't have that much farther to go.*

More lightening illuminated his way as he rounded the corner and with another flash he saw the door slightly ajar. He waited for more lightening. His heart sank. The next flare revealed a long flight of steps ascending into blackness. "I'll need the strength of a superman to pull my way up there." His body was shaking from fatigue and his arms and upper torso were bleeding from all the gashes and cuts.

I can't go on. Then he remembered his mom squeezing him in a big bear hug. He was six and had helped her carry in all the groceries. "You're my own little superman." He had felt so proud that his mother compared him to his favorite comic book character.

"Okay, Mom." His arms grabbed the railings and he began the long climb upward. "I am still your superman and I'm going to get up there."

CHAPTER TWENTY-FOUR

Like a professional thief in the night, Trixie carefully removed her shoes and opened the bedroom door without a sound. The red vigil light next to the statue of Jesus bathed the room in a soft rose. She tiptoed to the side of the bed and smiled. *So, this is the great Archbishop everyone admires, sleeping with his mouth open.*

She had been shaking the doctor's kit all along the route. *These critters should be good and angry by now.* She had checked earlier. They were still alive, no thanks to Elaine. Only twice had she thrown in a few dead mice and sloshed water over them. For weeks now, these reptiles had been stuck in that small case with no food or water.

Suddenly Elaine whispered in her lovely Southern drawl, "Wait, I want to be with him one last time."

"You can't do that, you bitch," Trixie whispered back. "How did you get here anyway?"

"I loved him as much as I could love anyone," She stifled a sob. "The other girls couldn't feel love any more than I could. They lied."

The Archbishop moaned slightly and turned on his side.

"Stupid fool, you're going to wake him." Trixie shoved at the empty space removing Elaine.

Turning back to the bed, she removed a plastic bag from her skirt pocket and took out a soaked rag. She held it tightly over the Archbishop's nose. He twisted a few times and then collapsed into a coma sleep. She opened the kit. The fowl stench almost knocked her over.

Something's wrong with my brother. Bastien bolted straight up in bed from a deep sleep. He jumped up and stumbled over the chair next to his bed. Pain jabbed through his big toe. "Son-of-a-bitch," he cursed. Still fully dressed, he mumbled, "It's the same feeling like the time he was drowning."

They were nine years old at the church picnic. Bastien knew that his brother was under water. He dropped the horseshoes and ran to the lake just as Andre's head popped up. He coughed up fried chicken and went under again. Bastien dived in, pumping his arms faster and faster. He grabbed Andre's hair and pulled him to the surface.

Andre cried out, "My trunks are snagged on something."

"Wiggle out of 'em them." Bastien shouted. When they got to the bank, Andre wouldn't stand up. "Bastien, I'm naked."

Bastien yanked a towel off a nearby bush. The next day at school a boy teased Andre about losing his swim pants. During recess Bastien broke the boy's nose.

Rudy rested his head on a stair step. *How many more can there be?* He saw a hairline crack of light from under the door and counted. O*nly six more.* With another spurt of energy, he heaved up the steps. He swallowed the sickness that kept coming up from his stomach. He wished he could scream, but the monster would hear him. Finally he pulled himself onto the small landing and reached up to feel for the door handle, but there was no knob, only a key pad. He jerked off the remaining shreds of his shirt and plaited it into a makeshift rope. He struck the panel as hard as he could, praying he'd activate an alarm. Tapping heels were approaching the wall. He tried to roll over to the corner. But he was too late. The wall-door slid open.

Trixie was not easily rattled, but when she saw Rudy she yelled. "What in the name of…!" She swung the kit at his head. It nicked his nose. He swung the shirt rope with all his power and hit her directly in the eye. She stepped back with a painful cry. Next, he grabbed her lower legs and yanked. She began to topple down the stairs, stiletto heels flying off. More than halfway down, she regained control and stopped the tumbling. She tugged her wig down over Elaine's hair and picked up her shoes and flashlight. The latex face looked back at Rudy and laughed. Rudy had never seen anything more frightening. She took a step up towards him. He turned his face to the wall and yelled as loud as he could. "Help, help." When he looked back, there was only darkness. She'd disappeared. He collapsed into unconsciousness.

The outside winds had completely stopped. Bastien stopped his limping run down the hallway spooked by a sudden eerie stillness. *I guess the eye is over us.* Then out of the silence came the cries, "Help, help." The sharp pains emanating up his leg from the broken toe didn't slow down his run. He tore into his brother's office, sprinted across the room and opened the bedroom door. He was nearly knocked over by an awful stench. "Snakes," he cried and shined his flashlight on the bed and saw the slithering movements under the covers. His voice cracked, "How the hell did she get in?"

He bolted across the room and grabbed the heavy wooden cross off the wall. He threw the covers back and began hammering the two water moccasins until they were lifeless. He raked a nonpoisonous snake onto the floor, picked it up behind its head and slammed it lifeless against the bed post, repeating with each swing, "It's all my fault. It's all my fault."

Brother Damien ran in. Making the sign of the cross, he gasped. "Dear God in heaven, have mercy on us."

"Get more light, a lantern and the candles on his desk. Then help me kill these bastards. I've gotten all the poisonous ones."

He shined the light on his brother and saw a reddish-yellow bite mark on his forearm and another on his neck. "I did this to you. May you forgive me." He picked up the soaked cloth lying next to Andre face and smelled it. *A blessing. He didn't feel a thing.*

Behind him, Brother Damien finished decapitating a non-poisonous one with the fireplace poker. "Have we got them all?" Brother Damien looked in the corners and under the furniture. In the bathroom, a small one was swimming in the commode.

"They must have come up from the sewers, which are probably flooding. One's still in the commode," Brother Damien explained.

"No Brother, these were intentionally put here by the witch across the street. How I don't know." He quickly said the Hail Mary prayer and then put his ear to his brother's chest. "He's still alive. Call the ambulance." The wind picked up and the metal shutters rattled. "Dammit, the eye has already passed?"

"Can't get through. The line's dead," Brother Damien called from the office.

Bastien stripped his brother and turned him over to search for bites on his back. "Bring that lantern. Seems to be only two bites but that's more than enough. The neck one's the worst. Bring the charcoal over by the fireplace."

Bastien gathered towels, a shaving cup of water and his brother's straight edge razor from the bathroom. Back at the bed, he dropped two charcoal pellets in the water, then slit open each bite. He put the wet charcoal directly on the wounds. "This should draw out some of the venom. Get some strong tape to hold these in place."

Brother Damien almost ran over Lanita on his way out. "I heard someone calling for help," Brother Damien ran past her saying, "The Archbishop's been bitten by water moccasins."

Terrified Lanita rushed into Andre's bedroom and froze. "It's awful, I know," Bastien said, "but can you help me?" Lanita nodded.

"Grind some of that charcoal down to a powder and mix it with water. I've got to get some of it down him."

"Okay," she headed for the door. "We island people always used echinacea oil for snake bites."

"I don't have any of that."

Bastien carefully examined his brother's entire body once again. There were only the two yellowish bites he had seen before. Just as he was covering Andre up, Lanita and Brother Damien hurried in at the same time. Bastien packed more wet charcoal into the wounds and taped them down tightly. Lanita stood by the bed with a glass of black charcoal water. Bastien pulled his brother up to sitting. "Lanita, when I open his mouth try to pour it down his throat."

"Are you sure about that?" Brother Damien helped to hold Andre while Bastien opened his mouth.

"I've cured many an animal with this."

"Wait." Lanita rushed to the bar in the study and came back with a handful of straws. "It will be easier to siphon this down his throat." She carefully inserted the straw down Andre's throat then took a sip and blew the water through the straw.

"That's much smarter," Bastien said. Lanita repeated the process several times. Then Bastien gently laid his brother down and once again checked his wounds.

Lanita surveyed the room. "I've got to clean up this place." As Lanita started to leave, Bastien put his hand on her shoulder. "Appreciate that. He never choked once and his pulse is steady."

After a glass of sherry, Ofelia had fallen asleep waiting for Lanita to decide her next move. She dreamed that Rudy was calling her for help, but she couldn't move. She woke up in a fright to find that Lanita was gone. "Lanita, are you in the bathroom?" When no answer came, she knew that something else had happened. Then the door from the kitchen opened. A flashlight beam moved over the bed and shone in her face. "Oh good, you're awake?" It was Lanita's voice. "I need your help. There's been another attack on the Archbishop's life."

Ofelia got out of bed. "We double-checked every door in this place. Was it one of the guests?"

"I don't have time to go over it now. Let's go."

"But how did you find out?"

"I heard someone calling for help and I decided to check without awakening you."

Ofelia grabbed her robe. "Why do you have that mop bucket filled with all that cleaning stuff?"

Ofelia followed Lanita. "You'll see."

"You know I dreamed that Rudy was calling for help."

"Well, I'm sure he's sleeping like a baby at the Elysian."

Before Lanita and Ofelia could start cleaning the room, Brother Damien and Bastien debated over the cleanup. "If you think this was intentional, shouldn't we wait until after the police can investigate the crime scene?" Brother Damien asked.

"The police have their hands full, and I'm not gonna let my brother lie in this filthy room." Bastien bowed his head. "Besides I know who did this and Leone already knows about the snakes and who got them. Now let's get to work."

On Bastien's command all four began the clean up. Twenty-five minutes later the bedroom was sparkling once again, and the fowl stench had been replaced by the fragrances of Pine Oil and lilac soap. Andre was breathing normally, but his pulse was beginning to weaken. Once again Bastien held his ear to his brother's chest. "He needs to be in a hospital."

He raised the window's outside metal shade a couple of inches. Electric lines were popping in the distance. The street was a river with at least a foot of rushing water. Shingles, boards, garbage cans and tree limbs were strewn about or flying in all directions. "Holy Mother of God, it'd probably kill us if we drove through this." He walked back in the study where everyone sat quietly in their own world of prayer and anxiety.

Bastien started for the bar then stopped remembering the yells he had heard. *That couldn't have been my brother. He was drugged.*

He began walking around the room. *It came from this room. I know it did.*

"Bastien, what's wrong?" Lanita asked.

"I don't know. Someone was screamin' for help. I thought it was Andre, but he was unconscious. I know it was coming from here."

"I heard those cries too," Lanita said. She walked over to the bookshelf and moved her hands over the books. "One time I was cleaning here and hit something that caused that opposite wall to slide open a crack. The Archbishop quickly closed it and said it led to an old escape route for slaves. He said he had intended to have it sealed off years ago and hadn't done it yet. In the meantime, he asked me to be careful and not open it again."

She continued pushing books to the back until the wall slid open a crack. Tossing the books to the floor, she saw the button. She pressed it down all the way and as the wall slid into its pocket. Rudy's upper torso fell into the room.

Elaine stood next to the mantel and looked up at her great-grandfather's portrait. Flickering from dozens of candles cut through the deep darkness allowing the shadows to dance throughout the room. The antebellum gown with the crinolines was draped across the chair where G-G-Daddy usually sat. "Here's a last toast to you." She raised the glass of sherry and drank.

"It's over." She shattered the glass in the hearth. "Your plans this time were about as successful as those from the War. Once again, you're going to lose."

She paced around the room. "You've been as bad for me as Trixie," she shouted. A bolt of lightning cracked a large oak in the front yard. The walls shook. "Oh, so now you're angry."

She took another glass and poured another sherry. "I killed all of them. I had to. But I saved your little darlin's dress. You can look at it and remember what a sweet innocent she was, always adoring you and so submissive." She noticed the magazine featuring her on the cover as a Southern belle. She snatched it up with a cry and began shredding it with her bare hands, tearing it into smaller and smaller pieces. "She's gone, you hear me? She too will die."

She sat back down on the couch and laughed. "Yes, even Elaine has to go. They may try to arrest her, pin false charges on her. And, as usual, you'd be incapable of doing anything."

Savoring the last drop in her glass, she sighed. "Well I'd better get going." She threw that glass at the portrait. "This storm will eventually be over. Only ten more gallons to go. The upstairs is thoroughly drenched. Yes, even Robert E. Lee's room. With all the rains, I hope it will be enough. But before that, Elaine will perform Antigone's death scene and hang herself." The Southern belle smiled at the portrait and said sweetly, "I hope you'll come to the performance."

She stood erect and projected her voice as if to the back of the auditorium. "Elaine had wanted to do Cleopatra's death scene, but then that awful Trixie used all the snakes to kill the Archbishop." She spat at the portrait. "Good-bye, G-G-Daddy."

CHAPTER TWENTY-FIVE

Rudy lay on a pallet in the middle of Andre's study. Though unconscious, he jerked about fitfully. Using bed slates and bed-sheets ripped into strips, Bastien had set Rudy's broken legs as best he could while Brother Damien, Ofelia and Lanita held him down. Andre's best Scotch didn't come close to numbing the pain and the rag Trixie had used on the Archbishop had lost its potency. Rudy cried out over and over, "I've got to stop her. I've got to stop her."

"It's okay Rudy. Listen to me." Bastien stroked his forehead. "I'm going to strangle the last bit of life out of her." Rudy relaxed and drifted off to sleep.

When Lanita heard this, she pulled Bastien over to the side. "You're going to let the law take care of Elaine. Andre wouldn't want you going to prison again. Especially not for him or Rudy. And I… I don't want that for you."

Bastien looked at the floor. He recalled his mother begging, "Bastien, put the ax back." Like his mother, Lanita didn't want him to get into trouble. Gratitude along with sadness overcame him. He replied softly. "Like they say in AA, I have to stop hurting myself." He looked at her. "I'll let the law take care of her."

Relieved, Lanita exhaled and went back to swabbing Rudy with alcohol. Ofelia placed icy towels over his swollen legs. "He's running such a high temperature in spite of the aspirin we've given him. If we can't get him to a hospital pretty soon…" She refused to say any more.

Everyone felt helpless. They could do nothing to halt the likely dying process of the two men they dearly loved. Time dragged by as the overpowering winds droned on and on in a hypnotic hum. Brother Damien left to make sandwiches, something to stay busy.

Bastien went to check on Andre. He redressed the wounds with new charcoal packs and siphoned more charcoal water down his throat. "Come on, Andre, you can fight that venom." He massaged his chest. "Put your mind to it just like you did with the books. There wasn't a thing you couldn't learn. I was always so proud of you." He wiped his eyes on his shirt sleeve. "Please, please don't die on me." He stepped back, thinking he saw Andre nod. He sprinkled holy water over Andre's entire body, took his hand and prayed. After several minutes he lightly kissed Andre's cheek and went back into the study and checked Rudy. "Let's put an ice bag on his forehead." He went to the chest refrigerator. "It might bring down the fever."

"Lanita got him to swallow more crushed aspirins with water." Ofelia said softly. "And he's not as hot or restless as he was."

She put a cold wet towel over his chest and began to tell everyone what she had been playing through her mind all night. "Elaine used the same snake to murder Andre that killed my mother. I think she planned it that way."

No one said anything. "You see, it makes sense in an insane way of thinking. Both my daddy and Andre took Shadow's Way away from her and the snake that killed my mother also in a way, killed my daddy. So she reasons that Andre should also die that way."

"It is insane, you're right, but it does follow and..." Bastien was interrupted by Brother's Damien's entrance. "Let's eat." He carried in a tray of ham sandwiches and sliced peaches. "We have to keep up our strength."

"There's a pot of hot coffee on the hotplate," Lanita said nodding towards the bar.

"I forgot to tell you." Brother Damien took a sandwich and sat down at the desk. "Leone called earlier before the electricity went down. Monsignor Rodin confessed to attempted murder as soon as he got to the station. He said that his Cardinal along with God had ordered him to rid Holy Mother Church of the evil Archbishop. Let's just hope the Cardinal is questioned about this."

Bastien held a coffee mug in both hands. "I'm sure both'll get off. At my trial, that priest swore I was lying. Said I was the one going after little boys. And everyone believed him because he was a priest and I was nothing." Bastien had never spoken of this before. "No one's going to believe something like this about a Monsignor or a Cardinal."

"Bastien," Brother Damien said, "perhaps the days are ending when people believe that Church officials are above the law."

"That's a hopeful thought." Bastien glanced at the clock and headed back to his brother's bedroom.

Ofelia adjusted Andre's easy chair all the way back. "I have to lie down for a few minutes. Suddenly I'm so tired, I just…" She closed her eyes and in an instant was asleep. She had become hysterical earlier when Rudy rolled onto the floor. "I can't lose my nephew," she cried over and over.

Lanita held her. "Rudy needs your help now. You've got to help."

Ofelia realized she was right. She stopped crying and got to work. Now her body could go no more. In her dreams her Grand-mere and mother were on either side of her. Grand-mere sang, "Oh, mon Cherie, you are safe. Go to sleep. Rest with God's Angels." Ofelia drifted deeper while her mother rocked her back and forth.

Lanita covered her with an afghan. She was now warm and safe and able to completely let go.

Bastien bent over the bed and placed his ear on his brother's chest. Andre opened his eyes. He slowly lifted his hand and gently stroked his brother's head. Startled, Bastien jerked upright.

Andre smiled at him and whispered, "You were always the better half of us. I deserted you, never helped, never tried."

"But I did this." A sob burst through Bastien's throat. "I got the snakes. I caught them for her."

"You didn't know…what she was going to do. But I knew. I knew what that priest was doing to you…and I hid." Andre gasped for air.

"Stay with me, brother," Bastien pleaded and lifted Andre up to help him breathe. "I'll get you to a hospital. The storm will soon be over."

Andre looked directly into his brother's eyes. "I'll never abandon you again." A moment later, his head dropped on Bastien's shoulder.

Outside, as on cue, all the winds stopped. A profound stillness rolled into the room.

"No, no," Bastien cried. He pounded his brother's chest with his fist. Lanita and Brother Damien ran in. Brother Damien stood beside Bastien. "Here let me." He pumped Andre's chest and blew into his mouth, but it was no use. Andre was gone.

Bastien dropped to the floor on his knees. He opened his mouth wide, leaned back and released a long cry of pain, the pain of losing a brother bound to him since the womb. Then another cry over the pains of molestations and helplessness. All had been stomped down into every recess of his body.

Lanita wrapped her arms around herself to control her trembling. She wanted to embrace Bastien, but her instincts held her back. This was his private grieving time. The clock showed only seconds after three o'clock. *He must have died at three like Jesus.* She made the sign of the cross and prayed, "May his soul rest in peace."

Brother Damien removed the bottles of holy oils from Andre's altar and administered the Last Rites. Bastien lay prostrate on the floor. Once Brother Damien finished the ritual, Bastien pulled himself up on the bed and held his brother in his arms. "I love you brother, always have, even when I said I hated you. May God forgive me."

Ofelia remained in her healing slumber and the guests who were lodged in a wing on the other side of the mansion slept quietly. However, the next day several said they'd dreamed that the Archbishop had come into their room and blessed them. That was followed by reports from others in the diocese who said the Archbishop had visited them with messages.

CHAPTER TWENTY-SIX

The winds stopped as if someone had flipped a switch. Elaine looked at the time. Three o'clock. Someone was in the room with her and it wasn't G-G-Daddy. In the dim light all she could see was a shadow. *The shadow of Shadow's Way?* She must hurry. In a few hours, it would be getting light outside.

She walked through the rooms, wishing she could cry, but any semblances to sentimentality had been ripped from her a long time ago. Unless she were playing a role, she had not shed a tear since she was six after her mother had herded her and year-old Gabrielle into the kitchen pantry. "There's stuff in there to eat in case I don't come back. I'll open this juice and leave a jug of water." She threw a pillow case filled with diapers and a bag of toys and books on the floor. "Elaine, if you have to go, use that can in the corner. Don't make a mess, you hear me?"

She flipped on the light switch and began to close the door. "Mama, mama, don't leave us," Elaine screamed and tried to hold the door open. Her mother shoved her back and slammed it shut. Elaine heard the lock click into place. She began to cry and kept crying until she collapsed into a sleep. When she woke up she saw that Gabrielle had opened a box of animal crackers. Crumbs soaked in spilt water were all over the floor. Gabrielle's diaper was sagging, and the smell of poop filled the tiny space. Elaine felt like she was being choked, when suddenly a new person was in her body. This person slapped her sister across the face as hard as she could, again and again. Gabrielle began to wail.

This new person didn't care. She had no feelings and she was powerful. Little Elaine liked having this person in her body. The new person was named Trixie and she told her, "You will never cry again, and no one will ever hurt you without pay-back."

Gabrielle screeched in pain as her cheeks turned red, then blue from the bruising. She held out her arms. "Sissie, Sissie," she pleaded desperately. Trixie pushed her across the pantry. Then the door jerked open and their father filled the doorway. Trixie was gone and Elaine ran to a corner to hide. Gabrielle tottered into his arms.

"That goddamn bitch," he shouted. "Hush, hush, my darling, Daddy's here and you are safe." He hugged Gabrielle close to him and began to walk away, then stopped and looked around. "Elaine. Oh, there you are. I know what you did, but with the mother you have I don't expect better." He turned away, kissing Gabrielle gently on her cheeks. He never kissed Elaine.

"You don't need him or anyone now that you've got me," Trixie whispered to her from the shadows. She loved this new person who, over the years had always taken care of her. Trixie may have hated Elaine, but Elaine loved her.

Little Elaine was still standing in the pantry when the doorbell rang. She heard a policeman talking with her father. "We found her trying to get on a train using a Tide coupon as a ticket." There was more talk, and then her father said, "I'll kill her if you bring her back here. Either put her in jail or the state hospital."

Her father then moved Lily Mae's family, her mother, father, and two sisters, into the servant quarters to take care of his daughters and the home. The quarters had already been refurbished with bathrooms. Lily Mae was the same age as Gabrielle. The two younger girls always played together and if Elaine came around, they ran away because she could be so mean. Impatiently Elaine would try to explain, "It's Trixie, not me."

As the years progressed, Elaine learned how to get what she wanted by using Trixie. Elaine loved watching Trixie fill people's faces with fear, the same fear she had felt years ago in that food closet.

Elaine shrugged her shoulders. "So much for the past. It's time to finish this up and move on. I wonder if they'll have a nice funeral for me." Elaine's laughter filled the house.

"Only one more room, G-G-Daddy. I saved the best for last." She yanked down his picture, threw her antebellum dress over it and soaked them in gasoline. She then splashed gasoline over the entire room and finally soaked the entry way and front door.

Lanita hurried down the second-floor hallway of the Archbishop's mansion and knocked on a door. Mrs. Clay opened it a crack. "Yes, dear, what's wrong?"

"We need Mr. Clay to help get someone to the hospital."

"Oh dear, it's not the Archbishop, is it? I had the strangest dream."

"No, it's someone else."

"Ernest, Ernest, get up. Someone's got to get to the hospital."

"And Mrs. Clay, I'll need your help getting breakfast for everyone." Lanita had decided to say nothing about the Archbishop's death. She'd reached her limit and couldn't witness the grief of others at this time.

At the top of the hallway leading to the main foyer, Lanita and Mr. Clay met Bastien and Brother Damien carrying Rudy on a stretcher of plywood taken from the wall by the stairs leading down to the tunnel. "Help us maneuver down the stairway," Bastien said. "And Ernest, we'll need that tent?" The Clays had planned on camping out farther up the state, but when the Archbishop offered them a dry room for the night they had accepted.

Mr. Clay nodded his head. "Yeah, it's in my car, if it hasn't been washed away."

"We'll put him in the back of my pickup and cover him with the tent. He's in bad shape."

Slowly they inched their way along the sidewalk and through the running water and debris. Rudy moaned with every movement. They set his makeshift gurney in the bed of the truck while Ernest held the tent over him. Bastien pulled out and drove slowly trying to avoid the pot holes. Several times, he stopped to let Brother Damien drag tree limbs from the road. They passed a group of people out searching for missing family members.

Once at the hospital, they waited thirty minutes in a hallway crowded with other injured people. Rudy moaned continuously. Bastien was alarmed by his swelling legs. *Please Holy Mother, don't let that infection get the best of him.* Once Rudy was taken into an operating room, the three men sat in the cafeteria and drank cup after cup of stale coffee. Every time the doors opened, they got up hoping for a report.

"How come the Archbishop ain't helpin'?" Ernest asked. "That's not like him."

Bastien felt the knot in his stomach tighten. He got up and headed for the coffee machine.

"He thought it best if he stayed behind in case other emergencies come in," Brother Damien lied. Mr. Clay was puzzled by the response but decided not to dwell on it. Instead, he picked up a hunting magazine.

Lanita shook Ofelia gently several times. "Ofelia, I need your help again." Ofelia opened her eyes and looked around, startled. "How long have I been asleep?"

Lanita glanced at the clock. "Forty minutes or so."

"You're kidding. It seems like days." Ofelia sat up. "I feel so much better."

She saw that Rudy's pallet was gone. "Oh my God, where's Rudy?"

"He's on his way to the hospital." Lanita took Ofelia's hand. "Ofelia, the Archbishop died."

Ofelia bent over dropping her head towards her lap. "On no. Oh God, no. May the Angels... oh, my dear God, God, God." Tears choked her throat.

"I need you to help me prepare his body," Lanita whispered. "I don't know how long it will take for the undertaker to get here."

Ofelia straightened up feeling the strength of her Grand-mere and mother whom she had just visited in the land of dreams. "Show me what to do."

Over the next hour, they washed the Archbishop's body with warm water and jasmine soap. The wounds from the snake bites had diminished to tiny slits. Ofelia covered them with makeup. Lanita rubbed his body with essential oils while Ofelia shaved his face. Sensing they were performing a solemn, holy ceremony, they silently prayed and moved about quietly and deliberately. After the cleansing they wrapped the body in clean sheets and draped fine altar linens over them.

Lanita put her palm on his chest and spoke, "You were so good to me, never a harsh word, only praise and encouragement. You never pried into my life. You were kind. Thank you for the good salary, the bicycle, the mattress, the refrigerator–I can't remember all the things you had delivered to my home. I loved you." Finally, she closed her eyes and gave herself permission to cry.

Ofelia had returned to the study to give Lanita privacy. She tidied up the room, putting things back in place and washing dishes at the bar sink. Finally, she decided to have a look at the outside world. It was a quarter past four. She pushed the button to open the outside shutter which stopped about half-way up because of the dents caused by the storm's flying debris. She expected to see darkness sprinkled with lights from emergency vehicles and maybe a rim of orange on the horizon announcing a new day, but what she saw anchored her feet to the floor.

Flaming fingers were curling out from every window and doorway of Shadow's Way. Despite being drenched by rain, the wood of the house burned like dried old timber and crackled with a hellish mirth. Even though it had once been her home, Ofelia felt joy, as if a part of herself she no longer wanted was being annihilated. *It's time it burned away.*

"Lanita," she called. Then a little louder, "Lanita, you have to come see this."

The women stood side by side and watched, each lost in her own thoughts. Finally, Ofelia said, "Evil is being purged right before our eyes."

Suddenly the car in the detached garage exploded, shooting sprays of flares high into the starless sky. Wild yellow tongues were consuming every structure on the property: the cottages, the honeymoon suite, the gazebo.

After one and a half hours, the doctor came out to talk with Bastien and Brother Damien. "He continues to move in and out of consciousness. He's been through a combat zone, but he's young and has remarkable strength. I don't know if you know this, but he was also poisoned. A real miracle that he's here." He looked down at his chart. "By the way, whoever set his legs did an excellent job." Brother Damien pointed. "That was Bastien." The doctor patted Bastien on the back. Congratulations, damn fine work. I could use you here." Bastien bowed his head. "I work a lot with injured animals."

CHAPTER TWENTY-SEVEN

For years people all through the South called it The Great Elaine Storm. Memories tormented the hearts and enfeebled the spirits of those in her path. "It was worse than when John F. Kennedy was assassinated," more than one person said.

The roiling waters carried away baby dolls, swollen dogs, beds, tables, couches, drenched family albums and the bloated bodies of men, women and children. The destruction caused lungs to collapse, stomachs to twist into ulcers, and four desperate souls to find strong rafters, tie nooses around their necks and jump.

Finding nothing left but meager bits and pieces of past lives, some gave up, got sick and died before their time. Some cursed God, others prayed, and still others became numb, but most picked up and went on, forever altered. However, nothing cut as deeply as news of the Archbishop's death. He had ministered to all, no matter which church one did or didn't go to, and he was admired by all. He'd roll up his sleeves and worked at the food kitchens, the women's shelter, the hospitals, the nursing homes, the local jail and the prisons. He made home visits, something no high-ranking Church official ever did. He helped poor people get legal assistance and he paid past-due bills for those in need.

Despite the respect, however, no one felt they knew him. No one ever said, "He's a friend." He was kind but aloof, authentic but mysterious. Even Brother Damien had tried unsuccessfully to establish a camaraderie with him, but after a while, gave up. Bastien had felt close to him because they had been bound together by one placenta. He had liked, loved and despised Andre to the same degree that he had liked, loved and despised himself.

Perhaps Lanita was closer to him than anyone besides the woman he had loved as a young priest. Andre confided in Lanita because she was safe. He knew that she was aware of his addiction, even though it was never discussed. Occasionally he sensed disapproval, but he never feared that she'd betray him. He would have been shocked to learn that she had divulged his secret to Rudy.

For two days after the storm, Leone and several firefighters sifted through what remained of Shadow's Way. Josh Conroe's charred body was found and shipped to Boston. A charred cotton bag was found, filled with wigs, dresses, jewelry and makeup. A partially melted hypodermic needle was retrieved, twisted and deformed, reflecting its sinister purpose. However, Elaine's body was nowhere to be found. "Impossible," Leone said, "it has to be here somewhere. Go again through every inch on the property."

"This fire didn't come about by lightning," the fire chief ruled. "Everything was soaked in gasoline and every building was set from the inside."

"She couldn't have gotten away," Leone said, "not in that storm. Besides her car is burnt to a crisp."

"We need to search the rivers and bayous," a policeman said. "Maybe some gator got her."

Leone smiled. "Hell, any gator would take one bite and spit her out."

A roll-away bed and recliner were brought into Rudy's hospital room for Ofelia, who stayed next to him until his dad could arrive. The local airport had been washed-out so Bernie took a flight to Atlanta and was driving the rest of the way.

Lanita was able to came for short visits only. She was occupied at the mansion caring for Bastien, who had become ill shortly after he had returned from the hospital. He was sitting at the kitchen table eating the lunch Lanita had prepared when he suddenly fell to the floor in convulsions. Mrs. Clay and Lanita managed to get him in bed. Chills as well as high temperatures attacked his body with harshness. In the deliriums, he'd shout, "I came in with my brother and I'm gonna have to leave with him. He'll get lost without me." The ramblings sometimes proceeded from animals to no-good priests to his mother's hardships. Around three o'clock on the second morning, he yelled out, "I got those snakes. I killed him. I killed him." Lanita was dozing on a cot in the next room and sat up wondering if she had heard correctly.

The next morning Lanita wrung her hands and asked the home-nurse, "Do you think he'll get his right mind back?"

"Oh yes, honey." The woman patted her hand, then turned back to Bastien. "Funny I never noticed before, but he's the spittin' image of the Archbishop." The gardener who dropped by added, "I never knew they were identical twins till now." Lanita had noticed it also. The anger lines and deep furrows created by the alcohol and indiginities seemed to be fading away.

The doorbell rang continuously. Brother Damien was patient, realizing that the sad and frightened ones needed to tell him how much the Archbishop had meant to them. He listened to all.

"He never once talked over my head, like some of them higher-ups do."

"He once told me that God loved me every bit as much as He loved him. That hit me like a ton of lead."

"I swear I think he healed my little girl, but he told me that was a foolish thing to say and not to repeat it, which I ain't, till now."

"He gave me money to get my boy out of jail, then paid for this lawyer who kept him from going back."

On the second afternoon, Brother Damien moved a small desk to the foyer, so he could get some work done rather than spend time walking back and forth from his office.

Lanita longed to check on her home. The devastation she had seen on her rides to and from the hospital had resigned her for the worst. "Well, the Lord giveth and He taketh away," she reminded herself when she thought of her little house. Then she silently added, "Thank you for letting me have my own home as long as I did. I won't ever forget that feeling."

On the third day, Bastien arose from his bed free of chills and fever and the thoughts of dying. "I feel like I've been given a new life," he told the nurse. Also on the third day, Andre's body was placed in a sealed casket before the main altar at the Cathedral. Long lines of mourners spilled from inside the Cathedral out to the courtyard, around the statues of the Virgin Mary and St. Paul and down the street.

After praying at Andre's bedroom altar, Bastien took a shower, shaved and dressed in a pair of his brother's slacks and one of his white shirts.

"Lanita, can you come help me with something?" he asked, walking into the kitchen.

Lanita was stirring a pot of grits. When she saw him, she jumped back from the pot, flinging a spoon of grits on the stove. "Oh, my dear sweet Jesus, I thought for a moment it was the Archbishop."

Bastien laughed. "I didn't bring no clothes and I can't find the ones I had on."

"Well, that's 'cause I didn't wash 'em yet. Here, sit down and have some food." Lanita put a cup of coffee on the table. "It's been next to impossible to get you to eat something these last few days. Tomato bisque and yogurt are the only things I could get down you."

"That's funny," he said. "I don't like yogurt or bisque one bit. But before I eat, there's somethin' I got to get done and I need you to help me, please."

He hurried from the room. Lanita turned off the burner and followed. Upon entering his brother's office, Bastien removed the letters from the top drawer. "Right after the Monsignor was hauled off, Andre made me promise to mail these if something happened to him. But I want to add something. Can you help me write it?"

"Bastien, I don't know how to write any better than you do. I only went through eighth grade."

"I could never learn to spell. Andre always said it was due to a learning problem, but I never paid attention."

"What do you want to write?"

"I want to make sure that Cardinal's name is mentioned along with Monsignor Rodin's."

"Leone and the police will report that."

"But not to the papers. Those boys are ruined for life and Andre wanted to help them."

Lanita saw the pain in his face. "Okay, I'll help." He felt for those poor children as he did for his poor critters damaged by people's meanness.

"Thank you, Lanita." She was like a cold glass of water on a hot day. He wanted to take her in his arms and hold her but was afraid.

"These letters that Andre wrote only explain what the priests did. I want them to know the full story."

Lanita she sat down opposite him and took a pen and paper from the carousel. "Tell me what to write."

Bastien began, "This is from Archbishop Figurant's twin brother, Bastien Figurant. On the night of the hurricane, Monsignor Rodin shot at and tried to kill Archbishop Figurant because Cardinal O'Hare had ordered him to do that. The Cardinal didn't want trouble for the Church and didn't want everyone to find out about all them priests molesting children. Later that night, the Archbishop was killed, but we don't think that was the Cardinal's doing."

He stopped, "Does that sound okay?"

Lanita nodded. "How many copies do we have to make?"

Bastien counted the envelopes. "An even dozen. I want to get these out this afternoon."

"Then you'll have to help me." She pushed some paper and a pen towards him.

CHAPTER TWENTY-EIGHT

Ofelia read aloud from *Oliver Twist* to a motionless Rudy. He occasionally squinted his eyes as if trying to open them. Since last night, he had awakened a few times, looked around and then lapsed back into sleep. The doctors had told her and Bernie to keep talking to him. When Bernie went down to the cafeteria, Ofelia decided to begin reading the book she had picked up from a shelf in the family waiting room. She had completely run out of things to say. "Don't talk about events that could be upsetting," the doctor had instructed.

Oh really. Well, that narrows the field considerably.

After a while her mind couldn't come up with topics. She'd exhausted praising the various hues of the fall colors, discussing ideas for new songs she wanted to write, or describing the delicious tastes of the gumbo her Grand-mere used to make. She wanted to tell him that there was only an ashy plot with a few blacked beams and rafters where Shadow's Way had once been. *That wouldn't be upsetting, would it?*

Shadow's Way had been Elaine's obsession and hers alone. No one else in the family really gave a damn about it. *Elaine was its jealous lover and she burned it to the ground rather than have someone else have it.* Ofelia wanted to tell Rudy that Elaine had vanished into thin air. "Well, that's damn good news." She could hear him say. "Hope she's been washed out into the Gulf."

Rudy often reminded her of his grandfather. The dad she had known before her mother died, before he had lost his way. Perhaps Elaine also saw similarities between him and their father, the man she blamed for the downfall of the great Chauvier family. Perhaps she had wanted revenge and figured that killing Rudy was the way to get it. She stopped reading and glanced over. Rudy was looking at her with a boyish grin. "I always liked Charles Dickens about as much as I liked spinach."

"Oh God, Rudy, you're talking, still like a brat, but you're talking." She hugged him. "You could say, 'thank you, Auntie, for reading to me.'"

"I've been able to hear for some time now, but I couldn't open my eyes or say anything." He paused, taking several deep breaths.

Lanita entered holding a red get-well balloon. "He's conscious," Ofelia exclaimed.

"Hello, beautiful," Rudy said softly.

Lanita leaned over, kissed his cheek and tied the balloon to the bed. "All the flowers in the garden have been washed away so all you'll get are balloons." She smiled and patted his cheek. "It's so good to see those baby blues, wide and bright again."

The nurse came in followed by Bernie with a bulging McDonald's bag.

"Oh great, a Big Mac," Rudy exclaimed.

His father was stunned. "You're awake, really awake."

"It's good to see you, Dad. When did you get here?"

Bernie leaned over the bed and hugged him. "Yesterday afternoon."

Rudy stretched with a yawn. "I'm sorry, but I'm really tired now." He instantly fell asleep. The nurse assured them this was normal. "He'll stay awake for longer and longer periods of time."

Lanita asked Bastien for the second time in one day if he would drive her out to her place. "I'm ready to see. Don't worry, I'll be able to take it."

Bastien gave in but asked if they could drive to his place first. He felt certain that her home no longer existed, and he wanted to put off seeing the unhappiness on her face. His cabin was on higher ground and had already survived several hurricanes. She agreed, looking forward to a drive away from the city. About halfway to his cabin, the lane was completely washed out. Bastien stopped the car, "I'm gonna walk the rest of the way."

"I'll go with you." Lanita jumped out of the cab.

"But you don't have on decent shoes. You'll ruin those canvas things." He went to the back of the truck and came back with two plastic bags. "Here, put these on and tie them with this twine."

She began to do as he directed, but then he bent down and secured the bags with the string, winding it around her ankle several times. Once again, she had the feeling of being safe and taken care of, a pleasant sensation.

As they picked their way through the mud and muck, they passed a fallen limb where several turtles were resting. "I hope we don't see any snakes," Lanita said.

"Oh yes, the snakes," he said sadly. "I'll go first." He stepped carefully, deep in thought, then turned back, his face full of distress. "I knew deep down she was up to no good. She said the venom was for medicine and I was drunk and let myself believe her. And I knew that she was Elaine, even though she looked like somethin' in a circus." Bastien sat down on a log and told Lanita the full story. When he finished, he buried his face in his hands.

"Bastien, you didn't put those snakes in his bed," Lanita whispered. She was afraid he would get sick again and prayed for the right words. "Leone told me you reported about those snakes weeks ago. You don't blame Leone for not doing a more thorough investigation, do you?"

Bastien was silent for a few moments, then he looked directly at her. "The last drink I had was the afternoon I gathered them for her. That liquor and them snakes is the reason my brother's not here. I'm never gonna have another drink." With that said, he got up and walked ahead.

Lanita followed him to the clearing. They stopped in their tracks. The home, the shed and the animal pens were no more. The land was cleared of everything. Not a board or car part or wire pen was there. "My brother, my home, all gone," Bastien said softly. "We grew up here, in that cabin. But I deserve this."

Lanita stroked his shoulder. "Andre would tell you that you deserve only good things. The past has been removed."

On impulse he did what he had wanted to do for such a long time. He took her in his arms and held her. Lanita whispered, "You'll rebuild."

Thirty minutes later Lanita nervously tapped her fingers as the pickup inched along, coming closer and closer to the corner. As soon as they made the turn, she would be able to see. A cry of joy filled the pickup. In the distance her little yellow and turquoise house sat, apparently untouched by the ferocious winds and attacking waters. Even the fence remained standing. Lanita whispered. "Tilly Marie and Mother Mary protected it."

Two neighbor houses were also intact. "We must not have been in the path."

"Well, I've seen tornados do that," Bastien remarked, "but never a hurricane."

"Elaine must not have hated me as much as I thought she did." Lanita giggled.

"I sure can't say the same for myself," Bastien replied good-naturedly.

When they got out of the pickup, their shoes sank into the soggy earth. Lanita was grateful the plastic bags were still tied on her shoes. Once inside the gate she saw that her garden and flower beds were gone. Bastien took the three steps up onto the porch. "It doesn't look like the waters got up to the porch. The inside shouldn't be flooded at all."

Lanita could hardly wait for him to remove the boards over the front door. Once inside the dank smell turned her stomach, but she quickly dismissed the discomfort. She was not going to complain about a little smell. As soon as all the boards were removed, and the windows were opened, the warm sun and fresh air would solve that problem. She was filled with nothing but gratitude.

A huge rat scurried across the floor. She screamed and ran from the room

"I'll find where it came in and plug it up." Bastien pulled the couch away from the wall. "All sorts of varmints are going to be looking for places to stay till the water goes down."

Even though Lanita had grown up on the edge of a jungle with every imaginable creature sneaking around outside and sometimes inside the house, she was still skittish. Many nights she would curl into a ball until her mother would come and sleep beside her.

"Jangles will take care of the rats."

"That one was almost as big as him." Lanita checked the corners for holes and then said hesitantly, "Bastien, now that you don't have a place you can camp out on my couch." She bit her lip, embarrassed. "Jangles and me need protection from the rats."

Bastien smiled, "Well, until everything dries out, you should stay at the mansion. Besides, that new Archbishop is going to need a housekeeper."

"No, I'm not working there anymore. Too much has gone on and I don't like the idea of those tunnels running underneath."

CHAPTER TWENTY-NINE

Seven days after his death, the Archbishop was laid to rest. Church and political dignitaries from inside and outside the state, as well as hundreds of common people attended. Chairs were crowded into the plaza and still more crowds streamed out into the streets. As requested in Andre's will, Father Garcia officiated at the requiem service. Father Garcia served the poorest parish in the diocese and had no political clout in the Church. Predictably, many of the higher officials were upset by this choice, but Andre's lawyer made sure that the wish was followed.

Bastien cried throughout the ceremony. Darlene handed him tissues from one side while Leone sat on the other side and patted his shoulder. Ofelia wished she could grieve, but her intense anger towards Elaine blotted out all other emotions. She tried hard to stay focused on the present. *Bastien looks so nice dressed up. Lanita had helped him pick out the new suit, shirt and tie for the funeral.* Ofelia smiled, recalling Bastien's comment. *I ain't had a suit since my First Communion and that one came from the parish's charity store.* She then became absorbed in the beautiful, but also sorrowful melodies coming from the organ which dispelled the anger and created worry. *Now what will become of us? Lanita doesn't have a job. Bastien doesn't have a home. Rudy may never walk again. What wickedness is Elaine up to now? Dear God, I pray a gator did get her.* At the thought she stifled a chuckle just as the priest was holding up the Eucharist. Lanita glanced at her with a frown. "Sorry," she whispered.

A catered meal at the Civic Center followed the service. The Bishops and Monsignors had expected to eat at the mansion; however, Lanita told Brother Damien that she couldn't cook for them as well as oversee the meal at the Center. Brother Damien rather enjoyed announcing to them, "The only meal will be at the center. We have a table set aside for you." Most left without partaking of the fried chicken, mashed potatoes and peach cobbler.

On the same day, seven newspapers published Andre's letters exposing the Church's sexual crimes and coverups. The letters detailed the names of accused priests and their parishes, and some also included Bastien's entry. "Monsignor Rodin had attempted to kill the Archbishop and was ordered to do so by Cardinal O'Hare."

Pandemonium broke out across the country. By the time the service was over, reporters were waiting outside the Cathedral to ask questions of church officials and the common people alike. Most parishioners replied that if the Archbishop had said it, then it was true. Some said they had been molested by a priest, so they knew it was true. Some vowed they'd never set foot in a Catholic Church again. Some said the Archbishop was wrong not to say anything sooner. Others said the Archbishop was wrong to say anything at all. However, within days the church counteracted by leaking rumors that the Archbishop had had several love affairs throughout his priesthood.

Some believed the rumors, but most did not. The more astute said, "Being a pedophile and committing murder are not the same as a man having sex with a woman, priest or no priest." Many people said they thought the celibacy rule made no sense and should be done away with anyway. "Hell, if I was a priest, I'd sure as hell would have a woman on the side," said the pharmacist. "Jesus had Mary Magdalene." Heads nodded in agreement. In general, the allegations failed at discrediting the Archbishop and in the end, the Church's reputation suffered far more than the Archbishop's.

Unfortunately, before the legal authorities could question Cardinal O'Hare about his involvement in a murder attempt, he was whisked off to the protected haven of the Vatican. He never returned to the United States for questioning or prosecution. After a short trial, Rodin was sent to a hospital for the criminally insane. Four months later he was murdered by an inmate devoted to the Archbishop.

Despite the blowback, the Church officials were strong enough to shift this scandal to the back burner. After all, the institution had covered up and protected pedophile priests, not to mention other atrocities, for hundreds of years. The manner of the Archbishop's death was never fully disclosed. Leone and the local authorities decided to keep it quiet. When it leaked out that he died from water moccasin bites, most laughed at the absurdity and chose to believe that Monsignor Rodin was the one who had in fact murdered him.

Two parishes in the state had to close their doors because of lowered attendance. In another diocese three priests were charged, but the cases were eventually dropped. The overall changes the Archbishop had hoped for never occurred. Years later, however, the scandals would once again surface and this time most people were no long victims of blind obedience and were beyond being brainwashed by the Church. The Archbishop was recognized by some for putting into motion the wheels of reform, a titanic achievement within an institution as powerful and insulated as the Catholic Church.

After the funeral, Darlene insisted that Bastien stay with them at her mother's home. "Leone's working night and day to repair our place from the hurricane."

Leone cut in, "I don't like livin' with her mama. You're welcome but I'll tell you she be the bossiest woman in all God's kingdom."

Bastien shook his head undecided. "Well, maybe but then I may just go to Lanita's once she's back to her place. She has a good couch." He nervously added, "She's awful afraid of the rats."

Darlene nodded with a smug grin. That night she told Leone, "I bet he's goin' to get more than rats and it won't be on no couch." Leone lowered the fishing magazine. "Woman, you've got the foulest mind I've ever seen. He's practically old enough to be her dad."

A week after the funeral, Andre's lawyer, Mr. Harold Ridale, ran into Bastien at the drug store. "Bastien, I've been looking all over for you. Have you checked your mail box?"

"It's been washed away."

"Oh, I didn't think of that. Well, can you come to my office this afternoon around three-thirty or so? The others are supposed to come at four."

"What others?" Bastien was frightened. *Am I in trouble for mailing those letters?*

"Ofelia Chauvier and Rudy Landon have been sent notices. But first I need to go over some things with you."

At three-thirty on the dot, Bastien was seated in front of the lawyer's desk. He felt weak and realized he hadn't eaten anything since breakfast. He had worked nonstop moving his brother's personal belongings into storage. The new Archbishop was due to arrive at the end of the week.

"Well, Bastien Figurant," Harold began, "your brother has taken good care of you."

"What do you mean?"

"Years ago, Andre inherited a sizeable amount of money, which he invested wisely. In his will, he designated that this sum was to go to various charities and certain individuals, while leaving you as the lion's share." The lawyer slid a paper across the table for Bastien to read, "he left you this sum."

Bastien squinted his eyes and stammered, "This can't be. There's something wrong."

Mr. Ridale chuckled. "It took me by surprise too. He was an astute businessman, no question about that."

"I need something on my stomach. I just had toast this morning. I'm afraid I might pass-out."

"Water's about all I got." Harold went to a corner dispenser and filled a paper cup. "Unfortunately, my secretary has the afternoon off or else I'd sent her out. I could call my wife to bring you something."

Bastien wasn't listening. "Are you sure this is right?"

"Yes, I am."

Bastien drank the water and looked out the window. "Whenever I'd run out of money he'd supply me with whatever I needed, mainly liquor. Elaine's daddy gave me that place, but my brother paid all the taxes. He even wanted to build me a nicer cabin, and all I ever gave back to him was..." His voice broke, "And now all this."

"I knew your brother pretty well and I think he'd want you to be happy and not remorseful." There was a slight knock on the door. "Come on in."

Ofelia and Bernie walked in. "Good afternoon, Mr. Ridale," Ofelia greeted him with a hand shake. "Rudy isn't able to leave the hospital yet, but this is his father, Bernard Landon."

"Can I sit in for my son?" Bernie asked.

"That's fine. That's fine. Have a seat. Here, let me pull in another chair from the other room." He got everyone settled and apologized for having only water to offer them. "Oh, I'm fine," mumbled Bernie. Ofelia nodded in agreement.

The lawyer opened a file and began, "Ofelia, as you know, Elaine Chauvier was never the sole owner of Shadow's Way. After you were born, your father drew up another will designating all three of his daughters as heirs. He also stipulated that if one of his daughters died, then her children were to get her share. If there were no descendants, then it was to be divided between the remaining two. However, Elaine doesn't—I'm assuming she may still be alive—own any part of Shadow's Way because she signed the deed over to Archbishop Figurant years ago. He procured her share by covering all the taxes, fees and renovations which, as you know, transformed the home into a money-making bed and breakfast lodging. Andre and Miss Chauvier had a written agreement that she would retain all the earnings from the business and would be allowed to live there rent free."

Mr. Ridale got up and refilled Bastien's cup. "Here Bastien, you're awfully pale. Once again, I'm sorry I don't have anything. You want me to call my wife?"

Bastien shook his head. "I'm okay."

Mr. Ridale opened a window, then sat down again and opened another folder. The deed to Shadow's Way had been properly signed over and witnessed, but just days before his death, the Archbishop drew up a codicil to his original will stating that Shadow's Way was to be divided three ways, between Ofelia, Rudy and Bastien. He never signed any document stating that the deed would go back to Elaine if he died first, even though it seems she may have believed that. She came here several months ago wanting me to get the deed back for her. When I told her that was impossible, she left pretty darn upset."

Mr. Ridale was silent for a moment. "She was, well a bit scary." He paused and pulled out a cigarette from his shirt pocket. "Do you mind?" No one said anything. "My wife allows me one a day and I feel I need it now."

He went to the open window, inhaled deeply and blew the smoke outside. "But that's not the only reason I've called you here. I already have an offer on the property, a very nice offer I might add. It's a valuable piece, more so without the home on it. You can be grateful it's been burned down. None of the historical societies would have allowed anything to happen to the structure, but now the lot's free to do with as one pleases and here's the good news. There's a large company that wants to build upscale," he put his hand over his head, "and I mean, upscale, high-rise apartments there. Luxury to the hilt. They've agree with the city council to follow the Southern architecture of the neighborhood and the Cathedral. I can proceed with the negotiations with your permission. So far, this is the offer and the terms." He handed each of them a manila folder.

CHAPTER THIRTY

Madame Claudine got off the train and looked around. She could see all the way down main street of the small French village. Boys were playing kickball on their way to school; storekeepers were putting out wares on the sidewalk; a farmer with a squealing pig in the back of a pickup stopped in front of the butcher's; a woman with a large basket of kale was entering the grocer's. Several housewives were out shopping for today's meals. Madame Claudine took a deep breath and smiled. *It is so good to be home, at last,* she thought in perfect French.

A Peugeot stopped in front of the depot and a young man jumped out. "Madame Claudine, my apologies for being late. You must be exhausted after your long trip."

"Hello, Karl, nice to meet you in person. Here's my ticket. Hope you can get my entire luggage into that small car. I have quite a lot."

"Oh yes, Madame. If needs be, I'll come back for the rest."

She smiled sweetly and allowed him to help her into the car.

"I suppose everything I've been shipping these past weeks has arrived safely?"

"Oh, yes, Madame, and it's already set up in your home just as you requested."

The cottage looked exactly as pictured in the brochure. Elaine had paid cash–or rather francs–for this place. Madame Claudine admired how clever Elaine had been with the money she had made over the years.

And thank goodness, she had paid attention to that awful nephew of hers and searched those tunnels.

Madame Claudine smiled thinking about the leather bag of gold coins and trinkets Elaine had found. Perhaps Elaine would have found more had she had more time. True, Madame Claudine detested having to bargain to get fair prices for the treasures causing an unwanted delay in New York. *If only Elaine had not killed Trixie. She would have been able to get the full price immediately.* Nevertheless, the bounty along with Elaine's savings would keep Madame Claudine very comfortable for the rest of her life.

It was sad that Elaine wouldn't be able to enjoy this new life. After all, she had made it all possible. Elaine had begun planning this move the moment her half-sister showed up with their father's second will. Elaine had bribed that old lawyer with persuasions he couldn't resist to destroy his copy of the second will. Little did she know that her father had given the original document to Grand-mere. She figured her senile father had locked it away in some long-forgotten safety deposit box. So with a heavy heart she began planning even though leaving Shadow's Way would destroy her. Perhaps if Ofelia hadn't changed the lock on her cabin, she could have gotten the original and destroyed it. Or if Ofelia had died from the poisoning, then maybe.

Madame Claudine silently thanked Elaine who had made numerous sacrifices. She had burned her birthright, her passion to the ground. She had abolished her beloved G-G-Daddy, who had been with her since age seven; and ultimately, she had given up her own life so that she, Madame Claudine, would be able to escape the fire and have a good life. A tear trickled down Madame's face as she remembered her beautiful girls and even Trixie, all of them lost in the fire. Such tragedy.

Karl unlocked the front door and handed her the keys. As she walked into the parlor, she smiled thinking how much Elaine would have loved this room, so beautifully and tastefully decorated. Then Madame Claudine recalled that Elaine had given very detailed directions as to how each room should look. *Elaine was always so good in making plans, in running things,* Madame paused to reflect. *Take, for example, my getaway.*

Elaine had shown her the tunnel that led to the edge of town. While Shadow's Way burned to the ground, Madame Claudine ran underground until she came across the ladder and pick. Elaine had thought of everything. For twenty minutes Madame hacked her way through wet packed dirt until a beam of daylight greeted her. She crawled out of the hole and began the tramp through two and a half miles of slush and mud. She waded across a knee-high stream, holding a canvas bag high over her head. By the time she reached the bridge, she was shivering all over from the cold and wet. She removed the towel and clean clothes from the bag. After cleaning and dressing herself, Madame Claudine threw the bag with the dirty clothes and towel into the churning current. Elaine had arranged for suitcases to be waiting in a storage bin in New York's Grand Central Station. Madame Claudine scrambled up the embankment just as the sun arose in the Eastern sky. She stood on the side of the highway waiting for a car heading towards the northern part of the state.

"Honey, you need help," said the woman in the car packed with kids and sacks of clothes and food.

"My trailer done washed away and I don't have no money to get to my uncle's." Once again Madame was grateful to Elaine, this time for teaching her how to use different accents. She sounded just like the poor white trash from around these parts. The woman saw Madame's black eye and knew that like her, she was probably running away from some no-good-son-of-a-bitch man.

"Well, come on, Ma'am, we'll make room for you. Move over, Johnny and Timmy so's that Louisie and Clara Mae can sit in back. Just put them sacks on the floor."

"Thank you kindly," Madame Claudine repeated several times as she squeezed into the passenger seat beside a sack of potatoes. The inside of the car stank with dirty children and the grime of poverty, but Madame was aware that she had to endure these discomforts if she were to survive.

Finally, the woman pointed at the swollen eye, "Ma'am, did he do that to you?" At first, Madame didn't know what she was talking about and then remembered Elaine had gotten a black eye, "Yesim, he did it with a knotted-up shirt. You can't tell nobody you done seen me." The woman promised that no one would ever know a thing.

"Hello Madame. Welcome to your home." Madame Claudine's thoughts returned to her new location and the face of the petite maid bowing towards her. "I hope you find everything to your liking. I have prepared a little meal. Perhaps you eat and then rest from your trip." Elaine had even thought of hiring a maid. *I can already tell that this one will be better than that indolent Lily Mae.*

"And you must be Angelique. A meal and rest sound wonderful. Thank you so much."

"Your French is very good, Madame."

"Well, why shouldn't it be? I was born here," she said rather sharply.

Angelique took a step back. "Oh, I'm sorry, Madame."

Madame Claudine inhaled, surprised that she would react so rudely. That was Elaine's behavior, not hers. "Oh, forgive me, my dear child, for being so unkind. I'm worn out from my days of travel but that's no excuse for rude behavior."

"That's alright, Madame. I understand. All I knew was that you were coming from the United States." Angelique curtsied, "If you'll excuse me, I'll finish your meal preparations."

Madame Claudine sat down in the overstuffed chair and took several deep breaths. She had spent too much time with Elaine. *I just pray I didn't acquire her unstable, sometimes mean temperament.*

After four months, the storm site was beginning to settle back into a sort of normalcy. Twenty-three people had lost their lives, all identified, but Elaine Chauvier was not among them. Some came to believe that the fire had consumed her completely, leaving no trace of a skeleton even though the officials had said that was not possible. Leone was quoted in the papers, saying, "She burnt it down, then escaped somehow."

Shortly thereafter, a farmer cleared up part of the mystery when one of his new-born calves fell into a hole in the middle of his pasture. The hole was the end of a tunnel that led all the way back to what had once been the basement of Shadow's Way. Days later, some boys were out fishing and snagged a garbage bag of dirty clothes. They were confirmed to be Elaine's. A most wanted bulletin immediately went out asking for any leads.

The woman who had given Elaine a lift was mailing a package at her post office when she saw the notice with a picture. She debated as to what to do but decided against going to the authorities. She too was a battered woman and knew how those no-good men could lie and how the law believed them and didn't give a damn about the woman's side. *They end up sayin' it was the woman's fault.* She had seen the black eye and how frightened this woman had been. She would keep quiet and say a prayer that she was never found.

As Rudy's days in the hospital undergoing rehabilitation dragged on, he became more and more difficult. One afternoon, Ofelia casually said, "I just hope that one day I can forgive Elaine. At times I feel sorry for her and want to pray for her." Rudy glared at her in disbelief and flung the dinner tray across the room yelling, "How could you even consider such a thing? She damn near killed both of us." He cursed several times and swung his wheelchair around with his back to her. "Even though I don't believe in prayers, I could never pray for the likes of her."

"I'm sorry. Perhaps you're right." Ofelia said softly. He didn't move. "Listen Rudy, she's done enough harm. Don't let her to come between us." He nodded slightly, but remained silent, grinding down on his teeth.

With each passing day, Rudy continued to retreat farther back into a cave of self-pity and hatred for Elaine. The doctor had told him that he would be able to walk with a cane if he kept up his exercises, but that did nothing to heighten his spirits. His sleep was fitful and full of nightmares. He often dreamed that he was strangling Elaine, but no matter how hard he squeezed he couldn't break her neck. She refused to die. He'd wake up, exhausted and sweat-soaked.

Bernie had left to make his home wheelchair accessible while Ofelia continued to come daily, no matter how painful the visits were. Lanita and Bastien dropped by as often as they could, but soon gave up trying to bring any cheer his way.

"I guess you're finished with me now that I'm a cripple," Rudy said one afternoon as Lanita was leaving. She hesitated at the door, then sat down next to his chair and took his hand. "Rudy, your present condition hasn't changed my mind. I wanted to say something earlier but didn't have the courage. Let's be honest. We come from very different lives and have little in common."

"I see," he scoffed, "you already got it all figured out."

"You were getting ready to go to Europe, Rudy. Within a month you would have forgotten my name."

"But I loved you," Rudy's voice broke.

She moved closer to him and spoke softly, "And I loved you, but it was not the kind that lasts. After a few years you'd get so bored with me you'd want to run away, and I'd end up hating you." She leaned over and tenderly kissed him. "You gave me lots of good times and I'll always carry a love for you." She wiped some tears from her eyes. He put his arms around her. "I'll always carry a love for you too," he said with a deep sigh.

A week later Rudy was able to board a plane to go home. On the way back from the airport Ofelia stopped at a small church and had a private service. She lit several candles. "Dear God have mercy on my sister and please don't let her hurt anyone else." She bowed her head. "And please give me and Rudy the grace to forgive her and not be filled with hatred." She left feeling somewhat better.

When Lanita was finally convinced that her home was free of rats and other creepy things, she moved back in. "I guarantee it." Bastien assured her. "And in town, I found a room to rent, but I appreciate the offer of your couch."

Lanita was relieved. Once she had regained her composure, she realized she wouldn't be comfortable having him stay at her place and had dreaded telling him that she had changed her mind. She wasn't willing to share her home until she had lunch with Ofelia. "I'm so sick of that hotel." Ofelia complained. "But I don't want to go back to New Orleans until everything here is settled." She leaned over and spoke just above a whisper. "I want to have that check in hand when I first see Grand-tante again. I can just imagine her face."

"That will be fun. But I just had an idea. My place is tiny, but it'll be better than a hotel and I'd love for you to stay with me."

Ofelia wasn't expecting that. "You mean it? That would be great. The closing's scheduled for any day now, so it shouldn't be very long."

"Isn't it great to have money?" Lanita said. "I haven't told anyone, but the Archbishop left me what amounts to more than two years of my salary."

"That's so wonderful," Ofelia said. "Now let's be sensible and invest some of it. If we're smart, it could last us a long time. I can help if you like."

Lanita motioned for the waiter. "Let me think about that. For the first time since I was thirteen, I'm not going to work. First Tilly Marie gives me a home, then the hurricane doesn't destroy it, and then I get this money. I feel so blessed. I may use it to go back to school and become a nurse."

They ordered desserts and coffee and talked on and on about their futures and their plans. "I hope you keep up with your singing," Lanita said. "You're really good, you know."

Ofelia leaned back in her chair and smiled. "Well, with all the craziness in my family, I thought maybe I should become a psychologist. It would be fun to see if I would ever come across anyone crazier than my sister."

The women laughed, relieved to be free of Shadow's Way and its inhabitant.

Bastien wasn't comfortable being a rich man. He didn't feel worthy. *It's too damn much for an ex-drunk like me.* Plus, that much money frightened him. Leone told him to get a financial advisor, but he didn't know if he'd trust anyone besides Leone or Lanita with all that money. But he was embarrassed to let them know how much he actually had.

He intended to rebuild his cabin and get larger cages attached to indoor shelters for his animals. Beyond that he didn't care about much more. He longed to take care of Lanita. When she told him that she wouldn't have to work for a while, thanks to his brother, he wanted to say, "I'll gladly give you enough money so you don't ever have to work." But he was afraid she might get insulted. She had told him once she didn't want to be with him because he was a drunkard, and yet he couldn't bring himself to tell her that he was determined never to have another drink. That might not make any difference.

Bastien derived happiness from his money when he could help others. Leone and Darlene were beside themselves when a custom Craft house boat, almost twice the size of their old one, was delivered to them with a note, "to the best people in the world, Bastien." Darlene bawled like a baby when she saw his gift. "You know she's gonna spend the rest of her days fishing on that fancy deck," Leone complained. "I just hope you're ready for gumbo, come morning, noon or night."

Bastien also anonymously helped the poor in his area. After Andre's funeral, he and Father Garcia developed a close friendship. Father Garcia, who had been sober for six years, became Bastien's AA sponsor and then a liaison for his charitable acts. Father Garcia knew better than anyone who needed help. Boxes of school clothes and supplies were left on front porches, bags of groceries appeared on back porches, overdue electric and hospital bills were mysteriously paid, and rents were covered for months, sometimes longer, depending upon the situation. "Father, there's a saint somewhere around here." The priest pretended ignorance.

Of course, everyone continued to wonder about the whereabouts of Elaine. Leone never let a day pass that he didn't do some work to solve the mystery. He was in communication with a detective in Boston. Rudy called every few days and became increasingly agitated with the lack of progress. It did no good to tell him that they were doing all they could.

CHAPTER THIRTY-ONE

The woman walked slowly down the quiet street looking in every store window. Her lips moved in a barely audible conversation with the invisible friend by her side. A couple of locals passed her and smiled. No one paid much attention to her any more. They had grown used to this eccentric American who claimed she had been born in a French province somewhat to the north. They had grown to accept and even cherish her.

She was entertainment, the topic of many conversations. At that very moment, a village woman was hanging out her wash while her neighbor leaned over the fence. "Ah, but Margit told me that when she delivered her groceries, the Madame told her about this Archbishop in America who bedded down with all sorts of women, but all he wanted was her. Yet she never once let him enter her boudoir and you'll never imagine why." The story teller couldn't keep from chuckling. "She said it was great-grandfather's wish that she remain a virgin."

The listener turned away from the line, leaving a shirt dangling from one clothes pin. "Mon Dieu, she may think she's Mother Mary and her great-grandfather is God." They laughed so hard they bent over and held their sides. One spurted out, "She might indeed. I hear she's at Mass every morning praying so loud at times the priest has to stop and ask her to whisper."

It was true. Every morning well before the daily champagne and pastries had crossed her palate, Madame Claudine received the Holy Communion wafer at the tiny St. Joan of Arc Church, two streets down from her home. One morning she walked into the sacristy after Mass. "Father Elie, would you be so kind as to allow me to entertain you this evening with dinner and light conversation?"

Father Elie was baffled by the request and the giggles which followed. *She sounds like a little girl, spoiled and manipulative. Nevertheless, she does give a nice stipend to the church every month.* As he placed his vestments in the wobbling wardrobe, he smiled. "That is very kind of you, Madame. I wholeheartedly accept.

A little after seven, he rang the doorbell. "Oh dear, Madame told me nothing about having a guest," Giselle, her new housekeeper, said as she greeted him. "Nothing is prepared except one poached egg with asparagus in cheese sauce."

"Did I hear the doorbell?" Madame Claudine stood in the doorway, a surprised look on her face. "Father, why in the world are you here? I'm not in need of the Last Rites." Once again, the childish giggle.

Red-faced, the priest began, "I was under the impression that you had invited me to dinner tonight and …"

"I have no intention of being the mistress of any priest."

Father Elie stared at her in shock. Dumbfounded, he apologized and turned to leave.

Madame held the door for a moment, blocking his exit. "I know you desire me. They all do. But I won't ever let her do that again."

Straining to hear every word, Giselle eagerly looked forward to the next morning when she could share this conversation with the women in the market. New rumors were soon flying everywhere. "Madame Claudine as much as admitted that she had been a priest's mistress. She may have propositioned that poor young priest at St. Joan's, but I can't imagine that he'd want sex with her. I've heard she talks about her sex life all the time."

Late one morning Madame entered the florist shop. "General Robert E. Lee is coming for a three-day visit," she said. "I need to have twelve large bouquets of your finest seasonal flowers delivered to my home by three this afternoon."

That evening the florist's delivery man held court at the village's favorite drinking establishment. "I crammed those twelve arrangements in every nook and cranny of that cottage. I swear I had to skip and leap to get out the front door. As fat as she is, I bet she's knocked every one of them over just moving about." He had to stop and wait for the laughter to die down. "And the whole time the Madame was talking about some Robert E Lee. I didn't know who the hell that could be."

"Good thing you didn't," Simone shouted out. "He's some hero or something from that Civil War in the United States. She lives in that time, you know?"

More jeers and laughter rocked the small bar before one shopkeeper changed the tone. "Well, she always pays cash and never haggles over prices, so what do I care if she's touched in the head."

"Yes, and she brings us lots of laughter," the butcher lifted his mug of beer, "so here's to the town's oddball, Madame Claudine." Everyone joined him in the toast, "To Madame Claudine."

"Only God knows all the secrets she's carrying around," piped up the Madame's laundress. "She said her friend had killed an Archbishop and gotten away with it. 'I had to help her,' she cried, but she was so full of liquor I didn't really pay attention. My husband wants me to stop working for her." The woman clicked her tongue, "She's harmless and kind and sweet most of the time, but then there are time she does make me a little uneasy the way she goes on."

Madame Claudine added to the rumors almost daily. "I had to abandon my country manor in a northern province because of the climate. My doctor, who also attends to Catherine Deneuve, advised me to live in a warmer place." Most people laughed, but some also wondered if she did, in fact, know Catherine Deneuve. Hadn't she also been an actress?

In moments of clarity, Madame Claudine would realize that she was getting careless by allowing Elaine's stories to become her own. Sometimes she had the sense to correct herself, "I mean one of my closest friends was an actress and I was with her, and so I got to meet those famous people."

In the twenty-six months that Madame Claudine had been in the village, she had gained eighty-five pounds, completely abandoning her once disciplined eating habits. She enjoyed champagne, fine cheeses, pastries and rich sauces at every meal, even breakfast. In the beginning she had considered maintaining Elaine's beautiful figure, but Elaine was dead. Now she, Madame Claudine, could eat what she wanted and could do as much or little as she wanted.

Her first maid, the shy young woman named Angelique cried to her mother, "I never know who'll be coming into the kitchen. One moment she's talking about her no-good father, the next she'll be a ten- year old girl wanting me to make her a custard and then she's back to being the kind Madame Claudine." Angelique's nerves were unraveling, and she was afraid Madame's craziness might harm her unborn child. After five months, she took her weekly pay, left and never returned.

The next housekeeper, Giselle, was much older and almost deaf. She paid little attention to Madame's peculiarities. In the beginning, she had thought that Madame Claudine was constantly talking to her. She would stop what she was doing and say, "Sorry, Madame, do you mind repeating that?" Madame would reply speaking as loud as she could. "I wasn't talking to you. I was rehearsing for a new role." Then one day Madame gave Giselle the large red scarf and a new amplifying hearing horn. "Whenever I wave this scarf," she shouted, "put this in your ear and listen." The arrangement worked well. Giselle went about her business of cooking and cleaning, stopping only for the waving red banner. Giselle would see her chattering away. *She's communing with all the ghosts of her past.*

Over the years Giselle had grown accustomed to the strangeness of rich people, yet Madame Claudine was not just strange, she was also kind and considerate. Giselle was being paid more than any maid in the area and the work load was light. Madame appreciated the older woman and relished her deafness which left her free to entertain whomever happened to drop by. Giselle never interrupted the conversations with her imaginary guests as that silly little Angelique had done. For the most part, Madame was quite content. "No longer is anyone trying to cheat me out of my home. No more working girls to take care of and no more demanding guests," she told Catherine Deneuve, then heaved herself up from the sofa, zigzagged to the table and poured another tall glass of champagne. She turned and smiled. "My dear, you haven't touched yours. Would you prefer brandy?" She weaved over to the liquor cabinet. "Sadly, the only gentleman caller I ever had, I mean Elaine had, was Andre, the Archbishop. No, it wasn't Elaine, it was the others." Giselle happened to glance into the room just as Madame was handing a brandy to an empty chair. She smiled. "Pickled up one side and down the other."

Madame's dress sizes climbed up and up. "Disgusting," she could hear Elaine scolding her, "look at those rolls on your waist." Madame would blush, then remember and shout, "You're dead." The jet-black hair became salty and unkept, but Madame simply tucked it under a lacy shower-like cap. Her dressing table, once covered with jars of creams, bottles of oils and vials of serums, was now bare. Madame Claudine's daily routine in the back garden would have been the last straw for Elaine. She luxuriated on a chaise lounge for hours sipping glass after glass of champagne in the hot sun while her smooth, creamy white skin reddened and deteriorated into a leathery roadmap of lines and creases.

CHAPTER THIRTY-TWO

The Elaine Chauvier case was becoming a cold one at the Boston Police Department. The posters, the news stories and the Most Wanted bulletins across the country resulted in a dozen calls, all of which led nowhere. Those who had known her believed that she'd probably taken on another identity. "She's off playing another role, I bet you anything," Judge Harris said.

Lanita had told the police of a conversation she'd overheard between the Archbishop and Elaine. "I was cleaning the hallway and I heard her shouting that Madame Claudette was very upset. I think she said Madame Claudette. The Archbishop just laughed out loud. 'She's one of your characters,' he said back. 'You take care of her.' It seemed so strange to me."

When Ofelia was interviewed, she too had very little to offer. "I did hear her say on several occasions that she wanted to die in France, the home of her ancestors." As an afterthought, she added, "She spoke French quite well and often used it around me." Interpol was then contacted but so far, nothing had come of that.

The partially burned bag of wigs, makeup, and costumes didn't provide any clues except to confirm Rudy's account of Elaine's bizarre behavior during his night of terror. "She went from being one person to another, with different voices and everything," he had stammered out.

Bastien had difficulty coming to grips with his brother's shadow side. At first, he denied that Andre would have ever had Elaine, no matter what role she was playing, as a mistress. However, a few days later he admitted to Leone, "Ever since we were kids he was totally taken with her. Sort of like he was possessed." Bastien took a few deep breaths. "She was a devil from the start."

Local police investigators discovered that two months before her disappearance, Elaine had begun closing out various banking and savings accounts. She had sold valuable pieces of art, sets of china, crystals, lamps, and furniture through a New York broker. Lily Mae had told them, "Yassir, I seed some things missin', but I knowed better than to asked or say inything."

"She's smart, that's for sure." The lead detective leaned back in his chair. "And she's thoroughly covered her trail."

Rudy cursed his condition. "Man, you got to change your attitude," said the young physical therapist while flexing and adjusting his shattered leg. Rudy wished he could kick him across the room. "Would you like to change places with me?" he asked.

The therapist smiled. "I think what you need is a little romance. You're a handsome man and you told me yourself you've got more money than you know what to do with."

"I don't want a woman going to bed with me because I have a lot of money," he mumbled, "or worse still out of pity because I'm a cripple."

"Man, you got to stop thinking that only ruthless gold diggers or woeful Mother Teresas would be interested in you. And stop with the cripple bullshit."

"Your time is up." Rudy glared at him. "Leave," he yelled.

"Listen, it could be worse," the therapist said. "You damn near lost this leg."

Rudy picked up the decanter of scotch and aimed it at the therapist's head. "Put that down or I'll rebreak this leg." Rudy lowered the decanter. The therapist began to gather up his things. "I'll be sending you the final bill. Call me when you can stop feeling sorry for yourself." He left. Rudy took a big swallow of scotch, not bothering with a glass. He had no reason to get better. His life was over. Then to make matters worse, Lanita and Ofelia showed up a few days later, all bubbly and excited about seeing him.

"How are you doing, dear nephew?" Ofelia hugged him. "I hope you'll cook up some of that famous clam chowder you were always bragging about."

"You came for clam chowder? You sure you didn't come just to gawk at the handicapped?" Ofelia and Lanita were too shocked to speak.

Bernie stepped in. "Rudy, you've been through a lot, but that's no excuse for this kind of behavior. They came because they care about you." He then faced Ofelia and Lanita. "I'm really happy you came. Let me show you to your rooms and then let's go out for some of the best clam chowder in the world."

He turned back to Rudy. "I'd love to have you join us if you can be civil."

Rudy hated treating his father and others so badly, but his anger was in control most of the time. He swung his chair around. "I'm really sorry. I'd like to go with you guys."

He talked a little during the meal and even managed to smile once. Then for the next two days, he accompanied his aunt and former girlfriend on trips to see various sights. Neither had ever been in Boston. They managed to get his chair in and out of the van and roll him across gardens, parks and into museums. At times he wished he could be happy and have a good time, but he knew that the ability for that had been destroyed in the basement of Shadow's Way.

After Ofelia and Lanita went back, Rudy refused to see visitors or talk to anyone who called. He sat in the dark, shades drawn, drinking Scotch. Depression became his only friend. "I'd rather be dead than like this," he muttered to the emptiness. Despite the surgeries, his left leg was crippled beyond repair. The other leg healed from the two clean breaks, yet every time the weather changed, biting shocks of pain ran up and down the bones. He brooded over his misfortunes for hours on end. Then one evening as the shadows crossed from one side of his room to the other, he decided that rather than kill himself, he would find Elaine and kill her. Revenge was the only cure. He slept better that night than he had since the attack.

Two days later his father invited a psychiatrist friend over for dinner. Rudy knew his father wanted to help him, so he listened to the doctor, especially when he talked about establishing new goals, new purposes for his life. Rudy smiled, "You're right. I must get on with my life. I have a terrific goal in mind." The doctor left feeling quite successful and Bernie was overjoyed.

Rudy grabbed his walker and wobbled with great effort to the shower. "Vengeance is mine sayeth Rudy," he sang to the tune of "Strangers in the Night." He called his physical therapist. "I'd like you to come back. I'm serious about getting better and I apologize for being such an asshole."

Daily, for the next months, Rudy endured painful therapy with a clamped jaw while visions of Elaine begging for mercy played out on his mental screen. Twice a day for an hour and a half, he lifted weights. Before long the flabby weight began to disappear and rippling muscles appeared in his arms and upper body. He lived on high-protein drinks and ate rare steaks. He pushed his way through strenuous exercises to strengthen his legs, often with tears of agony clouding his vision. He graduated from the wheelchair to a walker to crutches and finally to a cane. Then the day came when he flung the cane from his second-floor window into a patch of weeds that had once been a bed of his mother's pansies.

His limp, however, tenaciously hung on no matter how many exercises he did, and this fueled his vengeance to the point of complete obsession. *Elaine will pay for this.* The once charismatic and handsome man with the light brown curls and mischievous blue eyes had always been center stage in any gathering. Now he avoided attention and sought to be alone, constantly planning his revenge.

Believing that an avenging angel was guiding him, he gave free reign to his intuition. He hired one of the most recommended private detectives in the state and gathered all the police files he could obtain. Ofelia's statement about France peeked his interest because he remembered Elaine's fascination with what she referred to as her "homeland." He also sensed that the name Madame Claudette given by Lanita was a lead. Perhaps she was another one of Elaine's personalities. He sent the detective to France. Then he, once again, became fluent in French, an easy chore since his mother had begun speaking to him in this language while he was still in her womb. They had often conversed in French when they were alone, but after her death, he had never again used it.

Now that he had formulated a new mission in life and was rid of the cane, Rudy developed a façade of cheerfulness which delighted his father and friends. "He's getting back to his old self," they said with enthusiasm. To complete the charade, Rudy began to party, dated and even took a few to bed. Little did anyone know what lay beneath.

Ofelia was happy to be back in New Orleans. She had always loved the city. Once she was settled back into her old home, the owner of the club where she had previously worked offered her the ten to one slot on Friday and Saturday nights. Once again, she was singing and gathering fans as well as a reputation. A recording company had sent scouts to hear her perform and she felt that a contract was on the way. During the week, she wrote songs, looked after her aunt and edited her father's books, which had been returned by the publishing company with the note: *please resubmit after a thorough editing*. Ofelia enlisted the help of her college English professor, Sister Margarete. For several hours each week they determined what should stay and what should go and what should be rewritten. Sister Margarete insisted that Ofelia do all the rewriting, "You're a good writer and you know your dad's voice."

Occasionally she fantasized about getting a degree in psychology. "I can't help but feel sorry for people like Elaine and would like to help them," she told Tante. "How miserable they must be."

"You're not cut out for that kind of work" Tante said with a sigh. "Be content with the gifts God has given you." Yet Ofelia felt like she needed to be doing more. "I could teach piano and voice once a week in our living room."

Her aunt had had her fill. "What's your problem?" She had been stirring a pot of fudge candy at the stove and stopped to wave the wooden spoon at Ofelia. "You got enough goin' on. Besides, I won't put up with all that screeching and piano banging in my house. It almost drove me up the wall when you were little." Her aunt removed the pot from the stove. "You don't have to be busy every minute of the day. You got to learn to relax, to do nothing." Ofelia knew she was right but Tante wasn't finished. "In the name of Mother Mary, you got your singing, your song writing, your dad's books."

"Okay, Tante, I didn't mean to upset you. You're right." She was grateful to have this dear aunt to set her straight and decided she was ready to tell her the secret that was keeping her in a state of restlessness.

"Like you know, I went to Shadow's Way to mend my shattered heart and connect with a sister I didn't know," Ofelia exhaled deeply. "Instead, I ended up in hell." She sat down at the kitchen table and wondered if she should go on.

Tante broke the silence. "Well, from what you've already told me, it sounds like you learned the truth about your blood sister, but were blessed with a new sister named Lanita. And God showed you that you don't need a man to lean on. What more could there be?" She poured the steaming candy onto a cookie sheet. "That's not exactly what I'd call hell.

Ofelia blurted out, "Elaine tried to poison me. I almost died." Tante leaned back on the cabinet counter. "Oh sweet Jesus save us all. I did get an awful feeling in my bones and I prayed." She sank down in a chair. "Oh, how I prayed every single day." Ofelia took hold of her hand. "And that's why I didn't die." Tante put her arms around her. Ofelia began to sob, "It still frightens me so much and when I'm busy doing something, I don't think about it."

"Listen Baby, when it comes up," Tante said softly, "you remember your mama and Grand-mere taking care of you and you pray. That fear is like a spoiled child. If you don't pay attention to it, it straightens out."

That evening at the club, Ofelia looked up from the piano keys and saw a man, a young version of Harry Bellefonte, staring at her. She quickly looked down again, confused, *that couldn't be Harry Bellefonte, could it?*

When the set was over, Harry Bellefonte got up from his table and walked towards her. She almost stumbled over the piano bench getting up. As he approached, she realized that he did in fact resemble the famous singer. *He must be an island man. Maybe from the same one as Lanita.*

Was she ready to meet someone new? One week after she had arrived in New Orleans, her old flame, Roderick showed up on the front porch. She was preparing a cake and had the mixer running. Tante came to the kitchen doorway. "That doorbell keeps ringing."

"Well, can't you answer it? I've got my hands full."

"It's for you." Tante turned and walked off.

When Ofelia opened the door she caught her breath. There he stood on the porch with his flashy clothes and wide toothy smile. "Hello, baby, I'm back."

She just stared. He laughed, "Why you're so happy to see me, you can't talk. I know you missed me," His cockiness and self-assurance made her skin crawl. *Once upon a time, that attracted me.* She felt nauseous.

He stepped forward as if to enter the house, but she blocked him and pulled the door tighter to her. "You not gonna let me in? Aww, come on, baby. You mad at me?" He leaned over to kiss her. She backed off. "I'll make it up to you baby, I promise. Just give me the chance."

Suddenly she realized how shallow and selfcentered he was. So much like Greg. *How could I have been so blind?* "Roderick, I'm in the middle of something so I don't have time to talk." She began to close the door, then stopped. "Listen, I won't ever have time to talk to you so please don't come back." She closed the door in his face and collapsed on the couch. She could hear Tante in the next room praying, "Thank you, Jesus. Thank you, Jesus."

She sat there for a long time, assessing her life and how she had gone from one mistake to another, always the little girl looking for her daddy. A daddy who protected and pampered her, but then became someone she couldn't count on. She was determined to change that.

"After all, you're a grown woman now," she mumbled towards the piano.

"I really enjoyed your singing," the Harry Bellefonte man said and held out his hand. She took it. He had a firm yet gentle grasp and his voice was like velvet.

"If you're finished for the night, I'd like to buy you a drink. That is, if you're not with someone else."

Ofelia looked at him and smiled. "I appreciate the offer, but I have to get home."

"Oh, you married?" He was obviously disappointed.

"I'm not available at this time. Need to be all by myself for now." She smiled again, nodded a goodbye and began to leave. He called after her, "Maybe in a few months?"

She turned back. "Maybe."

On the drive home, she experienced a new sense of freedom. "I know someday the right man will come along, but for now I'm going to learn to be okay all by myself."

Lanita stood back and watched the workmen. Bastien wanted her input on every detail that went into his new home. It was situated much farther up the incline, away from the water. It was considerably larger than any cabin, and the foundation extended three feet from the ground. "Don't take any chances of getting flooded again," she advised when he first asked for her suggestions.

Initially Bastien had planned to build another cabin, similar in size and location. When he ran that by Lanita, she dropped her jaw. "Another cabin? Bastien, from what you've told me, you have enough money to build a really nice home. Why act like a poor man when you're not? There's nothing wrong with being rich."

He thought about that for a few days and realized she was right. "But I don't ever want to get high and mighty," he told her. Then he added timidly, "You know ever since I was little I've wanted an airplane, wanted to fly one. You think I'm smart enough to get a pilot's license?"

"You'll never know till you try," she said with a laugh. Then her attention shifted, "A split-level at the top of that incline with lots of windows facing the river would be so pretty."

Two days later he introduced her to an architect and instructed him, "Do whatever she wants." Bastien wanted this to be Lanita's home. He wanted her and a family, despite the doubts that clouded his hopes. *I know she can do so much better. I'm at least fifteen years older and a recovering drunk.*

Lanita never thought of the age difference. What mattered to her was Bastien's gentle kindness, his constant attention and his determination to be better. He had not had a drink in well over a year which had completely altered his temperament. He didn't get angry any more except when Elaine came to his mind. When the police officer in Boston told him they had done all they could, he fumed for hours. "They said she's dropped off the face of the earth. They're just not tryin'." He often felt that Andre was telling him to forget Elaine, but so far, he didn't want to.

Lanita had lived a life of leisure for five months following the Archbishop's gift. She learned to sleep past nine o'clock and go to bed at midnight. She replanted her vegetable and flower gardens and repainted the inside walls of her home and all the outside trim. She hired a tutor and passed the exam for a high school diploma. To celebrate, Bastien gave her a bottle of Cartier perfume and took her to dinner at the nicest restaurant in the city.

Over dinner she told him she was ready to get back to a regular sort of life. She had applied for her old job at the nursing home and was enrolling in classes to become a nurse's aide. Upset with his news, Bastien declared, "You don't need to work. Listen, I've thought of this before. I want to pay you for all the help you're giving me with the house."

Lanita put down her fork. "Bastien, that's kind of you, but I don't mind and besides I want to be a nurse's aide."

However, once the work and classes began, Lanita's life became hectic. Bastien wanted her input on every little detail: which flooring, what light fixtures, which counter-tops, what cabinets. One afternoon, she was exhausted and close to having a melt-down when Bastien called to say he was picking her up for a meeting with a landscaper. She had been at the nursing home all morning tending to a dying patient and was getting ready to study for a big test.

"Come in and sit down," she commanded as soon as he knocked. "Jangles move over." Bastien and Jangles nervously obeyed. Something was up.

She stood in the kitchen doorway across from him. "Bastien, you're expecting me to give more and more of my time. You can't seem to have a nail put in without first getting my okay. It's your home and I've got tests and old people to care for and I just can't do it all." She paused to catch her breath. *I sound a little off, out of control.*

Silence hung over the room. Jangles didn't dare purr. Lanita continued, "I know I brought some of this..."

"Lanita," Bastien interrupted her, "I don't want that home for me. I want it for you. I want it to be perfect for you because I want you to be happy there. I would like for you to marry me, to be my wife." He stopped, not believing he had just said what he had. Lanita remained standing with her mouth slightly ajar.

Bastien dropped his head and spoke more softly. "There's no question that I'm too old for you and I am and will always be an alcoholic, but I've quit for you. Well I've quit for myself too." His face reddened as he went on, "You're the first woman I've ever loved, and I promise I'll be good to you." He bowed his head a little lower.

Lanita collapsed on the chair next to him. She felt relief and joy rush through her. Ever since her mother had died, she had longed for someone like Bastien, someone who was there for her, helping her along, protecting and loving her. She pulled a handkerchief from her apron pocket and dabbed her eyes.

Bastien moved his hand to her shoulder, "I didn't mean to upset you. Just forget what I said."

Lanita pulled his arm around her. "Those are tears of joy, my lovely man. I can't wait to live with you as your wife in our beautiful home perched on our little hillside."

One week after their home was completed, they had a small ceremony near the bank of the river. Father Garcia officiated. Ofelia stood next to Lanita holding her bouquet while Leone was next to Bastien with the rings. Brother Damien and Darlene were in attendance along with Jangles.

The next day, the couple left for Niagara Falls, happier than they had ever been in their lives.

CHAPTER THIRTY-THREE

"I'm still haunted by that night," Rudy told his father one early spring day just as the snow was beginning to melt. "I want to go to England and France to heal my mind and soul." Bernie encouraged him, "That sounds wonderful. I want you to learn to enjoy life once again." As they were saying their goodbyes at the airport, Rudy handed his dad a check. "You retire now and build that sailboat you've always dreamed of." His father hugged him a long time. "You're so much like your mother," his dad said almost weeping. *No,* Rudy thought, *I'm not.*

He flew to London, got a flat and stayed there for several weeks waiting for his hair to get long. His investigator had found a village in southern France where an American woman had purchased a home over two years ago. However, her name was not Madame Claudette. It was Madame Claudine. Rudy's instincts assured him this was the one. Next, he became familiar with this town, learning the name of every street, church, school, store, bar, restaurant. He found out all he could about the local government and the small police department. He researched the median income of the households, the level of education of the inhabitants. He even found out names of several of the inhabitants. He became a walking encyclopedia of the village.

When his hair reached his shoulders, he was ready for his make-over. He walked into a beauty salon with long brown hair and walked out with bleached, tightly permed hair and shaved sides. A Gypsy lady at a side street kiosk pierced his ears and one eyebrow. Rudy chose a pair of dangling falcons for each lobe and a blood-red ruby for above his left eye. On a nearby street in the same area he was able to put together a wardrobe of silver studded leather pants and sleeveless vests embossed with emblems of wild animals: a panther, a bear, a snake, and a wolf.

Next, he visited an optician. "But sir, you don't need glasses." The perplexed man kept repeating. "Save your money."

"Sir, I need contact lenses to change the color of my eyes," Rudy countered. "I don't mind the cost of nonprescription lenses." After much going in circles, the doctor finally fitted him with contacts that turned his clear blue eyes into harsh black ones.

The dentist proved to be even more difficult. "But sir, your teeth are perfect as they are." Once again, Rudy argued, "Yes, but I need an upper set of clip-on teeth to go over mine." The dentist glared at him in disbelief. "My mouth had to stick out. It's for a part in a play I'm doing." Rudy didn't know of a play where a character had wide buck teeth and fortunately, the dentist didn't ask. He began measuring his mouth.

The last change before leaving for France took place in a tiny shop in the Soho district. A Tunisian lady drew henna tattoos on his arms and across his throat and neck. They depicted daggers dripping with blood, grotesque skulls, and a laughing Satan. "These should last a month provided you just wipe them with a damp cloth. Don't wash with soap or running water until you're ready to remove them. But before washing, loosen the ink with baby oil."

Back in his flat he looked in the mirror and didn't recognize the man who stared back. He was sure that Elaine wouldn't either. In the cab on his way to the airport he felt joy for the first time in years. *In a few hours I'll be in Paris. Then one more day and I'll reach the village where a Madame Claudine resides in her quaint little cottage.* He thumbed through the pictures his investigator had sent, one of her cottage, one of the bakery she frequented and one of the church she visited daily.

As Madame Claudine exited the church after morning Mass, she noticed the strange man leaning against a storefront across the street, one foot propped against the wall. He savagely bit into a baguette and chewed with his mouth open. His coal black eyes glared at her. Such flagrantly uncouth behavior repulsed and unnerved her as did the trashy tattoos covering most of his exposed skin. In a bit of a panic, she turned down a side street that circled back around the church. She would take a more circuitous route home. *If he tries to follow, perhaps I'll lose him with all the twists and turns.* This was the second time he had suddenly appeared in her life.

Just yesterday morning he was in the bakery where she went for her daily pastries. He stood just inside the door as if waiting for her. She didn't pay much attention at first, but then she could feel those pieces of coal glaring at her. When she turned to look, she drew her breath in. She had never experienced such naked hatred. He pulled his lips apart showing yellow oversized teeth. Horrified, she had to brush past him to exit and when she did, he yanked on her skirt. Once outside, she heard a strange sound and looked back to see that he was limping towards her, dragging one leg which made an unsettling scraping sound on the cobblestones. She pushed herself to go as quickly as she could, but at best, she could only waddle awkwardly. Suddenly the scraping stopped. She glanced around. He had vanished. *Has he gone into the hardware store?* Paralyzing fear kept her from checking to see if he had.

Now today once again she was lumbering along as quickly as she could in an overweight body unused to any degree of exertion. After she rounded the corner, she had to stop and lean against a cast-iron fence for support. Her lungs were burning and her head was light. She listened for his scraping walk but heard nothing. "You silly creature, he's not following you," she gasped. "Just imagining things." She held onto the railing and took a few steps forward, then paused. She felt anger coursing through her. "That damn Elaine made so many enemies along the way. Maybe he's the repairman she didn't pay because of some paint splatters on the sidewalk. Or the actor she insulted in front of the entire crew. A good actor could fake a limp." She pulled her floppy bonnet down to her eyebrows. "What am I saying? All those people are in the States, far from here. I'm safe."

She began to relax but then happened to glance across the street. Not more than fifty feet away, he was sitting in an old black Peugeot with badly dented front fenders. For a solid minute, his black eyes pinned her to the rail. She couldn't move or breathe. Then he floored the accelerator and sped away.

Somehow, she managed to stagger to a public bench. She whimpered as she dropped down on the seat, unaware of the two women beside her. "Trixie killed Rudy and that Boston detective and now they've sent someone to kill me," she blubbered. Startled, the women got up and hurried across the street. Madame realized she was talking out loud and became quiet, but her mind continued. *Rudy had knocked Trixie down those stairs, but she had gone back to check, even kicked him in his shattered legs, but he didn't move at all, and his mouth and eyes were open like a dead person's. He's dead, and that detective was so dead he was starting to smell. It's not them.* Madame clicked her tongue at the memory of the evil Elaine. During the short trek to her cottage she moaned. *Elaine, why did you kill Trixie? She could have taken care of this stalker.*

Madame rushed through her front door and collapsed on the nearest chair, exhausted and fearful. But as soon as she smelled Giselle's brewing coffee, she felt safe and reasoned that she had nothing to worry about. "Anyone from the past would be after Elaine. And she's dead," she shouted elatedly.

"You okay, Madame?" Giselle entered drying her hands on a dish towel.

"I'm going back to bed," Madame hollered into her ear. "Bring me a tray with pastries and champagne."

Two days later Madame ventured out once again to the church. After Mass she knelt at Our Lady's altar and took out her rosary. "Hail Mary, full of grace…" she abruptly stopped, terrified. She heard sneering laughter only a few pews behind her. *Mother Mary, take care of me.* Then she heard the scraping walk. He was inching towards her with sneering laughter, sounding like a dangerous devil.

The threatening chortles and loud scraping sounds reverberated through the empty church. Madame hoisted herself up and breathing heavily, stumbled towards a side exit. She hobbled outside and without looking began crossing the street. Annette, Giselle's niece, happened to be driving past and screeched to a halt just seconds before hitting Madame.

"Oh please, ma Cherie, take me home. He's going to kill me." Annette looked around but saw no one. She opened the passenger door. "I'll be happy to, Madame. Hop in." Madame always treated her aunt well and Annette would help her no matter how deranged she might be. The car stopped in front of the cottage. Madame thrust several francs into Annette's hand. "No, no Madame." But Madame was already out of the car and through the gate.

"Giselle, Giselle." She tripped going through her front door. Giselle dropped the feather duster and supported Madame to the couch. Ear horn in hand, she sat down beside the frantic woman. Madame Claudine got her story out in spurts, pausing every other second to catch her breath. "Oh yes, I saw that man yesterday," Giselle shouted back. "He was standing just across the street, looking in this very window. In black leather with silver dangles and long dirty blonde hair."

Madame grabbed a macaroon from a cut-glass dish on the side table and shoved the entire sweet into her mouth. Giselle continued, "I went to get a broom and when I got back, he was gone."

Madame swallowed the cookie. "I don't understand," she whimpered. "Why would anyone want to hurt me?"

"We need to call the police." Giselle got up and started for the phone on the kitchen wall.

"No," Madame yelled. "The police might learn that I was connected to that Elaine and might charge me as an accessory to murder. If only they could find her body."

"What?" Giselle stared at her, totally confused, certain that she had not heard correctly.

"Listen, Giselle. Put that back to your ear." She continued in a lower voice. "Contacting the police might provoke him into really harming us. He looks and acts like an insane man. As long as we ignore him, don't pay him any attention, he'll probably go away." Madame kicked off her shoes, laid back on the couch and put her swollen feet up on the pillows. "Make sure all the doors are locked and bolted, fasten all the windows, and draw the draperies leading to the streets.

Upon awakening the next morning, Madame sensed Elaine's disappointment in her. *You're letting this creep control you. You can't stay locked away forever.* Madame agreed. N*o one is keeping me from Mass. God protects me.* She would keep going to church and the market.

After Mass he suddenly appeared as she held on to the rail going down the outside steps. He stood just inside the cemetery fence waving her to come to him.

The tattoo of a knife dripping blood glowed in the sun and the blood seemed to splatter as he moved his arm. His black, dead eyes never blinked or looked away. Then he opened his mouth in a sinister smile exposing awful brownish-yellow teeth. Madame stepped down onto the ground as he unlatched the gate to the cemetery. Step, drag, step, drag resonated all around her. "What do you want?" Her screaming question was answered by a chilling demonic laugh.

"Don't you know, Elaine?" the monster hissed. "The devil has come for your soul." Madame turned away quickly and got her feet tangled. She tripped hitting her head on the edge of the bottom stone step. Her world went black.

Minutes later, the gardener saw her lying at the foot of the church steps. Like everyone else in the village, he knew who she was. Even though she weighed twice as much as he did, he was able to yank her up to a sitting position. He got his watering can and splashed water on her face. After a few seconds she regained consciousness. "Can you walk to my wagon?" he asked. "I'll take you to the doctor."

"No, no, no doctors. Please take me to my cottage. I'll pay you."

Luckily two boys were passing by and helped the gardener heave Madame into the cart. When they reached the cottage, Giselle threw up her hands in frustration. "I'm calling the police."

"No, you're not," Madame slurred her words. "He's not after me. He's after this terrible woman named Elaine." She removed the ice-filled towel Giselle had put on her forehead bump. "I will let him know that Elaine is dead. Now don't worry the police with anything."

From then on, Madame insisted that Giselle accompany her on the rare occasion she dared to venture out. Even then, he would appear, sitting on a public bench, examining vegetables in the market, standing by the confessional at church, drinking coffee at the outdoor café. Giselle often did not see him which made Madame furious. "He's over there by the fountain!" But when Giselle looked, he was gone.

Panic further unraveled Madame's nervous system already tattered from her years of living with Elaine. *The devil has come for your soul* looped through her brain night and day. Her hands had started shaking so much she had to drink her champagne from a large coffee mug, and her legs often buckled under after two or three steps leaving her in a heap on the floor. "You've gotten so fat, I can't pick you up," Giselle said and insisted that she get a walker.

"I could walk okay if the floors in this old house weren't so uneven." Giselle was close enough to hear and laughed out loud. "It's not the floors, but all the drinking making everything uneven." Madame threw a pillow at her, then demanded strawberries, chocolates and brandy. In addition to champagne she now consumed large amounts of brandy, especially each morning with her coffee.

To make matters worse, Madame began to see shadows floating past her at all hours of the day and night followed by hellish cries of pain and anguish. If she dared to open her front drapes for even a moment of sunshine he would be standing across the street, glaring with the black marble eyes and baring the yellow brown teeth. Finally she insisted that the drapes remained closed all the time.

Just after she had fallen asleep one bright moonlit night, she was awakened by a soft tapping on the window. When she opened her eyes, she cried out in horror. His monster face was pressed against the window, not five feet from her own. A low guttural laugh drifted into the room. She clasped her eyes shut and froze. The romantic notes of *La vie en rose* floated on the air. *He's whistling. For me? Serenading me? Is this nothing more than an obsessive lover?* Suddenly she was alive with sexual feelings. When the whistling stopped, she waited a few moments and then peeked out from the covers. He was gone. She relaxed. *He's a former lover, that's all.* She grabbed the half empty bottle of champagne sitting on the night table and emptied its contents in her coffee mug. Smiling coyly, she toasted towards the window, sipped slowly and recalled the days when men swooned over her. *What fun that was!*

But her mood shifted once the cup was drained. Her bedroom window faced her garden which meant he had climbed over the wall. *He's everywhere I am, day and night. He isn't wooing me, he's driving me insane, just as insane as Elaine was?* Tomorrow she would send Giselle to purchase drapes for this window. *Those teeth. Those earrings. That awful dragging walk.* She sat upright clutching the bed linens to her neck. Only when she heard Giselle in the kitchen preparing her breakfast did she dare lie back down and close her eyes.

Rudy sprawled on his bed and watched the ceiling fan slowly make its rounds. He was having a great time, sick as it was. Oh yes, revenge was sweet. When he first saw his aunt four weeks ago, he thought maybe he had been led to the wrong woman. Her once lovely face was now a mass of tanned creases, her attractive figure was hidden under layers of fat and her lustrous black hair was faded, matted and stuffed under a worn lacy night cap.

And since I've arrived she looks even more outrageous. It was true. Her eyes constantly darted about in fear while her lips moved in inaudible mumbles. The fronts of her dresses were usually spotted with food and drink stains. It was apparent to Rudy that she was becoming more and more unhinged, more and more terrified. He relished her expression of abject terror when he hissed,

"The devil is coming for your soul." What a joy it was to see that she was suffering as he had that night in the tunnel. Yet despite his avenging acts, there had been one or two times when he had felt a little sad watching her hurry to get away from him, wobbling from side to side, staggering, unable to catch her breath. "Stop that," his shadow side shouted. "Remember you're crippled for life because of that bitch."

He was no longer worried about any reprisals. *If she hasn't called the police by now, she's not going to. She won't expose herself.* But now he didn't know what to do next. He hadn't planned much beyond the stalking and terrorizing. He wanted her dead, but how to accomplish that was a mystery. *I don't have the nerve to murder someone.* He had envisioned that she'd get so frightened she'd have a heart attack or maybe kill herself. He sprang up. *Well that could still happen. Mustn't give up yet.*

The next day, he walked around the outside wall surrounding Madame's garden and spotted a small hole in the masonry. He chipped at the stucco until he could see inside. There she lay, like a beached whale, flabs of body hanging over the lounger. *She was once so beautiful. Hard to believe.* An ice bucket with a bottle stood on a stand beside her. A half-eaten tray of cheeses and salami rested on her stomach. She seemed to be dozing.

He cupped his hands around the hole. "You killed them. Killed them all and now you must pay," he said in a low, menacing voice.

Madame jerked upright. "What?"

"You killed them. Killed them all. Now you must pay."

She tried unsuccessfully to get up but ended up having to roll off the lounger. She crawled like a baby to the cottage's open doorway wailing, "He's here, he's here." Giselle ran out and looked around the patio for an intruder. Seeing no one, she pulled and heaved Madame inside and locked the French doors.

Madame spent the next three days on the living room couch afraid to go to her room or the patio. The heavy drapes Giselle had ordered hadn't arrived yet. "I can never go to the garden or anywhere else. You'll have to do all the shopping." She picked up her rosary from the side table. "Tell Father I'm sick and can't come to Mass anymore." She walked from room to room. "I must remain inside the rest of my life with all the doors locked and all the windows fastened and draped. You'll need to order fans for circulation, one for each room."

Giselle felt sorry for her mistress. Even though she hadn't seen the stalker in well over a week, she didn't think Madame was lying about her encounters. "You are a prisoner and still you don't want me to call the police?"

"It would only make things worse. Now bring me the small safe under my bed." Madame ordered.

Madame worked the combination. Once the door clicked open, she removed a wad of bills and peeled off franc after franc. She held them out for Giselle to take. "Oh Madame, you pay me very well and give me a lovely room. This isn't necessary."

"Promise you won't leave." Madame shoved the money into Giselle's hand. "Stay and take care of me until I'm gone, then take the rest of the money in this safe and leave. Others will come for the house."

Loyalty and devotion for her eccentric employer overpowered Giselle's own fears. "Madame, I won't leave you. I shall follow your orders," she said, feeling apprehensive. The next day, Giselle saw to it that Madame's bedroom window was boarded up and then coaxed her to go back to her comfortable bed with its adjustable settings. Over the next days, she made it a point to cook delicious meals, tried to supervise the amount of alcohol Madame consumed, and even watered down the brandy a bit. After her baths, she rubbed oils on Madame's cracked skin and shampooed her hair with herbals. Although there was little if any transformation, one day Madame happened to glance in the hall mirror. "Oh, Elaine would be proud of how good I'm looking."

Rudy was tired of stalking. He had been at it far too long and was beginning to feel disgusted. His aunt's horrified reactions no longer gave him the same satisfaction. But what to do next?

The following day, he caught sight of Giselle walking towards the farmer's market. He darted into the book store, not wanting her to see him. He glanced towards the children's section and froze. She was seated on a low bench looking through a picture book with a small boy, maybe five-years-old. Something began to tighten in his heart, squeezing out the hatred and revenge he had cherished for so long now. The gentleness, attentiveness and love shown to the boy made him gasp. *That's me and my mom twenty something years ago.* How could he have forgotten her and what she would want for him?

The woman glanced his way with the same clear, blue eyes that were his mother's. Soft freckles dotted her face. He remembered sitting on his mother's lap, counting each little reddish-brown dot. *For each one I love you a thousand times,* she whispered in his ear.

The young mother turned back to the boy, "Okay, we'll get that one too." Rudy couldn't understand the boy's comment. "Yes," replied the woman, "I think the hippopotamus is a most interesting animal."

Rudy staggered towards the door. A vise was pressing the air from his chest. As soon as he was outside, his heart began to pound so loudly he thought it might erupt from his chest. He ran as best he could to the hotel. *Oh Rudy, you are my loving boy and you always will be.* His mother's soft voice furled around him.

Back in his room, he dropped down on the bed and began to weep, raining out all the vileness that had poisoned his body for much too long. After thirty minutes, he fell asleep, totally exhausted. He awoke late in the afternoon, renewed and feeling once again like the son of Gabrielle. He jumped up and began shedding the stalking identity, stripping off the black leather pants and flinging them in the trash can. Next, with silver buttons darting in all directions of the room, he ripped at the black sleeveless vest and tossed it.

He walked into the bathroom and looked in the mirror and removed the earrings and brow ring. He slid the black contacts out of his eyes and spit out the brownish teeth. He removed his black nylon briefs, smeared baby oil over his tattoes and stepped into the shower. The hot water beat into his flesh and, once again, Rudy felt the tears flow. *I don't want to be like this anymore.* The months of animosity washed down the drain along with the henna colors. He wasn't a murderer. He was the son of Gabrielle, the kindest and gentlest of mothers, with the clear blue eyes and the freckled face, who spoke softly and read about the hippopotamus and all things wonderful.

After his shower and shave he called downstairs and requested a barber, a bottle of wine and a hot beef sandwich, all to be sent to his room. His brown hair had already started coming back, and a short cut would get rid of most of the yellow. Rudy was thankful that he had brought a set of regular clothes. He removed the pair of wrinkled khakis and Oxford shirt from his suitcase and called the desk again to get them pressed.

A few hours later a transformed Rudy went downstairs and out onto the street and lifted his face to the sun. He felt good again. Even his leg felt better, and the limp didn't seem to be as obvious. He strolled to the post office and sent two telegrams, one to the Boston Police Department and one to Bastien. *Elaine Chauvier, using the name Madame Claudine, is in Bernais, France 31, Rue de Calour. I'm at the Le Minu Hotel but shall be flying back to the States tomorrow. Rudy Landon.*

Rudy left the office certain that he never wanted to see or think of Elaine again. She would become a bad memory, a distant bad memory and then forgotten for the most part. He was going to rejoin life. He thought about becoming a teacher. *I think I might enjoy teaching little ones about hippopotamuses and the other wonders around them.* At heart, he'd always been a kid himself. "Rudy, will you ever grow up?" his mom asked on several occasions with a warm smile. He watched a dove fly to its home in the eave of the hotel and mumbled to himself, "I've gone from being a self-centered, fun seeker to a self-pitying victim to an avenging monster and now to a person I don't quite know." He realized that all he knew for sure was that he was different. *Perhaps I have Elaine to thank for that.*

"He's gone," Giselle said. "I haven't seen him anywhere. I've walked up and down every street and I've looked in every store. For three, four days now."

"I believe you, Giselle. I feel it. I knew he'd grow tired and leave." Madame was so relaxed she directed Giselle to open the draperies and the windows. "The fresh air will feel so good." She so looked forward to going out again into her sweet village, which is what she did that afternoon. It was wonderful to visit with the local people again. They were all delighted to see her up and about. "So sorry you've been under the weather" and "Good to see you back picking over the strawberries." On and on the comments went. Madame felt cherished.

The next morning, she hummed a merry tune, happily anticipating her warm croissant and coffee before Holy Mass. She pulled back the parlor drapes just as a police car came to a stop at her gate. A French policeman got out. Then from the back seat Bastien and another man, a Boston detective, emerged. "No. May God have mercy," she said faintly clutching the cream colored drapes in both hands to keep from falling over. The drapery rod broke under her weight and crashed down, shattering the porcelain statuettes on the window seat.

"What's going on?" Giselle hurried in. Then she saw Madame's drawn white face. "Is he back?"

Madame didn't answer. Instead she announced, "Elaine must do it now." She turned towards her room and weaved down the hallway, bumping from one wall to the other, struggling to steady herself.

From the parlor window, Giselle could see the officer ringing the bell. A sense of devotion kept her from answering. She heard the loud slam of Madame's bedroom door. She didn't move in either direction. A forceful pounding on the door moved her forward.

"We are here to speak with Elaine Chauvier," the French policeman briskly said.

"What? I don't hear good."

The policeman repeated much louder.

Giselle frowned, "You have the wrong house. There is no Elaine Chauvier here."

Bastien stepped forward, "No, it's Madame Claudine." The policeman repeated what he had said, afraid that Giselle might not understand Bastien's dialect.

Giselle paused. *I can't let myself get into trouble.* "Oh yes, a Madame Claudine lives here." She stood back and let the men enter the cottage.

"Where is she?" Bastien spoke loudly.

Giselle pointed down the hallway.

When Bastien flung open the door, he saw Elaine swallowing the last of a greenish-yellow liquid. He ran over and knocked the vial from her hand, then stood back stunned. Had they come upon the wrong person? This couldn't be Elaine. She looked up at him, somewhat alarmed. "Oh, my darling Andre," she said in the perfect Southern English drawl. "I knew you would come for me."

"Call an ambulance and get some sour milk," Bastien ordered. The policeman left the room.

Bastien grabbed Elaine by the shoulders and began shaking her. "I'm Bastien. You killed Andre." Her head flopped back and forth like a rag doll's.

"No, Bastien." The detective pulled him away. Elaine fell back on the bed. Her mouth twisted as if she were about to issue a curse. Before she could form the words, the detective spoke, "Elaine Chauvier, you are being arrested for two murders and two attempted murders.

She laughed, "You silly boys, do you think I care about your arrests? I'll be dead before an ambulance can get here."

"Where is that sour milk?" Bastien yelled.

"We don't have any sour milk," Giselle cried.

"I'd spit it all over you if we had some, you bastard man of God." The snarl was followed by two quick ear-splitting screams as deadly pains curled and doubled-back through her intestines. Once the pains subsided, she smiled at the two men. "You see once again, I've outsmarted the lot of you." She threw back her head and laughed until another convulsion of agony arched her back several inches off the bed. Staccato shrieks bounced off the walls. When she lay flat again, she exhaled moans and then whispered, "Just so you know…" another weaker moan, "it wasn't me…Trixie's the murderer…but you never knew...Elaine was so clever."

Her face turned a reddish purple and perspiration seeped from every pore. She cried out again pitifully, but as soon as the pain subsided, she turned her face to Bastien. "Andre, I really did love you. I tried to show you through the girls. They were so lovely, weren't they?" She winced. "I wanted to give myself to you, but G-G-Daddy wouldn't allow it." With that she said her last words.

Then she shrieked almost continually as her body jerked about from one side of the bed to the other. Giselle ran in with an iced towel and put it on her head. Elaine yanked it off as foam began to come out of her mouth.

Bastien couldn't witness such misery, even for the person who had killed his brother. He walked outside into the garden where the agonizing cries were muffled but still audible. Suddenly a presence was at his side. *Forgive her.* Andre was asking him to do something he didn't think he could do; nevertheless, he sank onto the nearest chair and bowed his head. "Merciful God, I wish to forgive her and ask that she be delivered from this suffering." After many long minutes of saying the same prayer over and over, the cries stopped. Bastien stood up. A stillness settled over everything, a stillness he had never before heard.

ABOUT THE AUTHOR

Barbara Frances has plenty of stories and a life spent acquiring them. Growing up Catholic on a small Texas farm, her childhood ambition was to become a nun. In ninth grade she entered a boarding school in Our Lady of the Lake Convent as an aspirant, the first of several steps before taking vows. On graduation, however, she passed up the nun's habit for a college degree in English and Theatre Arts. Her professors were aghast when she declined a PhD program in order to become a stewardess, but Barbara never looked back. "In the Sixties, a stewardess was a glamorous occupation." Her career highlights include dating a very gentlemanly Chuck Berry and "opening the bar" for a planeload of underage privates on their way to Vietnam.

Marriage, children, school teaching and divorce distracted her from storytelling, but one summer she and a friend coauthored a screenplay. "I never had such fun! I come from a family of storytellers. Relatives would come over and after dinner everyone would tell tales. Sometimes they were even true." The next summer Barbara wrote a screenplay solo. Contest recognition, an agent and three optioned scripts followed but, weary of fickle producers and endless rewrites, she turned to novels. *Shadow's Way* is her third book. Her first, *Lottie's Adventure,* is aimed at young readers. Her second, *Like I Used To Dance,* is a family saga set in 1950's rural Texas. Barbara's fans can be thankful she passed up convent life for one of stories and storytelling. She and her husband Bill live in Austin, Texas.

Barbara welcomes questions or comments about *Shadow's Way* at barb@barbarafrances.com .

If you enjoyed *Shadow's Way*, please go to Amazon.com and write a review.

Other Books by Barbara Frances

Like I Used To Dance

"Our kids, my, my, Gracie" laughed Bud. "Where did we go wrong? One marries God, another a Jew and the last one, the devil!"

Texas, 1951. The Wolanskys—Grace, Bud and their three grown children—are a close knit clan, deeply rooted in their rural community and traditional faith. On their orderly farm, life seems good and tomorrow always holds promise. But under the surface, it's a different story. http://likeiusedtodance.com.

Lottie's Adventure: Facing The Monster

an action-packed children's book written especially for ages 8 through 14. Children will enjoy this exciting read while also improving their reading skills. Twenty nine chapters filled with twists and turns keep kids reading to discover the outcome.

Lottie, a lively ten-year old Hispanic girl, longs for something new and different in her life. Her summers up to this point have all been, more or less, the same. Then the arrival of a magical letter and a TV newscast transforms her vacation time into high adventure. http://lottiesadventure.com.

CPSIA information can be obtained
at www.ICGtesting.com
Printed in the USA
BVHW070047151218
535403BV00009B/51/P